# EROTIC FICTION?

HANNAH LYNN

Text copyright © 2020 Hannah Lynn
First published 2020

**ISBN-13:** 979-8610025230

**Imprint:** Independently published

**Cover design by** Jake Lynn
**Edited by** Charmaine Tan

*To Paddy and Bart,*
*for all the joy you bring.*

# CHAPTER 1

S arah sat on the sofa and scrolled down the page in front of her. *Four-bedroom detached house with a substantial garden. Four-bedroom semi with two en-suites. Three-bedroom townhouse in a sought-after area with a large garden.* She clicked on the photo. Perfectly decorated, tastefully decked out, and with a kitchen that could fit the whole family without the worry that someone was going to pull a pan down on themselves. The whole house was beautiful. Modern yet classic. Ideal for families like hers if only it wasn't a million miles out of her price range. Her living room, with its peeling walls and stained brick fireplace, looked practically derelict compared to those she fantasised about. The carpet, which had once been cream, was now very definitely taupe. Grubby little fingerprints dirtied everything up to a height of three feet, and the whole place, no matter how much she cleaned, seemed to hold on to a weird aroma of unwashed children and over-boiled pasta. She shifted her gaze to her husband, Drew, as he mindlessly darted his fingers across the screen on his phone. Just a standard night; Drew on his computer games and Sarah dreaming of a home and life she would never be able to afford.

They had met at a party in their second year of university. Drew had an ineffable ease about him; at least that was what Sarah had thought as they chatted all night about very little; bands, places they had visited, places they both wanted to visit. Half a dozen times, she took her phone out as a subtle hint that maybe he might want to ask for her phone number. It was a hint he didn't get. In the end, she had bitten the bullet and suggested they go for a drink later in the week. Needless to say, she was more than a little surprised when she turned up at the bar to find he'd invited three of his scruffy, long-haired flatmates along too.

'I thought we were going on a date?' she hissed, as they stood at the bar waiting to be served. 'Why did you bring them?'

'This is a date?' Drew looked horrified, although whether it was because he was on a date or because he had invited his friends, Sarah wasn't quite sure at the time. 'Oh my God. I'm so sorry. I'll get rid of them. I'll make them go.'

'You can't do that,' she said, secretly hoping he would anyway. He didn't.

In the end, the five of them, Sarah, Drew, and company, all got food together. Drew spent almost the whole night apologising. Still, it hadn't ended too badly, really. Just perhaps not quite how she had expected it to.

The truth was that sometimes it all got a bit too much. Sometimes, she needed to rant. And it was hard to do that without feeling like an utter bitch. How many of their friends had struggled to get pregnant? How many were struggling still? How many conversations had ended with friends weeping into her shoulder after yet another month of disappointment after failed IVF or acupuncture or whatever alternative route they had gone down? Sarah and Drew were amongst the lucky ones. She knew that. It's just some days she had trouble remembering it.

Her eyes drifted back from her fireplace to the computer screen and images of perfectly manicured gardens and beautiful bay windows – ideal for a covered seat or reading nook. She barely had room for a bookshelf now, what with all the children's toys. Not that she had time to read anyway. The last time she had had any real time to read was on her honeymoon. She definitely looked back on those two weeks in the sun with mixed emotions.

Three days in and Sarah had already got the best tan of her life.

'We should start trying now,' she had said, grinning as she sipped the dregs of her fourth mojito and gazed out over the crystal-clear Maldivian waters. 'It'll probably take us years. It takes most people years.'

'We should definitely start practising,' Drew replied. 'I think we should get in as much practice as possible.'

Caught up in the endless sun and the rainbow-coloured cocktails and being sickeningly in love, they had been oblivious to reality.

'It took my mother years to conceive.'

'Then the sooner we get started, the better.'

And so, on the third day of their holiday, they had started practising on a pristine hotel bed decorated with origami towel swans. They practised all week; morning, night, and even sometimes in the afternoon after a brief siesta and even more cocktails. Only when they got home and back to the real world did they discover they hadn't been practising at all.

George arrived nine months and ten days after that once in a lifetime trip. His room had been painted and decorated a month before his due date and, despite knowing the gender, Sarah and Drew had gone for neutral colours; yellows, greens, and browns. Part of it was idealistic first-time parenting, so very conscious of not wanting to create any gender bias. The other part of it was practical parenting as they could keep it the same for the next one. They definitely wanted two. That had always been the plan. Although, perhaps not quite as quickly as they had imagined.

'How does that even happen?' Drew said, staring at the pair of blue lines on the testing stick, just eighteen months after George's arrival. 'I don't even remember having sex.'

'Your birthday, remember?' Sarah replied. 'Your mum took George for a couple of hours. We said we were going to go out for dinner, but in the end, we just got takeaway.'

'From the dodgy kebab shop.'

'That's it. And then your mum rang to say he'd fallen asleep, so she'd keep him for the night.'

Drew rubbed his temples in a circular motion.

'Do you think I have some kind of super sperm? For it to happen again that easily?'

Sarah gave him a look that suggested it was probably best if he stopped talking.

'Think of it this way,' Drew had said, wrapping his arms around her and trying to make amends for the super sperm comment. 'We always wanted two. Now we've got them. And on the bright side, this means, by the time we're in our mid-forties, they'll both be packed off to university, and we'll have the house to ourselves.'

'As long as we don't have any more,' Sarah replied.

'Don't worry,' Drew promised her. 'We are not having any more.'

The realisation that she was expecting yet again had occurred during their daughter, Eva's third birthday party. The carefully curated buffet of chicken nuggets, crisps, chocolate biscuits, and jelly sweets was perfect for sending children into sugar-crazed highs, although Sarah had also ensured a small plate of rapidly drying cucumber and carrot sticks took centre stage on the table, just so people wouldn't judge her parenting skills too harshly. As Drew hung up the birthday banner, she grabbed a chicken nugget. Two chews in, and she spat it out into her hand.

'Here,' she'd picked up another and handed it to Drew. 'Does this taste funny to you? I think they're off. Perhaps I can take them back to the shop. We can't give everyone food poisoning.'

'I don't think there's anything wrong with them.' Drew climbed off the chair and put two more in his mouth at once to prove his point. 'They taste fine to me.'

That was when she realized. Only twice in her life had Sarah not been able to stomach chicken nuggets, and both of those times, she'd been pregnant.

*Shit* was the only word that rattled around her head for the rest of the party. *Shit,* and every other expletive of a similar meaning. She wanted to wait, though. She wasn't going to tell Drew just yet. Not until she was certain.

Even when her period was late, she failed to accept what was going on. After all, she had a lot on her mind. She'd been trying to get into freelance translation again. It was an ambitious task, attempting to set up a website, emailing all her old contacts, brushing up on her German and Italian, all with a toddler on her heels all day. And periods could be late. Stress did that. Only when she attempted to fit into her biggest, pre-baby, pair of stretchy elasticated jeans, and discovered that they would no longer go up past her thighs, did she break down on the bedroom floor and, while unceremoniously weeping, announced to Drew that he was going to be a father again.

'I just don't see how we're going to cope,' she had sobbed into Drew's shoulder 'I can't do it, I can't. What if it happens again? What if I…? If it…'

'It will be fine.' Drew said, his shirt getting wetter and wetter by the second. 'You are going to be absolutely fine.' Though as she lifted her head, Sarah couldn't help but feel he looked unfeasibly pale as he spoke.

# CHAPTER 2

On the television, someone playing piano with only his elbows and toes was claiming he had *got talent* whilst a mean-spirited judging panel mocked and ridiculed him. Sarah put down her laptop and turned to Drew.

'I am so glad George is at school now,' Sarah said. 'I went to give Eva and him lunch on Sunday and realised it was nine-thirty. Nine-thirty in the morning, and it felt like I'd already done a full day.'

'Uh-huh.' Drew didn't look up from his phone as his fingers swiped at the screen.

'It's like they suck me into some kind of vortex. Like dog years, but in reverse.'

'Uh-huh.'

'Drew, are you even listening to me?'

'What … what's that?' He lifted his eyes momentarily, away from the screen.

There was no point trying to explain it to him, Sarah decided as she turned back to the television. He'd never say it, but Drew still thought that looking after the children day in day out was just one cushy game of knights and princesses, all fun and games. Despite the fact that he would need a two-hour nap after one afternoon with them. Now twenty-two weeks pregnant, she had managed the entire summer holidays on her own, dragging them from one playdate and outdoor playground to the next.

'Some days, I don't know why I bother,' she said, then with a heavy sigh, Sarah turned her thoughts back to the pages upon pages of unattainable dream houses. A moment later, she put her laptop down by her side and leaned back on the sofa.

'You okay?' Drew looked up from his phone for less than a second.

'Fine,' Sarah said, in a tone that clearly indicated otherwise. Drew carried on staring at his game. Sarah let the pause elongate between them. 'I just don't see how we're going to make it work, that's all.' She rested her hand on her bump. It wasn't really a bump, more an expansion of the belly she hadn't lost since the first two. 'I just don't know how we're going to make ends meet. We already have so much debt.'

'Everybody has debts, Sah.' Drew put his phone down and looked at her properly for the first time all night. 'And they're not real debts. Not like gambling debts or debts from crack-addiction, or bankruptcy. We have a mortgage and a car loan. That's what normal people have.'

'And two credit cards,' she added.

'That have hardly anything on them. Everyone has credit cards. Honestly, you are stressing about nothing.'

From upstairs came a familiar-sounding whimper. The

pair stopped the conversation, waiting to see if it died down. It didn't.

'Did you put a nappy on Eva?' Sarah shuffled herself onto her feet.

'She said she didn't need one. She just wanted to wear her knickers to bed.'

'And you let her?'

'She sounded pretty certain about it.'

'Brilliant. Just brilliant.'

Upstairs, she lifted Eva out of bed.

'You're soaked through.' She needlessly patted the pyjamas. 'Let's get you changed.'

Sarah pulled off her daughter's sodden underwear and chucked it into the washing basket, then stripped the bed and put the sheets straight in the washing machine.

They didn't have a clean set. George had managed to spill milk over his sheets two nights before, and he'd got the spare flowery set on his bed already. She had washed his cover, but the tumble drier had packed up, and it had been pouring with rain for the last two days, and there was nowhere in the house to hang things. As such, his recently-cleaned bedclothes spent two days festering and were now once again back in the washing machine.

She pulled a clean nappy up over her daughter's now dry behind.

'I guess this means you're in our bed tonight.'

After tucking a grumbling Eva into the bed, and padding out the sides with cushions, Sarah trundled downstairs, unable to contain her yawns. The night was a bust. She knew it. There was no chance Eva would stay down in their bed unless she or Drew were there with her. Even if she did, there wasn't much point in Sarah staying up. She had learned through the years that trying to translate a piece of High German when your brain was filled with thoughts of school holiday activities and credit cards was damn near impossible. Besides, Drew would probably end up putting on some unnecessarily gruesome film. What she needed was sleep. What she had needed for the last five years had been sleep.

'Are you okay to do George's school snacks for tomorrow?' she asked Drew from the doorway. 'I'm beat.'

'Course I can.' His eyes stayed down. 'Have we got some biscuits or something?'

'He's not allowed sugar, remember? We got the email last week. Fruit or vegetables only.'

'That sounds a bit militant.'

'Well, that's the rule. There are some grapes in the fridge, although they might have gone mouldy. If they're no good, there are some carrot sticks. The pre-cut ones were too expensive, I'm afraid. So you're going to have to peel them yourself.'

'I think I can cope with that.'

'Are you sure? I don't mind doing it.'

Finally, his eyes came up and met hers. 'Go to bed. I'll do it.'

With a grateful smile, she leaned forward to kiss him on the forehead, yawning again before she even made contact.

'Thank you. You're a star.'

'I won't be long,' Drew said as he put down his phone and picked up the television remote.

Almost every book Sarah had read about parenting made co-sleeping sound like the most comforting and rewarding thing a parent could do. Being snuggled up with your little one all night. Their gentle little breaths in your ear and the feel of their soft touch as they snuggled up against you. What bliss. What tenderness. What rubbish.

Every morning, Sarah expected to wake up to a black eye or a broken rib. Never, in the existence of mankind, could she have imagined this pint-sized child could need so much space to sleep. If it wasn't Eva's foot kicking her in the boobs, it was her tiny fist coming straight down on her jaw. And always her, never Drew. Never did Eva seem to heel him right in the groin. Sarah considered it a good job she didn't have to go to work anymore, as she had lost count of the number of split lips she had had. However, despite it all, she remained optimistic. Eva would grow out of it at some point. It wouldn't go on like this forever. Maybe tonight would be the night they all got a good night's sleep.

Upstairs in the bedroom, Sarah reached up and flicked the bedside light off, deciding she was too tired even to read. She pulled up the duvet, closed her eyes, and began to drift off. A fraction of a second later, one of Eva's fingers somehow went straight up her nose. Tonight, apparently, was not the night.

# CHAPTER 3

A bad night was followed by a worse morning. Eva was up before the crack of dawn, desperate to play dragons, a game in which the only actions involved her screaming, 'Dragon!' at the top of her voice and repeatedly whipping the duvet off the bed as she dived underneath it. And while George started the morning in his generally placid mood, it was only while pulling on his trousers that her phone beeped with a reminder message from the school.

*Book Day,* Sarah read from her screen, a sickening feeling rising its way up through her stomach. 'How the hell is it Book Day? Drew. Drew! Can you get Eva? She's unravelling the toilet roll again,' she said to nobody in particular.

Drew appeared at the top of the stairs. The last three years had seen him go from consistently clean-shaven to anywhere between light stubble and a full-grown beard. His hair had gone from short back and sides to some nondescript style, and his expression from one of eternal optimism to one who now took life with a heavy dose of scepticism.

'What's up?' he appeared at the top of the stairs. 'What can I do?'

'Stop Eva from blocking the toilet, for one. And work out what the hell I'm going to do for Book Day.'

'Book Day? On the second week of term?'

'Apparently so.'

Drew plucked the toilet roll out of Eva's grasp, which resulted in her dropping to the ground and hammering her hands and feet on the floor.

'Do you want me to have a look in the dressing-up box?' he asked, ignoring Eva's meltdown entirely.

'Yes, see what you can find. Anything will do. See if you can find him a striped jumper, and I'll send him as Where's Wally.'

'Do we have a striped jumper?'

'No idea.'

Minutes later, Drew returned with a Policeman's helmet and a pair of plastic handcuffs in his hand.

'Will these do?'

'Who's he going to go as? We need a character. We need to be able to say he's someone. Otherwise, they'll think we just picked some random outfit out of the dressing up box.'

'But we did. Can't we just say he's dressed up as PC Plod?'

'Is that a real character?'

'I don't know. Hang on a sec, I'll Google it.'

So as Sarah struggled to get a wriggling George out of his school trousers and into some blue tracksuit bottoms – while simultaneously stopping Eva from giving herself a concussion through her tantrum – Drew tapped away on his phone.

With George now dressed, next came the job of trying to

tame the children's unfeasibly frizzy hair into something remotely presentable. Of all the things to inherit, frizzy hair was, in Sarah's book, only one step above her Aunt Greta's moustache.

'What do you need me to do?' Drew held down Eva so Sarah could brush.

'You need to go. You don't want to miss your train.'

'I've got five minutes still. Tell me what to do to help.'

Sarah looked around at the chaos. Every day since Eva had been born, her life had been a manic rush from one place to the next, and yet it still managed to surprise her exactly how chaotic it was.

'Could you just grab his school bag and make sure his snacks are in it?'

'Sure. What snacks does he want?'

Sarah stopped with the hairbrush in mid-air. 'What do you mean, *what snacks?* The ones you made last night. The carrot sticks.'

Drew's eyes shifted from one side of the room to another. 'Shit,' he said.

Sarah's jaw locked. 'Please tell me you're joking.'

'It's fine. He can just take biscuits.'

'He's not allowed biscuits. Or crisps or any type of food we have in the house.'

'Surely we have some fruit or something?'

'Have you been shopping?'

'I thought —'

'It's fine.' Sarah returned to brushing Eva's hair with a newfound vigour. 'Just pick through the grapes. See if you can find a dozen that look remotely edible. I'm sure he can steal someone else's if he needs to. Philomena always has a full organic buffet with her.'

It took another ten minutes before Sarah had finally bundled Eva and a poorly dressed policeman into the back of the car. In George's backpack were the most insipid, wrinkled selection of grapes anyone had ever seen. It was just for one day, though, Sarah reminded herself. She would do some shopping in the afternoon. Just as soon as she'd washed the vomit and urine-soaked bed-sheets. And, she recalled with a shudder, survived toddler group.

Drew sat in his office. He'd only been at work for four hours, but it felt like he'd done three days straight. He rubbed his eyes and stared at the screen. This new programme was taking some getting used to. He'd worked as an analyst at Home Crew, an online supermarket, for seven years now, and each time he thought he had everything sussed, they would throw another spanner in the works, almost always in the form of a new operating system. What was it with the need to change computer programmes the minute the staff had got the hang of the old one? Who made these decisions? And who created these stupid platforms, with shortcuts that required you to hit five different keys in the exact right order to do one simple task? Did they ever think about asking the people who actually used the programmes what would make life easier? Maybe he'd retrain and become a programmer. Maybe that would be a solution to their money problems. Although, he had enough trouble trying to programme the washing machine, let alone anything more complicated. Besides, he still liked their little house. It was true, they didn't exactly have a lot of room to do things, but it was theirs, their family all snuggled together under one roof. Deep down, Sarah thought the same. He was sure of it.

Looking away from the screen, he pushed the heels of his hands into his eye sockets. He hated it. This wasn't where he imagined his life. Not yet, at least. He had thought there'd be more time for adventure. More time to spend outside with his children. And he was only at the beginning. He had another eighteen years of this to go at least.

A rap on the doorframe woke him from his thoughts.

'Good weekend, eh?' said a cheery face.

When Drew had started work at Home Crew, Barry had already been there five years. Surprisingly, well actually not that surprising when he really thought about it, Drew had been promoted ahead of him and had been moved out of a cubicle and into an office, which he wasn't convinced was any bigger than his previous cubicle. The shift in power had done little to change their relationship, the only real difference being that at least Drew now got paid for cleaning up Barry's messes. As such, he knew there was no point beating around the bush.

'What do you need, Barry?'

'Oh… well, now that you ask… I don't seem to be able to log on to that new platform. You know, the one we're meant to have sent through all our predictions on?'

'And you want me to come and show you?'

'Well, it's just —'

'Here.' Drew lifted himself off his seat and stepped back, clearing the pathway to his desk and computer. 'I'm already logged on. Just fill in your numbers on mine, and I'll sort the rest out.' He had learned over the years that it was easier to let Barry have five minutes at his computer than try and work out how the heck he had messed up the system on his again.

'Thanks boss.'

'No problem. And I'm not your boss. I'm just a junior supervisor.'

Two minutes later, Drew shuddered as he snuck a glance over Barry's shoulder while he tapped away at the screen. Already, Barry had managed to close two windows, open a dozen different tabs, and was about to open a game of solitaire.

'Why don't you just send your numbers to me in an email? I can input them for you.'

'No, no,' Barry continued to flash up one screen and then another. 'I'll just be a minute.'

Gritting his teeth, Drew stared out the office window that overlooked the dozen or so cubicles and tried not to think about how long he was going to have to spend sorting out whatever Barry had done. Or all the jobs that awaited him at home. He still had to put Eva's new toddler bed together so the baby could take her cot. Sarah was a thousand times better at those types of things than he was, particularly when it came to making sense of page after page of ridiculous instructions that all these things came with. Perhaps he would see if she wanted to put the bed together instead, but then again, judging by the mood she'd been in lately, perhaps he was better off doing it himself.

Only when a hand went up in front of the glass window did Drew realise he had been staring at the same point throughout the whole of his internal dialogue.

'Morning,' Polly mouthed from the other side of the glass.

Flushed, Drew raised his hand for a half-wave before hurriedly looking away.

Polly was one of three graduate interns at the company. Rumours had been rife that her position had been gained merely because her uncle was on The Board, but if there was any preferential treatment going on upstairs, Drew had seen no evidence of it. And there was certainly nothing about her work to give cause for complaint. It had only been a short time, but she was already far more on the ball than Barry. Besides, from what he had seen, her uncle, Casper Horton, didn't give preferential treatment to anyone.

'Men only say things like that when women are attractive,' Sarah had responded when Drew had first told her of the interest around his new intern. 'They can't possibly believe a woman can be both highly intelligent and highly attractive.'

'That's not true.'

'Well, is she?'

'Is she what?'

'Attractive?'

Drew had waved his head a little from side to side in a decidedly non-committal manner. 'Possibly.'

'See,' Sarah had replied. 'My point exactly. It would be so much easier for you men if intelligent women came packaged in frumpy tweed skirts and glasses.'

Slipping his hands around her waist, Drew had pulled Sarah in towards him.

'You're intelligent, and you're attractive.' He'd begun to nuzzle his nose into her neck, with thoughts of nuzzling other places coming to mind. 'Besides. I think you'd look good in a tweed skirt and glasses. My sexy secretary.' His lips had barely made contact with skin when she pushed him away.

'Really! That's really how you're going to objectify me?' She had stepped back and placed her hands on her hips. 'I have jobs to do, and so have you. The nappy bin hasn't been changed all week, and I need you to get all of George's old clothes out of the loft. I want to see if Eva fits into any of them now.'

Drew's arms had fallen to his sides in defeat. 'Oh, the glamour.'

'Thanks for that. I'm all done.' Barry's voice once again brought Drew back from his thoughts and into the office. 'Although, there's something going on with your screen. It appears to be flashing.'

Clenching his teeth as he forced a smile-cum-grimace on to his face, Drew nudged Barry out of his seat.

'No worries,' he sighed, wondering what Barry had managed to screw up now.

Barry smiled gratefully before stopping at the door. 'So, you coming for lunch?' he asked.

Monday's lunchtime fry-up had been a tradition at the Home Crew office for years. Thoughts of crispy bacon and fat sausages were the only thing that made getting out of bed on a Monday morning almost bearable. By the time twelve o'clock came around, Drew would be salivating ravenously.

'I'll meet you there,' Drew said to Barry as he watched the rest of the staff heading for the door. 'I just need to get some money out first.'

Having given up trying to fix the computer almost immediately, Drew left the building and turned right as he made the short walk up the road toward the ATM.

Dreaming of hash browns and fried mushrooms, Drew slipped his card into the machine. After a quick hesitation, he checked the balance then blinked repeatedly at the number on the screen. It was only the sixth of the month, he thought, checking his watch to make sure he hadn't unknowingly fallen into a coma for a fortnight. How could so much money have gone already? He took a moment to do a quick scan of purchases in his head. There were the new shoes that George had needed, and Sarah's car had had to go in for a service. They'd also taken his mother out for her birthday. But could those things really have made such a dent? Feeling decidedly less hungry, he selected a small amount of cash, took back his card, and headed over to the greasy spoon.

The rest of them had taken over their normal table in the corner where the waiter was already taking their orders.

'Just in time,' Barry said as Drew pulled out a chair and took his place. 'I ordered you a full English and an Americano.'

Drew glanced at the menu on the table. The place was good value, with a full fry up for a tenner. And while it didn't quite reach the standard of *legendary*, as was written in several places on the menu, it was damn good. Normally, he didn't think about the cost. Ten pounds was hardly a lot to spend on lunch, especially when it was only once a week. However, if you took into account the bank balance he had just seen, it *was* a lot of money. Particularly with over three weeks to go until their next payday. He could just imagine Sarah's face when she found out how much he'd spent on one meal for himself.

'Actually,' he grabbed the waiter's attention before he could leave. 'Could you swap one of those full Englishs for a bacon sandwich?'

'Course, no problem.'

'What?' Barry looked at him with disgust. 'Are you wimping out on me?'

'I'm just not that hungry. I had a big breakfast with the kids this morning,' he lied.

'But we always have a fry up.'

'Next time. Really. I just don't think I could eat it.'

'Well, don't try stealing any of my hash browns,' someone else around the table said.

Drew forced out a laugh. He was going to have to come up with another excuse for next week's outing.

CHAPTER 4

Toddler group had been an unmitigated disaster.
After dropping PC Plod off at the school amid a
myriad of perfect Harry Potters and Wimpy Kids,
Sarah drove the car back home and transferred Eva into her
pushchair. At three, she was just about old enough to walk
the mile journey there and back, but that meant going at
such a lethargic pace that the local OAPs would be tutting
behind her on the pavement trying to get her to speed up.
Plus, given how much they had paid to get the car serviced
already this month, she'd rather they never used it again.

The walk there was brisk and pleasant, and exactly what
Sarah needed to clear her head a little, although sadly, her
optimism didn't last long.

Eva was on form in the worst possible way. Continuing on
from the toilet roll mayhem of the morning, she decided to
start the day by stealing everyone's toys at toddler group and
then screaming like a banshee with a throat infection at
anyone who tried to get the items back off her. She snatched
another child's drink box, and then proceeded to squeeze the

juice all over the table and said child. During the 10 seconds in which Sarah thought her daughter was actually behaving, Eva was using a permanent marker to add a little decoration to the newly painted walls.

All of this was made a thousand times worse by the fact that Justine Simmons was watching it all.

Sarah had first encountered Justine at her antenatal classes with George, and no matter how much she tried, she just couldn't bring herself to like the woman. Justine was one of those women for whom everything arrived on a silver platter. Her hair was perfect, her figure was perfect, her skin was smoother than that of an antique porcelain doll, and her teeth could put any Hollywood A-lister to shame. You went camping in Snowdonia, she went trekking in the Himalayan foothills. You took the kids to the zoo, she took hers on a bespoke, environmentally-sustainable safari, where incidentally, she helped rescue an orphan baby elephant from a mudslide. And if you managed to find a nice dress, which you actually felt reasonably attractive in, then you could guarantee that Justine would wear the exact same one as you to the same party and look a thousand times better than you did. It had happened twice now.

Her husband, Hugh, like Drew, worked up in London, although he worked in finance and was easily able to maintain their family lifestyle of exotic holidays, mani-pedis, and designer outfits. As such, it had come as a huge shock to Sarah when Justine enrolled her eldest, Philomena, in the same local primary as George.

'Honestly, with the way some of these private schools are growing, there's hardly any difference in class sizes. Then you add in the commute, and we'd obviously need help with the long school holidays. It just doesn't seem worth it at this age. Of course, they don't have the same range of peripatetic teachers in the state sector, but we can compensate for that.'

Sarah nodded mutely, wondering if peripatetic was a word she was supposed to know the meaning of.

'This means I'll have to see her every day,' she had said to Drew that evening as she'd wept into her glass of wine. 'Every day. Forever. What have I done to deserve this? School plays, parents' evenings. Everything.'

'It won't be forever,' Drew assured her. 'Doesn't primary school only last for seven years?' What she would give to swap lives for just a day.

Less than fifteen seconds after Sarah had managed to yank the permanent marker out of Eva's hand, Justine appeared at her side.

'It's so difficult when they're like this, isn't it?' Her hair was clipped back in a perfectly coiffed manner and would have looked more in place on a film set than in an environment where it was at constant risk of attacks from anything from PVA glue to pine cones. 'Demetrius has been going through a terrible phase, too, if I'm honest. Sometimes, I don't know how I get through it.'

Sarah glanced across the room to where the two-year-old was sitting perfectly, making pasta necklaces, in exactly the same manner he had been doing for the last forty minutes. In fact, the only time Sarah had seen him move was when he lifted his hand, to ask in the politest way imaginable if he could 'possibly have a small glass of water, please?'

Sarah grunted her response. 'Hopefully, they'll grow out of it soon,' Sarah said. 'I don't ever remember George being like this.'

'It's the second child. They just need so much more Are you sure she gets enough attention? It's so easy to neglect one and focus your attention on the other. We all do it. Last night, I was so preoccupied with Philomena's spellings, that I actually cooked Demetrius whole wheat pasta. With gluten! Can you imagine?'

'No,' said Sarah flatly. 'I couldn't.'

'Well.' Justine flashed her luminous teeth. 'I'm always here if you need to talk. You know what they say, a problem shared is a problem halved.'

'That's very kind,' Sarah said through gritted teeth and a forced smile. 'I'll bear that in mind.'

By the time it was over, Sarah and Eva were equally exhausted. Toward the end, the little girl's whines had risen an octave in pitch, and she could barely walk for rubbing her eyes and yawning. All Sarah had to do was make sure that Eva didn't fall asleep in the pushchair on the way home. That way, she would get a solid two hours to get all her jobs done, including two loads of washing, writing the shopping list for the week, and replying to at least one email about the possibility of a book translation job.

As she wheeled the buggy out of the hall, Sarah glanced up at the sky. The weather was perfect for the walk back. A little overcast, but at least the chill woke them both up a little. Sarah refused to be one of those mums who wore workout gear everywhere she went, mainly due to the hypocrisy. She would be hard pushed to count one aqua aerobics session and two yoga classes over the past five years as a regular fitness regime. There were now two levels of hips where there used to be only one, and bulges in places she was sure shouldn't bulge.

With George, she had felt so great being pregnant, and even with Eva, she had had her good days. But with this bump, she felt terrible. Her growing belly, her veiny legs, and the grey hairs that infiltrated the once uniformly brown ones. Every day, there would be another one. She was in her late twenties for crying out loud; what kind of woman in their twenties had grey pubes?

Sarah was busy thinking about stray grey hairs and whether she should just take the plunge and dye them all when Eva's pushchair bumped awkwardly.

'Please don't do that, Eva.' Sarah said, assuming her daughter was kicking the footrest the way she normally did. She pushed on the handlebars to resume their journey. Nothing moved.

'Not again,' she groaned and moved around to the front to have a proper look. The front left wheel was now pointing a full seventy degrees in another direction to all of the rest of them. Sarah gave it a quick kick before trying to push again. The back wheels lifted up, while the front ones stayed fixed to the ground. Eva flew forward.

'Shit!' Sarah lunged forward and caught her daughter before she hit the gravel. She kicked the wheel again, harder. Still, the buggy refused to move.

'Oh, for crying out loud. You have to be kidding me.' She tried again and again, but each time, the same thing happened. The dodgy wheel was now acting as the strongest brake in the entire history of pushchairs.

She was still busy hammering the wheel with the heel of her hand when a brand new SUV drew up behind them and the driver beeped the horn.

'See you at pick up time,' Justine called through her open window before doing her best impression of the Royal wave.

'See you at pick up time,' Sarah said with her most perfect smile. As the SUV drove away, her smile dropped and was replaced by two middle fingers in the air.

In the end, Sarah managed to lift the pushchair, with Eva inside, over to the path, where she got down on her knees to try and see a way to fix it from down there. Perfect, she thought to herself. This is exactly how I thought I'd spend my life; twenty-two weeks pregnant and crawling on the floor trying to fix a cheap bloody pushchair wheel. Then, just to add insult to injury, it started to rain.

In the end, the only option she had was to take Eva out and force her to walk while she carried the broken pushchair beneath her arm. For the most of the way, Eva screamed, mostly from tiredness, but occasionally because of Sarah swinging around without thinking and accidentally clobbering her in the head.

'I don't want to walk. I want the car. I want the car!' she screamed at what seemed like a thousand decibels.

'We don't have the car, sweetie,' Sarah repeated for the umpteenth time.

'I want the car.'

'So do I, my love. So do I.'

Nearly an hour later, and with a soaking wet toddler so tired she was practically sleepwalking, Sarah finally opened her front door.

The extra time it had taken with Eva walking resulted in further disasters for the rest of the day. Eva, understandably, collapsed on the sofa the moment they got in the house, meaning – due to the close proximity to the washing machine and Eva's supersonic bat hearing – Sarah still couldn't put the dirty washing on. The shopping, which Sarah had planned on buying hadn't happened due to Eva's extended nap, meaning that when Eva did eventually wake up, there was no food in the house. After rummaging through the back of every cupboard, Sarah finally managed to find a packet of breadsticks –she deliberately avoided looking at the sell-by date – and a tin of sweetcorn, which Eva scattered everywhere from the kitchen to the downstairs toilet. By that point, it was time to pick up George. Sarah rang Drew before she left.

'Hey, what's up?' he said the moment he answered.

'A lot. I don't suppose you could do a quick shop on the way home, could you? I haven't managed to get it done, and I honestly don't think I could face it with the pair of them.'

'What do you need?'

'Everything. I'll send you a list. Bread, cereal, milk. And do we have a screwdriver?'

'You want me to pick up a screwdriver?'

'Only if we don't already have one.'

'We've probably got one in the garage somewhere. What do you need it for?'

'The pushchair. The front wheel's gone again.'

A sigh rattled down the line. 'I told you we should have got a new one.'

'Really? With what money?' Sarah could feel her tone sharpening. She closed her eyes and took a deep breath in. 'I'll send you a text, okay? If you can just pick up whatever you can carry. I'll take the car tomorrow and do a big shop. Or I can go tonight, and you put the kids to bed if that's easier?'

'Whatever you think's best. Don't worry, I'll get enough stuff to get us through tonight. Just send me the list. Oh, there might a screwdriver under the sink. Although I can have a look at the pushchair when I get home if you want.'

A slight pause lingered down the line during which Sarah tried to work out if there was a polite way of saying that their twenty-two-week-old unborn foetus was probably more naturally inclined at DIY than her husband. Fortunately, he got the message in the silence.

'Maybe it's just best if I leave it to you,' he said.

'I'll see you later.'

# CHAPTER 5

D rew hated supermarkets. Hated them. He hated the fact that things were never in the aisle you thought they should be in. He hated the fact that the chillers were so cold you felt like you needed to dress for winter. And he hated the fact that people happily rammed their trollies this way and that way with no regard for who was standing in front of them. If you tried that in a car, you'd get sent to prison, or at the very least, lose your licence. But try it at Tesco, and no one bats an eyelid. Fines for irresponsible trolley drivers. That's what they needed.

Sarah had, as promised, sent through a shopping list. It was fairly standard; milk, cereal, beige freezer food – perhaps not the most useful instruction – a bag of salad – which he was certain would be left in the fridge until the leaves began decomposing at the bottom of the bag – fragrance-free wet wipes, and a few other sundries. At the entrance to the shop, he moved to grab a trolley, only to change his mind and pick up a basket instead. After all, the list wasn't that long. Two rows in, and he was regretting the decision. The thin plastic handle dug into his fingers as he tried to fit everything into the tiny basket. It was the message's fault. The comment about freezer food had stumped him. *Did pizza count as beige freezer food?* he asked himself. The bottom of it was beige. He picked one off the shelf and threw it in the basket. What about spring rolls? They were definitely beige. Inside and out. He scanned up and down the cabinet and picked up a few extras, such as spicy chicken kievs and mixed vegetables. Satisfied with his haul, he moved on to the cereal.

When George had first started weaning, as conscientious parents, he and Sarah had been so picky about what he ate. No processed food. Organic where possible and always made from scratch. There was a full checklist to go through, including salt content and country of origin, before deciding whether or not a certain item was allowed to pass between their precious baby's lips. Now there was only one criterion on that checklist; would they eat it?

'Why the hell do they need so many cereals?' Drew wondered out loud as he looked at the rainbow display ten feet long. It seemed like every animal on the planet had been turned into an advertisement for sugary breakfast treats. Some, of course, he recognized; Tony the Tiger had probably been around longer than he had, and then there was that monkey on the chocolate cereal. But now there was everything else too. Mermaid cereal, unicorn cereal. Cereal with frogs on. How did frogs sell cereal? Were children really so fickle?

His eyes wandered up and down until they fell on a large red label.

*Two for one,* it said.

'Perfect.' The boxes were already fairly cheap, but with

the two for one deal, it was a bargain that even Sarah would be pleased with. Feeling smug with his accomplishment, Drew dropped two boxes onto the top of his already full basket and headed towards the checkout.

The evening air was cool and crisp on his walk back from the shop. Summer was giving way to autumn. He strolled easily now, with the shopping more evenly distributed across two hands and a couple of the tins in his backpack, taking in the aromas and enjoying the quiet. It wasn't very often he got two minutes to himself like this. He had the commute, of course, although he often wished he could use the time more productively. People tapped away at their computers, firing off emails or else doing something equally productive; he could barely keep his eyes open. Occasionally, he would just grab one of the free magazines to flick through. That was about all he had the energy for.

He turned onto their road and gazed up at the street. Narrow, with minimal parking and dubious calibre of neighbours, it wasn't the ideal location to live in, but it wasn't all bad. There were great transport links to start with. And it was easy. What would be the point in moving somewhere bigger? A bigger mortgage that he'd have to pay. More space to fill up with crap. No, they had it good where they were.

'Why are you so late?' Sarah was on him the moment he stepped through the front door, without him even having a chance to put the bags down.

'I went to the shops, remember? You asked me to pick some things up.'

'What shops did you go to? I thought you'd be quick. And how much did you buy?'

'Just the things on the list. That's all.'

Her hands were currently juggling a collection of dirty plates, cuddly toys, and washing.

'Can you stop George chewing on the wrong end of that pencil?' she asked, taking the bags and hauling them into the kitchen before he'd had a chance to object.

'Is there a right end of a pencil to chew on?' Drew called after her, removing the offending item from his son's mouth.

'The one that doesn't give him lead poisoning.'

'You know it's not actually lead?' he said, wiping the pencil dry and placing it out of his George's reach on the bookshelf. 'And I'm pretty sure the other end would be worse if you got splinters.'

'For Christ sake, Drew!'

'It's fine. I've done it.' He looked at his daughter, who was currently taking very precise deep breaths in an attempt to stay calm. 'What's wrong with Eva?'

'We've lost Mrs Cat.'

Drew's eyes widened. A swell of panic surged through him. 'What do you mean, lost her? Where did she have her last? Have you looked in her bedroom? She can't go to sleep without Mrs Cat. She won't go to bed without her.'

'I am aware of that.'

'Where have you looked?' Memories of the last time Mrs Cat had gone AWOL flashed through Drew's mind. Punching and biting and wailing until sunrise.

'I've looked everywhere that I had a chance to look.' Sarah said as she came out of the kitchen, arms overflowing with a mass of toys and clutter. 'Please, can you just take her upstairs for a minute? Read her a story or something. Just give me a minute to sort myself out, and I'll find it.'

'Are you sure you don't want me to look instead?'

'No. Can you just take them both upstairs and get them into their pyjamas? I'll be up in a bit.'

'What about putting the shopping away?'

'I'll deal with that when I've found Mrs Cat.'

After hesitating just a fraction longer, Drew bent down and picked up Eva.

'Come on, you two.' He reached his spare hand down to George. 'Time for Daddy to pick a book.'

With Drew having taken the children upstairs, Sarah retraced Eva's steps since they had got back from picking George up from school. After a snack on the sofa, they got the LEGO out. That play had lasted nicely for twenty minutes, before Eva decided she had to have every red and blue brick, which George also desperately needed to complete his ice castle. After a close call with an irate Eva and the mantelpiece, Sarah sent George upstairs with his own selection of LEGO bricks and kept Eva down with her while she tried to sort out the washing. That, she realised, was the last time she had seen Mrs Cat.

Sarah walked through the kitchen and clicked open the washing machine door. There, dripping wet and twisted between a tangle of bedsheets, was Mrs Cat.

'That's the first part of the problem solved,' she said to the sodden, stuffed feline. 'Now to get you dry.'

She probably spent longer using the hairdryer on Mrs Cat than she had needed to, but there was something relaxing about the white noise and its ability to drown out whatever bangs and wails were going on next door in the children's room. It wasn't a productive use of time, and she contemplated that fact several times. However, after each brief consideration, she kept on going. She should dry her hair more often, she thought. Twice a day, at least. After all, Drew had his commute in which to simply sit and be. An exquisite hour on either side of the workday that was entirely his own, where he didn't have to worry about what was going on at work or at home or anywhere else in the world. Maybe she would make hair drying her commute equivalent. God only knew she needed something. When Mrs Cat was nearly dry, Sarah moved her over to the radiator and headed down to the kitchen to unpack the shopping.

'How's the soggy moggy doing?' Drew asked, appearing in the doorway. 'Any chance Eva will be able to take her to bed tonight?'

'Probably. It just needs another half hour on the radiator.'

'Thank God. You know, I really think we should get a spare one of those, you know, in case we lose it for real?'

'We did that with the penguins for George, remember? They cost us a fortune, and now he doesn't even look at either of them.'

'True, but that was George. Eva's really attached…'

Sarah had stopped listening. Bent double over the shopping bag, she scrunched her face at the contents. She reached in and pulled out a cardboard box of cereal.

'Fyberflakes?' she questioned. 'Why did you get Fyberflakes?'

'You told me to get cereal.'

'Yes. Cereal. Cereal our children will eat.'

'They'll eat this, won't they?'

'No.' Sarah crinkled up her nose and scratched her eyebrows. How was it possible to miss the mark by such a large degree? 'They will not eat Fyberflakes.'

'Have they ever had them?'

'Of course not.'

'So, they might enjoy them?'

Sarah pinched the bridge of her nose.

'They won't eat the edge on crustless bread because they think it's too dry.'

'Well, there'll be milk on it, so it won't be that dry, will it? They're not going to eat them without milk on.'

'Did you get milk?'

Drew's lips disappeared into a flat line from which his tongue protruded ever so slightly.

'Great,' Sarah huffed. 'So not only have we now got a box of cereal that nobody will eat –'

'But it was two for one,' implored Drew, desperately trying to defend his choice.

'Oh, I see. Well, that makes all the difference. So not only do we have two boxes of cereal that nobody will eat, I've still not got any milk for Eva in the morning.'

She pulled on her coat and grabbed her keys from the bowl by the door.

'Are you heading out? Where are you going?'

Sarah rubbed her forehead with the palm of her hand. 'I'm going to get milk, where else would I be going? And cereal.'

'Do you want me to go?'

Sarah moved her eyes from the Fyberflakes to her husband and back again.

'No,' she said. 'I don't.'

As she moved to pass him, her eyes fell on the second shopping bag. She stopped and inhaled deeply. 'You bought spring rolls?'

'You said to get beige freezer food?'

There were no words.

CHAPTER 6

Getting out of the house on her own felt good. While it pained Sarah to spend yet more money, she decided to get the bumper family pack of cereal, on the account that it would save money in the long run. After picking up four pints of milk and having a quick rummage through the reduced section, she made her way to the checkout via the wine aisle.

'Oh, how I miss you,' she spoke aloud as she stared longingly at the bottles of Pinot Noir and Merlot. Several of her friends had continued to drink while pregnant. In fairness, she had had the odd glass too in those first three months when she was living in complete denial. But there was always so much guilt associated with it. After a sad sniff goodbye, she ambled down the aisle and stopped in front of the selection of non-alcoholic beers, picking up the cheapest bottle she could see. Even in a glass, it looked insipid. Besides, there was no way she could justify spending three pounds fifty on one bottle of lager, particularly when it was bound to taste like dishwater. With another heavy sigh, she planted it back on the shelf and turned back around to her trolley.

'Oh, I do not blame you.'

Perfectly even eyeliner, a pair of meticulously curated eyebrows, and skin with fewer pores than a marble bath blocked the way. 'I couldn't stand that stuff. Honestly, when Philomena was born, the first thing I did was crack open a bottle of Moet. Really, the very first thing. I was still in the birthing tub. It's the way all the Europeans do it. Fortunately, Anton goes over to Paris every couple of months. They have a much better range of non-alcoholic beers. They got me through my pregnancy with Demetrius. Honestly, the French just know how to do these things better, don't you think? Not that I'd go through it a third time. My goodness, I think you're insane. In the nicest possible way, of course.' Justine emitted a high-pitched laugh, which rippled down Sarah's spine.

'Justine, how funny bumping into you here.'

'It is, isn't it? You know what it's like. Sometimes you just need to pop out for a few of those last-minute necessities.'

Sarah's lips tightened as she glanced in Justine's trolley; a selection of organic cheeses, a bottle of champagne, and another bottle of wine with an ochre-coloured label, clearly costing well over the maximum six-pound limit Sarah allowed them to spend on wine, even when they were celebrating. There was also a pack of smoked salmon, a jar of artichoke hearts, and an expensive box of chocolates.

'Have you got a special evening planned?' she said, nodding to contents that looked like perfect dinner party accompaniments.

'Oh goodness no, just the usual. Anton's away again next

week, so we like to make the most of the time we get together. You know how it is. Once the children are asleep.' Justine gave an exaggerated wink. 'You have to keep the marriage alive, don't you?'

'Oh yes, quite.' Sarah recalled the night before of internet browsing and computer game playing. Her marriage was still alive, just in a borderline comatose type of way. 'Well.' She shuffled through the gap between Justine's trolley and the wine racks, trying not to hit either with her bump en route. 'I'd better be getting home. George will be waiting to read me a bedtime story.'

'Really? At this time?' Justine lifted a perfectly plucked eyebrow. 'You know, I admire your ability to be fluid as a parent. If mine ever stay up this late, I just don't know what I'd do. I need my me time. It's selfish, I know, but it keeps me sane. I admire you so much for throwing out the idea of routines like that.'

'Yes. That's us. Just throwing our routines to the wind.' Sarah made to move before hesitating. In one graceful turn, she twisted around, picked two insipid looking non-alcoholic beers off the shelf, and popped them in the trolley. That was throwing something to the wind. Most probably their bank balance.

'Did they go down okay?' Sarah called through from the kitchen as she put away a selection of more sensible, kid-friendly freezer food.

'George is still waiting to read you a story,' Drew called

back. 'And Eva wanted double milk then asked to go to bed without a nappy on, so I said that was fine.'

Sarah burst into the living room, dropping the cereal boxes on the floor as she went. 'You are joking, aren't you?'

A cheeky grin twisted on Drew's lips. 'You see,' he said. 'I do listen sometimes.'

'Very funny.'

When all the stories were read, and Sarah had checked Eva's nappy for potential leaks – just because Drew put it on, it didn't mean he put it on properly – she headed downstairs and collapsed on the sofa.

'Sorry I got stressed about the food,' she said as she lifted her legs up onto the sofa and placed them on Drew's lap. 'It's just another expense. Another load of wasted money, gone on nothing.'

'It's not wasted,' Drew assured her, as he put down his phone and began to rub the soles of her feet. 'I'll eat the cereal.'

'You don't like cereal.'

'I'm sure it's not bad.'

Sarah smiled gratefully before leaning back, closing her eyes and trying to find a delicate way to start the conversation she wanted to have.

'I know what you said before,' she started. 'But I was thinking about it again, and I think you should ask your parents for a loan.' His eyes rolled before she'd even finished her sentence. 'Please listen to me.'

'Sorry, but there's no point. I'm not doing it, Sarah.'

She gritted her teeth against the use of her full, two-syllable name. She was always *Sah* to Drew unless he was about to say something she didn't want to hear.

'Why not? What's wrong with just asking?'

'Because we don't need it. We're perfectly all right as we are.'

Sarah clenched her jaw and reminded herself that hitting him over the head with a saucepan was not a good idea, no matter how it felt at that exact moment.

'We are not fine, Drew. We are cramped. We are cramped and miserable, and that's with four of us. When this thing is born, we're going to have even less room. You know they've got plenty of money. Just ask.'

'I'm not asking them for a loan,' Drew said. 'And will you please stop calling our baby a thing?'

'I will stop calling it a thing when it stops being a thing. Right now, that is what it is. A thing, draining all my energy, stopping me from eating all my favourite things in life, and leaving me scared witless of what it is going to put me through. I could call it a parasite if you'd rather? That would work fine.'

Drew grunted into his beer. 'Thing is fine.'

She took his hands and forced him around to face her. 'I know you don't want to do this, but please, can you think about it? For me? I feel like I don't know who I am anymore, other than the mum who does really terrible costumes for Book Day. I used to want to write books, now I barely even have time to read them.'

'You'll find the time again soon.'

'Will I? When? When will I get a chance? When will I go back to work or do something for me? When will I stop having to come second to everybody else?'

It was an unfair question, and she knew it. Drew did what he could. She just needed him to appreciate her a bit more, that was all. Appreciate what it was she was going through day in, day out.

'Look, do you want to put a film on?' Drew suggested, sitting up, snuggling into her shoulder, and completely ignoring the questions she had lambasted him with. 'You can pick.'

Sarah considered the idea momentarily, before shaking her head. 'No. I'll just end up falling asleep. I'll head to bed a bit early and read my book for a while instead.'

After kissing Drew good night, Sarah trundled upstairs. As quietly as she could, she pushed the door open and peered in on the children. If this was a film, Sarah thought while watching her little ones spread eagle on the bed, the loving mother would go into the room, kiss the children gently, pull the blankets over them and tuck them tightly in. However, this was real life, and she had quickly learned that any act that involved the possibility of waking them up was utter stupidity. So instead, she pulled the door closed and headed into her own room. She was asleep before she had even read half a chapter.

# CHAPTER 7

Drew was feeling less than pristine the following morning. He paced the platform, waiting for the train to arrive so he could sit down and sort himself out. He had slept well enough, got out of bed with his alarm, and the kids had been reasonably cooperative while getting dressed. Eva had been in an exceptionally giggly mood, and while George had insisted on wearing his sister's pink unicorn socks to school as they were hidden under trousers – meaning his sister wouldn't notice – Drew decided there wouldn't be anything wrong with that. In general terms, most of the morning had gone far smoother than usual. The problem was with the cereal.

It was now evident why Fyberflakes breakfast cereal was not only on offer but also cheap to begin with. Fyberflakes, Drew was now aware, tasted of nothing except pure, unadulterated dryness. Every mouthful was like having all the moisture sucked directly from his mouth and tongue, made worse by the fact that every half-filled spoonful lasted approximately

200 chews. Only two spoonfuls in, and his jaw had started to seize up. But Sarah had been watching him with her hawk eyes since the moment he poured his overly generous helping, so he'd had no choice but to finish it. Still, there was no way he could eat two boxes of the stuff. Not a chance. He would have to start putting them in the outside bin when she wasn't home.

On the platform, the tannoy dinged above him. His train was on time too. At least that was another good thing. Grabbing one of the free papers as he boarded, Drew selected a seat at the back of one of the carriages. He sorted out his backpack and checked his phone before settling into the seat and flicking open the magazine.

Despite the image of an OAP in suspenders and a leather corset being at the centre of the double-page spread, it was the title of the article upon which he opened that caught Drew's eye.

*Naughty Nanny makes 10K a Month* was written in a bold font that crossed the double page. Naughty Nanny dressed in a black leather ensemble winked at the camera. 'Ridiculous,' he said, starting to turn the page to find an article on the housing situation in London. Hesitating, he cast a quick eye around him before turning back to Naughty Nanny and beginning to read. His immediate feeling of absurdity at the title began to change into something else. Ten grand a month. That was an unthinkable amount of money. And it certainly sounded like Naughty Nanny had more fun making ends meet than Drew did.

As they passed stop after stop, Drew read the article twice, word for word, including all the picture captions. And the end of the second read, he took one more lingering gaze at the image before rolling the paper up and slipping it into his backpack. It was brilliant, he thought, leaning back in his seat. Perfect. This would give Sarah everything she wanted; financial security, a chance to explore her creative side again, and an ability to forge an identity for herself away from the children. All day long, he was buzzing at the thought of telling her his new master plan. She would love it.

'Are you insane?' During the split second of silence that followed, Sarah considered if there was anything else she should add to the comment, but it seemed to sum up her thoughts succinctly enough, so she said it again with only a minor addition. 'Are you *completely* insane?'

Drew stood in the kitchen, the top buttons of his work shirt undone, his tie loose, and the newspaper in his hand, clearly unable to respond. Rolling her eyes, Sarah simultaneously shook her head and massaged the small of her back. It had been a frustrating day, to put it mildly.

With her house now smelling continually of damp and certain that some form of toxic mould was quite likely lurking in the paintwork, she had tried to rectify the broken tumble drier situation by finding a second hand one online. Despite her low expectations that she would find anything within a reasonable distance, it took only a few minutes of searching the internet to discover exactly what she was after only a couple of streets down.

'Come on, Eva,' she'd dragged Eva away from her mid-morning bowl of cereal, despite it being only half-finished. 'Let's go. The nice lady with the tumble drier said she's only going to be home for twenty minutes, so we need to move.'

Still pulling Eva's coat on as they had walked out the front door, Sarah raced around to the house. However, when she arrived, she quickly discovered that the nice lady's tumble drier was in no better condition than her own.

'I thought you said it was working? It says in the advert it is working.'

'Well, it could work,' the woman had shrugged. 'You just need to get it fixed.'

'If it was that simple, don't you think I would have done that with my own?' Sarah had seethed.

The owner shrugged again.

Back home again, with forty minutes of her day completely wasted, Sarah attempted to get on with the housework. Eva trundled along behind her, *helping*, which ostensibly meant creating a wake of destruction, pulling clothes out of the drawers, and plastering sticky fingerprints over clean surfaces. Essentially, undoing all of Sarah's hard work. The day went from bad to worse when she picked up George from school. With his bag strapped to his shoulders, he thrust an A5 paper notice into her hand.

'Someone's got nits,' he had announced proudly. 'We all have to shampoo our heads.'

'Why do you all have to do it? Surely just the person with nits should have to do it?'

'We all have to do it. That's what the teacher said.'

Sure enough, the letter clearly stated that it was the new school policy. All children to be treated for lice on the discovery of an infestation. It also went through the procedure of what you were expected to do if your child was found to have nits, including contacting the school nurse and ensuring they were not sent into school until the situation had been fully rectified. 'Great. More money.'

After a back and forth debate in her head, and a thorough scour of George's scalp, Sarah was still undecided about forking out ten pounds unnecessarily on nit lotion when her phone vibrated.

*Need a break from work. Come for coffee.*

After three years as university housemates, Nelly was the closest thing Sarah had to a sister.

'Try not to break anything. And if you need the toilet, make sure you flush it properly,' Sarah had warned as she pulled up outside the only individualistic house on an estate of three hundred carbon copy new builds. 'And we are not staying for food, so don't even start asking.'

'Pretty. It's so pretty.' Eva clapped her hands at the rainbow-coloured fence outside her car window.

'Why doesn't our fence look like that?' George asked, climbing out of his car seat and grabbing his LEGO action figures. 'Our fence is rubbish.'

A small smile curled on the corner of Sarah's lips. It was a truly spectacular fence, perfectly painted in a full array of colours. There was also a wide variety of garden gnomes, in various undignified postures, occupying the small patch of grass that was their front garden, and a large welcome mat saying, *I like it dirty*, outside the front door.

'I like to think of it as in-law repellent,' Nelly had told Sarah on her very first visit to the house.

'In-law repellent?'

'Uh-huh. They said they'd only lend us the money for a deposit it we moved to somewhere around here. They're a three-minute walk away, you see. When we moved in, they were doing my nut in, popping in whenever they fancied it. Even got themselves a bloody key cut.'

'So you painted your fence?'

'Genius, right? It's the effect of the whole vibe, really. They're terrified of being seen here. That mat worked a treat too. Now they're seriously worried we could be swingers.'

Sarah had chuckled to herself. No matter how bad her day seemed, at least she had never gone to those kinds of extremes to avoid people.

'Ask your dad,' Sarah said to George, unclipping an orange gate and pushing the children past a pair of fornicating gnomes. 'Ask him if he'll paint it for you.'

'But dad can't paint anything.'

'Then I guess you're stuck.'

'Do you want a drink?' Nelly said as Sarah took off Eva's coat and hung it with hers on the back of an armchair.

'I'd love one.'

Nelly disappeared into the kitchen, returning a few minutes later with two mugs of tea and a selection of nibbles on a garish pink plastic plate which she placed on the table next to a pile of magazines. Sarah glanced at one of the cover stories; *I married my uncle, now my child is my cousin.* For all Nelly's intelligence, and the fact she managed to run her own successful graphic design business out of her spare bedroom, she did have the trashiest taste in magazines.

'I've only got plastic plates. Jeff and I are both boycotting the washing up. Until one of us caves, it's like we are on a permanent picnic.'

George was busily helping his LEGO figures torment Nelly's cat, and Eva was sitting in front of the iPad, playing on a German-language game that Drew had downloaded for her. Sarah was a hundred percent certain not a single word of it was going in – and currently, the only German word Eva had picked up was a very aggressive, very determined sounding, *nein* – but it made her feel less of an awful parent than when she just let her watch YouTube.

'God, I can't wait till I can have a real drink again,' Sarah said as she put down her tea and helped herself to a second biscuit. 'What kind of person advertises a broken tumble drier as working?'

'Someone who is too cheap or too lazy to get it removed.'

'I really hate people sometimes.' She took another bite. 'And I got a triple dose of Justine yesterday. School gates, toddler group, and the supermarket in the evening. Do you think she'd have me arrested if I slapped her?'

'Depends what she'd said.'

'I don't think she'd have to say anything, to be honest.'

'Go for it. I'll be right behind you.'

Sarah laughed and cast her eye over at Eva and George.

'So how are you and Jeff doing now?' Sarah asked, having finished her second biscuit and reaching down for her tea. 'Are things any better?'

Nelly half shrugged, half nodded.

'He's trying. I'm trying. I've been making an effort not to

spend so much time working when he gets home, and he has agreed to try and get home a little earlier. We've made a list of chores too, so we both know what needs doing around the house.' She gestured toward the plastic plate. 'As you can see that is going brilliantly.'

A slight pause interrupted the conversation.

'So,' Nelly sat back in her seat, smile firmly back on her face; every indication needed to show that the conversation about her flailing marriage was over. 'What about you and Drew? Has he finally accepted that you need to move to a new house?'

'I don't think he even notices. By the time he gets home in the evening, I've tidied away all the kid's things, put away the washing, cooked dinner, and done the washing up. The house doesn't feel that small if you're not trying to do anything in it.'

'But you've spoken to him about it?'

'What's the point? He's still convinced that it's fine. We'll live in that damn house our entire lives if he gets his way. I dread to think what it's going to be like when the new one comes along. He's decided he's not going to come to the birthing classes this time.'

'What?' Nelly slammed her drink down with such force that it spilled out over the edge. The children looked up momentarily. Nelly smiled at them, and they returned to what they were doing. 'He knows how you feel about it all, right? After everything you went through with Eva?'

With her fingers running around the edge of her mug, Sarah inhaled a noisy breath through her nose. There were very few things Sarah got truly mad at Drew for, but the way he was handling the whole birth of number three was probably highest on the list. 'He thinks going to classes will just make things worse. That it's better if I don't think about it until the time comes, otherwise I'll just spend my time working myself up into a state.'

'That's rubbish, and you know it.'

'You know what he's like. Once he's set his mind on something, that's it.'

Nelly reached over and placed her hand on Sarah's knee.

'Look, you need to sort this. If you're terrified, he needs to know.'

Sarah dipped her chin in the most minuscule of nods. 'Just when I think of what nearly happened with Eva…' she started.

'You know what? So what if he doesn't want to come to birthing classes. You don't need him there. You don't. You're the one who pushes the damn thing out. You could do that whole damn birth by yourself in the back of a bus if it came down to it.'

'I don't think that's exactly true.'

'Trust me. You're going to be fine. And this stuff with you and Drew is just a blip. You'll work your way through it. I'm sure you will.'

'Why would you think this is something I would want to do?' Open mouthed, Sarah glanced back down at the article about the Naughty Nanny. They had made it deliberately provocative. In the photo, *Nanny* was sitting in an armchair, glasses on the end of her nose, her grey hair in tight curls around her scalp, a whip hung over the back of the chair.

Resting on her stockinged thighs was a laptop. The title could have just as easily read *Porno for Pensioners*.

'This is it, don't you see?' Drew jabbed his finger at the page. 'This could be the answer to everything.'

'Have you lost your mind?'

Drew took her by the hand and stared earnestly into her eyes.

'Only yesterday you were saying how you wish you had more time to be creative and do the things you love. Things like writing. This woman makes a fortune writing. And I bet they're not even that great. I bet even you could write them.'

'Even me?' Sarah's eyebrows arched towards her hairline. 'Wow, thanks for the compliment.'

'You know what I mean.' He took the paper from her. 'I'm serious about this, Sah. I really think it could work. There's a massive market out there. What's to stop us from giving this a go?'

'If this is about the fact that I'm not earning anything, that was a joint decision, remember? You were the one who said it was better if I stopped work completely when Eva came along.'

'This isn't just about money, Sah.'

'No?'

'No.'

'Then what is it about?'

'You. Us. Doing something creative together.'

'Really,' Sarah's arched brows took on an even more impressive curve. 'Well, if that's the case, George has got a whole box full of colouring pencils and watercolours you can use. Knock yourself out.'

With one final glance down, she took the newspaper, folded it shut, and handed it back to her husband.

'I'm going to head to bed,' she said, taking a moment to kiss him on the cheek despite the fact she didn't feel like it at all. 'You're most welcome to join me once you rediscover your sanity.'

'Just think abo—'

'Honestly,' Sarah stopped him before he started again. 'Me writing erotic fiction. Like I have the time to do that.'

CHAPTER 8

D rew was gutted. Sarah's response to his suggestion that she rediscovered her creative nature through the means of writing erotic fiction had been the antithesis of what he had hoped. It wasn't about the money. He didn't expect the pair of them to make the same type of money that Naughty Nanny did, not at first at least, but even a little bit would help. Maybe with a couple of hundred pounds extra a month in the bank, Sarah wouldn't feel so inclined to whinge about the house the whole time. They could get the credit card debt sorted a lot quicker too.

She hadn't even wanted to entertain the idea. And from the look she had ended their conversation with, he knew there was no point in broaching the subject again for a while. The problem was, he just couldn't stop thinking about it.

Three days later, while on his commute to work, Drew's mind was still mulling over the idea of how to convince Sarah that the enterprise was a good one. Confidence, he decided. That was the issue. Sarah just wasn't confident in her ability to write that type of story. But if he could show her, if he could convince her that it really wasn't that hard, then maybe she'd get on board. Maybe then she would give it a try. Then again, what did he know? He had never even read any of these books. The train jolted to a stop at one of the stations, causing his phone to tumble out onto his lap. As he stared at it, a small glimmer of light flickered on in his mind. If he was serious about the pair of them giving it a go, then he was going to have to start somewhere. Nerves bubbled through his stomach. One minute later, and twelve minutes into his fifty-minute commute, Drew downloaded his first erotic fiction novel.

It was hard to settle into the storyline. Every second line, Drew looked up from the page, convinced people with x-ray vision could see through the back of his phone to read what was on his screen. He swore he could see their disapproving looks and hear the tongues tutting, and he knew full well that his cheeks turned crimson when he reached the first particularly explicit paragraph. Still, despite his continual nerves, Drew came to the conclusion less than one chapter into *Naughty Nanny and the Night Nurse, Book One*, that his initial instincts had been correct. They could do this.

The writing wasn't bad as such, but he hardly expected to see it shortlisted for the Man Booker Prize. Phrasing was repetitive, and the vocabulary no more elaborate than that of an average secondary school standard. With chapter one quickly under his belt, he carried on reading. Sarah could easily write something just as good, if not better than

Naughty Nanny. Heck, he could probably even give it a try
Of course, it wasn't like he had much time with work.

~

'You look focused.' A voice at the door brought Drew's head
up from his computer, 'What are you reading. Looks
engrossing?'

Blushing, Drew minimised the tab on his computer
screen. Lunchtime had just come to an end, and rather than
heading out and stretching his legs, Drew had been looking at
the earnings of the top erotic fiction authors. His head spun
at the numbers. There had to have been a mix-up in the
decimal places for some of these writers.

'Polly?' Drew's eyes went down to his computer once
again to double-check for digital evidence. 'Is everything
okay? What can I do for you?'

She smiled and stepped inside the room. 'It's fine. I just
had an email from Casper about the Christmas projections.
Have you seen it?'

Closing the internet tab completely, Drew flicked open his
emails. That was one of the reasons he respected Polly; it was
the fact that she never flaunted her relationship with the
CEO. He was never Uncle Casper, or Casp, simply Casper.
Sometimes he had even heard her refer to him as Mr.
Horton.

'I've got it,' he said, bringing up the message on the
screen. 'Don't worry, I can see to it. If you want to send me
through the rest of the team's data, that would be great.'

'And Barry,' she lifted her eyes upwards. 'What about
his?'

The pair looked through the window to where Barry was scratching the inside of his nose with the writing end of a Bic Biro.

'Don't worry. I can sort that,' Drew said. He had grown used to Barry's chaotic way of almost working. No doubt he would find half the figures he needed on the back of a Tesco's receipt. Or else, hidden in some encrypted folder on his desktop with no idea how they got there.

Polly smiled, lifting her cheeks just a fraction. 'You do way too much for him. You know that, right? You're a great boss,' she said.

Drew gave a short, one-breath laugh. 'Technically, I'm just his line manager, and I'm pretty sure a great boss would have made him better at his job by now.'

'You're not a miracle worker,' Polly laughed back. Half-way out the door, she turned back. 'Oh yeah, Stu asked if I could grab the accounts drive for him.'

Unable to hide his disdain, Drew unplugged the sleek external hard drive. Stu was the office weirdo. The one man at Home Crew who made Barry look like a member of the social elite.

'This is ridiculous,' he said, handing the hard drive to Polly. 'Who does he think will hack his work emails, for good-ness sake? How does he communicate with people in the outside world? Come to think of it, how did he even get this job?'

'I think it's sweet,' Polly replied. 'Think how much less complicated your life would be without all the palaver that comes with using social media. Not to mention the news. It must be great not to be greeted by bad news every day.'

'Then he should just stay off Facebook and the BBC. He could use the work intranet for crying out loud.'

'Apparently not,' Polly replied. 'Anyway, thanks.' She smiled, a hint of amusement glinting in her eyes before she turned around and headed back towards the door. 'I'll see you later,' she called back.

On the train back home, Drew shuffled deeper into his seat, pulled out his phone, and started where he had left off. By the time he arrived back home, he had already read all seventeen chapters of *Naughty Nanny and the Night Nurse, Book One*, with *Book Two* downloaded and ready for tomorrow's commute. The next time he mentioned writing these types of books to Sarah, he was going to make sure he was totally prepared. That way, there would be no chance she could say no.

It was ridiculous how one week could blend into another with nothing on the to-do list ever getting ticked off. George had already completed his first month in Year One, and the bump was well on its way to having its own gravitational field. Having managed without a tumble drier for over five weeks – and with the warmth of summer well and truly gone – Sarah had bitten the bullet and gone online to order one before they all ended up in frozen jumpers for winter.

'What the hell,' she said, as the credit card was declined for the third time. 'Is this one maxed out, too?'

Drew squinted away from his phone to look. He winced.

'I had to buy my new travel card last week. It's for the year, though.'

'Great,' Sarah replied. 'You can travel to work in wet clothes.'

Drew grunted some response, barely even bothering to look up from his phone.

George was preparing for the Christmas play – despite nine weeks to go – and every day, it felt like Sarah was being sent home with yet another piece of the set or costume that she was required to either make or buy. Not to mention various notes about charity raffles and other such obligatory philanthropy she could barely afford.

Eva had managed a total of two consecutive nights in a row in her bed in the previous four weeks. The sleepless nights resulted in zombie-like days, which had led to numerous errors, including sending George to school with an entirely empty snack box and walking Eva out of the house with no shoes on. Twice.

Drew seemed happy, though. He still spent most of the evening on his phone, but bizarrely, instead of playing the various shoot em up/car chase/football manager games he had been addicted to since getting a smartphone, he had gone back to reading for the first time in years. At first, Sarah assumed it was some fad, and the annoying waste-of-time apps that made her irrationally angry would be back any day, but a month in and reading was still his chosen activity for the evenings. Drew's passion for books was something that had first attracted her to him all those moons ago. Especially when he devoured her own amateur efforts. She spared a moment to wonder what might have been if she had pursued writing rather than going into the more financially stable field of translating. As such, it was with sweet nostalgia that she watched him so absorbed in the text.

A newly ignited love of literature wasn't the only change in Drew. Something about him felt more relaxed. Like the way he had come in and kissed her when he got home after work every day that week. And the way he gazed at the bump too, with excitement. She couldn't remember him doing that before, not properly, and not with this one. Then there was that other thing too. The other thing had definitely changed.

'We can easily do it on the sofa,' he said, having become abnormally frisky during an episode of *Strictly Come Dancing*. 'If you just sit with your legs like that...' He took her left leg and attempted to lift it up onto the arm of the sofa.

'You actually think I can sit like that?'

'I'm sure you can, can't you?'

'You do remember I have a baby inside me,' Sarah objected as she lifted her leg back down and pulled his hand away from her thigh.

'You just need to give it a try. What about if we just...' He attempted to manoeuvre her back between the cushions.

'Will you stop? It's not happening. You're going to wake Eva and George. And I'm not dealing with them. Not today. Eva spent all morning pretending she was a unicorn. She even put her lunch on the floor and ate it from the bowl on her hands and knees.'

'But she ate it?'

Sarah nodded contemplatively. 'Yeah. That's a good thing, I suppose.'

In one last-ditch attempt, Drew wrapped his arms around her waist. Sarah slipped away from his grip.

'Honestly. How can you want to do that now? When I look like this?'

Drew frowned. He moved forward and put his hands back on her waist. Sarah wanted to move them off her. She could feel the tension building down her spine. Maybe if she'd had time to change her underwear and put some makeup on. Or better still, switch the lights off.

'You look perfect.' Drew said, frown still in place. 'You know that, right? You look incredible. You always look incredible.'

The tension in her spine rose to a quivering in her lips. She hated feeling like that. She absolutely despised it. She wanted to be body confident and proud of her curves, the way she used to be. Not terrified of what her husband might be faced with when he pulled down her jeans and their elasti-cated waistband.

'I'm a bit tired now,' she said, slipping out of his grip for the second time. 'Maybe later in the week, when we've both had some proper sleep.' With that, she turned around and left before she could see the disappointment in his eyes.

CHAPTER 9

The level of nervousness Drew was feeling had previously been reserved for the more momentous occasions in his life, such as the birth of his children, asking Sarah to marry him, and his wedding day. Today, none of those factors were in play, and yet his stomach swarmed with butterflies of Amazonian proportions. His flustered state didn't bode well.

After much consideration – and test runs during the previous week's commutes to work – Drew had decided upon a rear-facing seat towards the back of one of the middle carriages. Rear-facing meant it was unlikely that someone would choose to sit next to him, at least until the train was full, although he had decided to forgo the luxury of a proper table. It would be more convenient to have had one, there was no doubt about it, but table space was at a premium, meaning there was a high chance of being overlooked. And today, Drew needed privacy. Placing his laptop on his lap, he flipped it open.

Already, his pulse was buzzing and his mouth as dry as

two-day-old bread. But it was time, he knew it. In the last five weeks, he had devoured all eighteen of Naughty Nanny's books and even had the next one on pre-order, set to download the moment it appeared on the virtual bookshelf. He didn't need it, though.

The last week had been spent procrastinating. There was the Sarah issue, of course. Deep down, he still thought she'd be great at doing this, but the fact that she wouldn't even let him put his hand down her bra unless she was under the covers with the bedroom light turned off meant she was unlikely to take kindly to him bringing up the idea again. It would be better, he decided, if he started it first, then he could bring her on board with all the crazy money talk he had been reading about. That, of course, meant the pressure was firmly on him to get the job done. For a full week, he had gone back and forth analysing certain scenes and looking at the use of language; but he could procrastinate no longer. The time was upon him. It was time to write.

The Adventures of an Air Hostess. That was the scenario he had decided upon. In his head spanned an unending series; *The Air Hostess Hits Hungary*, *The Air Hostess Hits Hong Kong*, *The Air Hostess Hits Honolulu*. He would probably have to shake things up a bit when he ran out of countries and cities that started with an H, but the idea had longevity to it, he was sure of that. Or at least it would if he could just work out how to start writing the damn thing. Five minutes after staring at the screen, and still, he had nothing. It was the country, he decided, that was causing the block. How could he write about a place he'd never visited? The last thing he wanted was to put off prospective readers by crappy descriptions cut straight from the internet.

After another minute of frustration, he closed his eyes, took a deep breath, opened them, and began to type.

*The Air Hostess hits the Hot Tub,* he wrote. Sure, it wasn't the most exotic place, but this way, he could be a bit vaguer about locations and not worry too much about getting things wrong. Now that the excuse was put to rest, he had focus.

*Raven kicked off her four-inch heels the moment she got in through the door,* he started, letting his fingers take the lead. *The flight had been delayed by two hours, and with the traffic backed up when she left the airport, she thought she might never get home. Fortunately, one of the passengers from First Class saw her standing in the rain while waiting in the cab queue, and offered her a lift in his limo, along with his number if she wanted it for later in the week.*

Two paragraphs in, and he started having fun with it. 'Names,' he said out loud to himself as he wrote. He needed a name for the first male to enter her life. Brad, maybe? Or was that too obvious? Christian, had that been used before? Deciding to go with a non-offensive Joe for his initial leading male, Drew carried on typing, finding himself more and more absorbed with every line. Only when the carriage emptied, and he was left alone, did he realise they had arrived. Tucking his laptop under his arm, he raced off the train. He would have to grab a sandwich to eat at his desk for lunch today, he thought. There was more work that needed to be done.

The first ten thousand words had flown by once he got into the swing of things. After realising that there was only so far the hot tub scenario could take him, Drew had fallen back on his original idea and was now four chapters into *The Air Hostess Hits Halkidiki*. He had visited the Greek Islands with his parents whilst growing up, and though his memory of the finer details was perhaps a little hazy, after a bit of time perusing images and watching a few *sunny relocation programmes* with Sarah, he was confident in his ability to capture the essence of Mediterranean heat and brightly coloured cocktails. There was no denying it; writing was fun. So far, the leading lady had managed illicit encounters in the taxi ride to the airport, at the airport itself, and on the plane. According to his plan – which he had jotted down after reading several online posts advising him to have at least an outline of his story – he still had several more misadventures for her to enjoy, including at the hotel, on the beach, at the beach bar, and the swimming pool, then a whole couple of extra chapters when she headed back to the U.K. for some time off work. He was storming ahead.

'Surely you don't have to work again tonight?' Sarah said as she sat on the sofa, legs propped up on the futon that used to be Drew's but had somehow changed possession to Sarah since she first fell pregnant with George. It was old now, squashed out of shape with almost all the firmness gone, but he still missed it. When Sarah was done with this final baby, he would work out a way to go about claiming it back, although he wasn't entirely sure how he would go about doing that. And it wasn't like it mattered at the moment. For the last week, he had been more than happy sitting at the dining room table, laptop facing the corner of the room as he continued to type away. At this rate, he would get the first book done well before the bump was due to join them. With a little bit of luck, he would then earn enough to jet them off to the never-ending list of H-inspired destinations under the guise of research and a well-deserved holiday. Which to go to first, that was the question on his mind? Honolulu or Hong Kong?

'Drew, did you hear what I said?'

'Sorry?' he looked up from his screen.

'I asked if you really had to work tonight. It's been every night this week. I thought you might want to watch something?'

'I will. I won't be long,' he said, glancing down to the chapter he had just started writing. Maybe just two hundred words. Two hundred more words and he would stop. His air hostess had just been given the key card to her hotel room. Little did she know, there had been a mix up at the check-in desk.

'What is it you're doing?' Sarah asked, breaking his stream of concentration before it had even begun to form.

'Sorry?'

'I said, what is it you're working on?'

'Oh, just some things for Christmas.' Drew tried to hide his irritation at the interruption and remember what it was he had planned on writing next.

'Drew?'

'Oh, just warehouse allocation.' He said the first thing that came to mind Sarah continued to stare at him, her eyebrows expectantly. 'That type of thing.'

Obviously not satisfied by his answer, Sarah heaved herself into a more upright position on the sofa.

'Surely they can't be expecting you to work every night like this. It's not as if you're paid for it.'

'It's just the Christmas period. You know what it's like. And we do get a Christmas bonus, remember?'

'I suppose.'

Thinking that the interrogation was over, Drew got back to work. A split second later, he saw Sarah was standing over him.

'Jesus!' He slammed the laptop closed. 'What are you doing? You scared the crap out of me.'

'I just wanted to see what you were working on. That was all.'

Drew could feel the clammy heat building on his skin.

'I told you. It's just work. A report,' he said.

'A report? On what?'

'For warehouse allocations. Like I said.' His throat was clamming up too now. And a cold sweat trickled down his neck. He hated lying. He was useless at it, but with her glaring eyes and already suspicious expression gracing her face, there was no way he wanted to risk the truth. 'It's a reflection,' he said, the lie out of his mouth before he had even thought it through. 'I have to write a reflection on all the current warehouses. Storage volume, refrigeration ability, ease of road access. That type of thing.'

'Is that a new thing you have to do?'

'Not particularly.' His sweating grew more profuse. He was worried now that slamming the lid shut would have stopped the work from saving too. If that was the case, he was going to be even more annoyed.

Sarah's eyes remained fixed, although the tension around them loosened by a fraction.

'Do you want some help?' she said finally. 'I'm a fast typer. You could dictate it to me if you like.'

'You don't want to do that.'

'I do. It'll be fun. It's not like I get to use my brain anymore. And it'll get you done a bit quicker. Let me help.'

The tightness in Drew's abdomen refused to let up as he watched the glimmer of hope flicker in Sarah's eyes. It wasn't a case of her helping him, he could see that. It was a request for herself. Her state of mind. And wasn't that the reason he had wanted her to do this? Wasn't this meant to be for her in the first place? His eyes went down to the top of the computer lid. He should show her now, he thought. But the flicker of hope in her eyes was met by a look of doubt in his own. Another week, he told himself. Another week, then at least he would have a little more to show for himself.

Avoiding his wife's gaze, he placed his hand on the top of the computer.

'Perhaps it would be best if I just worked on it myself,' he said.

CHAPTER 10

She knew Drew almost certainly thought she was being churlish. Three days had passed and not once had he even tried to apologise. They had gone through the whole weekend in a stalemate type of tension. He probably didn't even think he had done anything wrong. He never did. But the fact of the matter was, his silly little remark had made her feel even worse than before, and given her current state of mind, that was no small feat.

True, it wasn't like she worked at Home Crew even if she did feel like she knew the business inside out from all the evenings Drew had talked about it. And maybe there were some legal grey areas with her typing stuff up, but that had never bothered him before. There had been plenty of times throughout the years where he had *asked* her for help. Maybe not writing reports but reading out numbers so he could input them faster, checking spreadsheets, that type of thing. It had never been a problem all those other times. It was the way he looked at her. Like she was deluded and incapable of following some basic dictation. Not even worthy of secretary status.

'He's a wanker, of course. But it's genetic. You can't blame him entirely.' Nelly's way of comforting her was nothing if not blunt. Sarah hadn't planned on imposing on Nelly, she hated interrupting her workday, but she was still seething and snapping at the kids for nothing beyond the ordinary level of mayhem.

'Being a wanker is genetic?' Sarah said in response to Nelly's statement.

'Being male is. It's his type of nesting. You know, before the babies are born, women go into nesting mode, tidying the house, sorting the nursery—'

'I stocked up on frozen burritos and cheese strings.'

'Okay, well, lots of women do the whole tidying thing. Men's brains act differently. They go into this whole cavemen *must provide* macho mentality.'

'Is that what Jeff did?'

Nelly plucked the drink from the coffee machine. 'Jeff hired a bloody great chainsaw and nearly put a tree through our roof, but in a manner of speaking, yes.'

Sarah inhaled. As much as she didn't like to admit it, it made sense. After all, it wasn't like this was normal behaviour for him. 'So you don't think I should let it get to me?'

'Is it going to change anything if you do?'

The high road hadn't been an easy one to take, especially after three days of internal festering, but take it she would. After coffee, Eva had been in one of her limpet moods, where she clung to Sarah's leg all afternoon, and any attempt at separation ended up with screaming loud enough to rupture her eardrums. Usually, it meant she had a cold or something coming, and Sarah would have had a little sympathy. However, when she finally got away for two minutes to go to the toilet, she discovered that at some point in the morning, Eva had lodged one of her plastic ponies into the bottom of the bowl. That in itself would have been a mild irritation had it not been for the fact that Sarah only noticed after she had done her business and gone to flush it away. The whole contents – sans pony – floated up to the top and started to run down the sides. Of course, the plunger hadn't worked on the toy, and she had been forced to lower her hand inside – with no rubber gloves – and pull out the offending equine.

She was still trying to scrub the stench from her arm when Drew came in from work. With the children already in bed, he had barely even said hello before he was back, tapping away at his computer.

'Do you want to watch a film?' Sarah asked an hour later when she had done enough channel hopping to cause carpal tunnel syndrome. 'You can put a horror on?'

'What's that?'

'A film? Do you want to put one on?'

With a sad sense of nostalgia, she thought back to those few weeks when he was reading. Maybe if he sat on the sofa with her so that they could watch a bit of telly while he worked, she would have felt better about it, but he insisted on hiding himself away in the corner of the room, laptop hidden in the shadows like he didn't want her to see what he was up to. When no reply to her original question was given, she tried a different approach with her screen-possessed spouse.

'I'm going to go into town and grab a couple of Christmas presents tomorrow,' she said. Once again, all she received from Drew was a grunt of response. 'Is there anything you want me to pick up for your sister and her kids?' she added. 'They've got one of those discount book shops.'

'Sorry, what?' His eyes came momentarily up from the computer.

'I said I was going into town tomorrow. I thought I'd head to the cheap bookshop and get a few bits and pieces for Christmas.'

A crease formed in Drew's brow. 'You know it's only just November, don't you?'

'I am aware, yes, thank you. But if I wait till next month, everything will have gone up in price. And this is the only day your mum and dad could do before they fly off to France.'

'It's a Mum and Dad day tomorrow?' Drew asked, the furrow deepening.

'It is.'

'That's come around fast. Do you really need to use them again so soon? If you're just going shopping, surely you can take Eva? How hard would it be?'

'How hard could it be?' And just like that, Sarah felt herself careen off of the high road, down through the trees, and come crashing onto the low road.

His word choice was probably less than ideal. But in his defence, she was the one who insisted on making conversation when he was clearly working. The book was going so well, and the last thing he wanted to do was lose momentum. He was already onto chapter five and had gone back to the beginning just to have a read through and check that there weren't any glaring errors. This last page had been his fastest yet; with a little bit of luck, he'd have the whole thing finished in another fortnight.

Halkidiki was still proving a good setting, at least in Drew's version of the island. Secret beach-front caves, remote huts on cliff edges, and rooftop bars and luxurious hotel rooms with whitewashed walls and canopy beds. He had thousands of places that his air hostess could partake in a little bit of naughtiness. The possibilities were endless. The hard part was just trying to find time to write them all down.

Despite what Sarah believed, work really was crazy too. The build-up to Christmas meant having to employ hundreds of extra staff to work in the warehouses as pickers, getting all the food ready for home delivery. Then there was the need for the extra delivery drivers and vans too. And while none of those were Drew's direct responsibility – he was in charge of what and how much they stock of certain products – all the other managers needed his input on things to make their departments run smoothly. Several lunchtimes that week, he had had to hand over to actual work, as opposed to the task of finishing his book as he had planned to do. As such, his evenings had become precious writing time. Hence the less than perfect reply to Sarah's comment.

'All I thought is that maybe you and Eva could go together. Have a girly day.'

'What, because the other three hundred and sixty-four days a year where it's just me and her don't count? And what do you mean it's come around fast? The last time they had them was at the start of October. Is one day off a month too many now?'

A thin vein protruded along her forehead. Normally,

there were stages; shorter terse sentences, lip-smacking, deep inhales that flattened her nostrils to the side of her nose. The vein – a clear signal that she was about to explode – was normally stage four. Very rarely did it appear without some prior warning. And yet, there it was. Drew's stomach churned as he pushed his laptop lid all the way closed.

'I didn't mean that.' He pushed back his seat so he could at least look his wife in the eye. He tried to dig himself out from a different angle. 'I just meant that if you're dropping Eva off at Mum and Dad's, and you have a whole day, then maybe you wanted to do something a little more productive with your time than shopping.'

'A little more productive?' Her eyebrows were arched and butting her hairline. 'I guess I could mow the lawn? Re-plaster the bathroom? I do about every other sodding job in this house; I might as well add those to the list.'

'Sorry,' Drew said, more than a little taken aback from the sudden explosion and not too subtle insinuation that he did nothing around the house to help. 'Did I miss something?'

'Miss something? You mean other than me having to fish Eva's pony from a pool of my own shit?'

'And I was supposed to know about that, how?'

'Oh, I don't know, you could have asked about my day to start with.'

A grating sound buzzed through his skull as he tried to stop himself from grinding his teeth.

'I'm at work all day, Sarah. I come home, and I do work.' He pointed at the laptop, feeling entirely indignent despite the fact he hadn't really done any Home Crew work on it for nearly two weeks. There was very little point when his work desktop was so much faster, even for writing the book. Still, this was not the time to bring that up. Instead, he pulled his most outraged face. 'I barely get any time to myself as it is, Sarah. What more do you want me to do?'

'Oh, I don't know, some parenting.'

Baby hormones or not, Drew could feel his own vein twitching. He twisted his lips as his feet took a firmer plant on the carpet. 'You don't think I parent?'

Sarah was still standing up, hands on her hips, 'I think you do the fun parenting part. You come in late, read them bedtime stories, get to take George for a kick around at the park—'

'Deal with the tantrums. Bath Eva when her nappy explodes. Have you forgotten that one?'

'One time, Drew. She'd had diarrhoea for three days. Three days. And you changed one explosion. Congratulations. I guess your Dad of the Year Award got lost in the bloody post.'

'How was I meant to do more? I was at work—'

'I'll go to work, Drew. If it's that much of an effort, then I'll get a job. You can stay here day in, day out.'

His back molars ground together so hard that he could feel the vibrations buzzing all the way through to his skull. He flexed his fingers and took a long, deep inhale. This was his wife, he reminded himself. He loved her dearly. She was just going through a hard transition with the baby on the way. As much as he wasn't one of those men who like to use the word *hormones* as a blanket method to cover his wife's changing moods, he couldn't help but feel that this time, it was bang on point.

'Look. If what you want is a bit of time, maybe we should

look at putting Eva into nursery for a couple of days a week, then —'

'And where the hell would we find the money for that? Honestly? You go for your Monday fry up every week, your Friday donuts, or whatever the hell it is, and I'm here working out how the hell I can make dinner out of three wilted carrots and a bag of pasta every night.'

'Now you're being ridiculous. It's not like we're on the breadline.'

'No?' The vein was well and truly popping now. 'Then why the hell have I not had a night out in the last year? Why was the last time I got a new pair of jeans or a new top before Eva was born?'

'Then go out and buy something for yourself. Who's stopping you? I'm not. That's the whole point of a credit card, Sarah.' He hated raising his voice. He hated getting angry, but it felt like she was living in a parallel universe.

'It's more debt, *Andrew.*'

'Everybody uses credit cards. If you're that worried, I can get another job. There are plenty of evening picking positions going at warehouses. And delivery drivers. Maybe if I go straight from the office to the warehouse, it would give you less time in the day to be pissed off with me.'

'Maybe I'd be less pissed off with you if you just once asked me how my day had been when you got in each night.'

'What are you on about? I always ask you. Every day, I talk to you.'

'Really? Because I barely feel like I can remember what you look like, your face has been so damn glued to that computer.'

'For a week.'

'And the rest.'

'No.' He was putting his foot down on this. He knew exactly when he'd started working on the book, and today marked day eleven. It was close enough to a week to pass in his consideration. 'One week I've been working on my computer at night. One bloody week, Sarah. And I'm sorry. I'm sorry I have to do work when I get in. I'm sorry you have to stay at home and be with Eva and take George to school while I have to sit in an office listening to people drone on for hour after hour. I'm sorry I can't afford a massive house and a nanny like Justine, or that I'm not exciting enough to paint my fence like a stupid rainbow. But this is me, Sarah. This is who I am. And if you don't know that by now, then maybe we have a bigger problem than me being on the laptop in the evening.' And with that, he smacked his lips together, took three defiant strides from the table to the hall, and headed straight out the front door.

# CHAPTER 11

Sarah felt like crap. Not that she didn't think she was justified. The fact that Drew had stormed out and left her with the kids, despite the whole argument centring around the fact that she was always stuck with the kids, meant that she was, in her mind, one hundred percent justified in every comment that she made. Unfortunately, that didn't change how she felt. All she'd wanted was for him to sit next to her for a bit. Snuggle up maybe, without trying to get into her overly-frayed, never-to-be-seen-in-public knickers. All she'd wanted was for him to make her feel like she was a bit more human after a day listening to Eva and George go endlessly at it with one another. But now, she just felt like crap. And she was fairly sure her arm still stank of it too.

A brief sigh escaped from his lips as the cold beer hit the back of his throat, although it did little to alleviate the guilt that sat heavy in his gut. Not that he had anything to feel guilty about, Drew assured himself, hands still around the glass. Not really. He had been working, for crying out loud. Okay, maybe it wasn't the type of work he had told Sarah he was working on, but she didn't know that. As far as she was concerned, he could have been up against some extremely important deadlines. And she had attacked him for it. Although, he did feel guilty about storming out. It wasn't his proudest moment, he would admit that much. With another sip of beer, he attempted to dilute the sensation of guilt swilling around in his stomach. Following his dramatic exit, he had actually stopped for a second outside the front door, worried that the slamming and shouting had woken up Eva and that Sarah would now have to deal with it. Then again, he had considered, she was all about playing the martyr card. It would probably suit her just fine.

With the churning continuing in his stomach, he went for his pint again, this time swallowing back a good few mouthfuls before placing the glass down in front of him and staring into the amber bubbles. He would finish this one and then go back, he told himself. Just give her a little bit of time to cool down. The truth was, he couldn't really imagine being at home with them all day. Well, actually, he could. There had been one time before Sarah had found out about number three when she had gone away for two nights for a hen do. It had been Drew flying solo for a full 48 hours. Naturally, when Sarah returned, Drew assured her how everything had gone fine. Swimmingly. A breeze. The truth was, he had been on his knees. It wasn't so much that they needed entertaining, more like they needed entertaining, feeding, comforting, humouring, and disciplining and nurturing, all at the same time. Every ounce of his parent skills was drawn upon in that 48-hour period. Colouring, building blocks, jigsaw puzzles - before he discovered that Eva was chewing on the edge pieces that he was putting to one side. He had even attempted to make some cupcakes so they could use up some time decorating them. Only, shortly after they went in the oven, Eva had a toilet emergency, and he was forced to act as a poop doula while the cakes burned. When Sarah came through the front door, he had his shoes on and was headed to the pub before she had even taken off her coat.

The jolt of the memory was accompanied by another roll of guilt. Maybe the book writing had made him slightly more neglectful this last week, he considered. Maybe he would have to pick up his commute word count to try and get everything done. And then, because he knew there was nothing else he could do in the situation, he picked up his phone and messaged Sarah. *I love you.*

She was already in bed when her phone beeped out a message. *I love you, Sarah.* Followed quickly by, *Sorry I was an idiot. Just tired.* Tossing the phone aside, she tried to maintain her surly mindset, but the phone continued to beep, and the arrival of several sad-faced and heart emojis began to soften her resolve ever so slightly. She picked up her phone and considered what to reply, only to change her mind. Perhaps she had gone a bit too far. It wasn't like Drew didn't look after the children at all. He was as hands-on as he had time to be. A lot more hands-on than other parents she knew who worked full time, mums and dads both. Still, she would let him stew a little bit longer. Perhaps that way, it would get him off his bloody computer at night.

When he came home less than an hour later, he snaked his arms around her waist as he snuggled into her back.

'Sorry,' he said. His socks were still on. It was a foible she'd grown used to. 'Can we not fight, please? I hate it. I was just busy, that's all.'

She grunted, half to pretend she was asleep, half to show he wasn't completely forgiven.

'I'll try not to bring things home,' he continued. 'I will. No more sitting at my computer at night unless it's really important.'

Knowing he wasn't going to stop until she actually replied, Sarah shifted herself around and groaned, 'I just wanted to have a conversation, that was all. I thought it would be a nice normal thing to do, talk about each other's day.'

'I know, and I'm sorry. You're completely right.' He hooked his fingers in hers. 'As soon as we get through Christmas, things are going to change,' he told her. 'Trust me, okay? Things are going to be great.'

'Drew, Christmas isn't the —'

'Trust me,' he said again.

And because it was easier than saying anything else, she nodded her head and said, 'Okay.'

Morning came after a broken night's sleep. She and Drew had stayed up a little longer, putting the world to rights the way they used to when they were younger. Back then, they had talked about travelling the world, renovating their dream house, or maybe even building their own. Now they talked about whether the dark patches on the skirting board were mould, or Eva induced. Not long after they had fallen asleep, Eva had woken up, and while Drew was quick on his feet to deal with her – obviously wanting to make up for the lack of parenting she had commented on – it meant they had spent the rest of the night wrestling for the blanket and trying to avoid getting a black eye.

When morning came around, the thought of heading into town and finding a car parking space while working out how to cover the entire costs of Christmas without spending a penny over their typical monthly budget, sounded about as enjoyable as another episode of *My Little Pony and the U-bend*.

The problem was that Drew's parents would never offer to make up the day if Sarah cancelled. It was either using their token of generosity now, at its designated time, or wait for another thirty days to roll by before she was afforded the same luxury again.

While Drew's parents lived only four miles down the road, they were not what one would consider on-hand. They loved their grandchildren, of that there was no doubt, but every time Sarah went round, she could see her mother-in-law's face contort and twist as the children ran their grubby fingers along the walls and pulled the neatly arranged books off the bookshelves. They were not the type of grandparents that embraced messy play, dressing up, or any one of the general arrays of emotions and characteristics their grand-children displayed. And so, a couple of years ago, this arrangement was forged.

Once a month, Neil and Amanda took Eva, and back

then, George, for the entire day, giving Sarah approximately ten hours to complete all the errands she so desperately needed to do. Amanda and Neil, meanwhile, would endure ten hours of complete and utter chaos and maintain a perfectly curated home for the remaining twenty-nine to thirty days of grandchild-free peace.

'You can drop them off whatever time you want,' Sarah said as she handed Eva over on the doorstep of her in-law's beautiful Georgian semi. 'I'll be home for most of the day, so just give me a ring. And George has Coding Club activity, so he won't need picking up until four. But if that's too much trouble, I can always get him, then come pick up Eva too.'

'Don't be silly.' Amanda was dressed in black trousers and a black top – a marked improvement from the beige ensemble she had worn last time. 'We are going to have a wonderful day, aren't we? There's an exhibition I thought we might go to. What do you think about that, Eva? Do you think you'd like to see an art exhibition?'

'No,' Eva responded, walking through the door and dumping her shoes in the middle of the hallway.

'Oh, she gets funnier by the day, doesn't she?' Neil laughed.

'I did try to call you this morning,' Amanda said, waving Neil off to go and get the discarded shoes. 'I want to check whether she could eat avocados.'

'You did?' Sarah pulled out her phone and looked at the screen. 'I've not got a missed call.'

'Oh no, I tried the landline. You get a much better reception on them. I can never hear on the portable telephones.'

'I guess Drew must have unplugged it again, as it didn't ring.' Sarah replied. Amanda tutted with disapproval.

It was only a small lie, really, Sarah considered. Drew *had* been the one to unplug the phone. She had just asked him to do it. Besides Amanda and Neil, she couldn't actually remember the last time she had received a call on it that wasn't from someone trying to offer reduced-cost electricity or to sell them double glazing. As such, she had made the executive decision to leave it permanently unplugged.

'Eva.' Sarah called her daughter back to kiss her on the cheek, before thanking her mother-in-law one more time and bolting for the car before they could change their minds.

Now she had removed the Christmas shopping trip from her to-do list, her day was, if possible, more mundane than normal. There was the tumble dryer; that was number one to be seen to. After the failed credit card purchase and weeks of refusing to give up and rummaging through every folder and drawer in the house, she finally managed to find the manual, which included some basic instructions on maintenance. She had also got Drew to dig out every Allen key, screwdriver, and hammer they had, to ensure she was fully prepared to handle any situation. She may as well give the house a good once over too. There were so many brown patches on the carpet, she had started to forget what the original colour was, and the back of the sofa covers had begun to smell like an unwashed cat food bowl, despite the fact that they had never owned a cat. Then, of course, there was the mould on the skirting board.

*Cuppa this afternoon?* Nelly's message pinged up on her phone the second Sarah stepped through the front door.

*Jobs to do.* Sarah typed her reply with one hand while fishing around for her house keys. *I'll call later.*

Before tackling the tumble dryer, Sarah went into the

children's room. There had been a time when it had just been the three of them; when everything was so organised. George's clothes had been ordered not only according to type – shorts, jumpers, trousers – but according to size, colour, and season. She even had a separate drawer for things that still had the tag on so she could re-gift them if he didn't get around to wearing them before they were too small. Now, they were ordered in two piles; clean and dirty. And currently, the dirty pile was by far overshadowing the clean. With a heavy sigh, she lowered herself down to the ground and began to pick through the pile.

When the clothes were sorted and put away or in the washing machine, and all the sheets in the bedrooms changed, Sarah decided to avoid the issue of the tumble drier for a little longer by running the vacuum around the rest of the house. There was a time when giving the house a proper clean was satisfying. Now it was just frustrating, knowing that all her hard work would be undone within fifteen minutes of the children returning home. What must it be like to have someone clean your house for you, she wondered? Even if it was just twice a year to scrub off some of the strange stains from the sofa. Once the tumble drier and credit cards had been sorted, a cordless vacuum would be high on her list of purchases, she thought, switching her wish list to more attainable fantasies. She was sick of dragging Henry the hoover, with his smug face, around while he listlessly attempted to suck up the detritus of family life. She brushed various crumbs, dust bunnies, and other unidentifiable items into small piles before setting Henry on them, systematically cleaning the house, one corner at a time. She was working on the living room, trying to vacuum up the most visible crumbs when her eyes landed on something that had slid between two of the cushions.

'Great,' she said, pulling Drew's phone out of the gap. 'I guess there's no point sending you another shopping list for this afternoon,' she said aloud. Switching off the vacuum, she was in the process of reaching over to put the phone on the mantelpiece when the screen flashed with light. Instinctively, her eyes flicked towards the notice.

*Naughty Nanny Nineteen is now available online*, the notice said. *Your pre-ordered copy has been sent directly to your eBook app.*

Sarah stared at the phone. Naughty Nanny? The name rang a bell, although it took a minute of staring at the screen to remember why. Naughty Nanny, of course, the geriatric woman who was earning a fortune writing dirty books. She was happy she could remember, although why Drew would have notifications about it on his phone, was another matter entirely. She placed the phone on the mantelpiece and went back to the housework.

It was curiosity more than anything else, she told herself during the short deliberation that preceded picking Drew's phone back and typing in the code. After all, they had no secrets. She knew more of the passwords to Drew's bank accounts, emails, and social media platforms than he did. She had forged his signature on enough documents over the years that even the FBI would have difficulty telling the difference. It was just curiosity, that was the reason. She was just intrigued as to why he appeared to have a *Naughty Nanny* book on pre-order. Probably a glitch, she told herself, as she swiped open the phone and went straight to his e-books.

'Nineteen.' Her eyes bulged. 'How the hell can he have nineteen of these books on his phone?'

CHAPTER 12

He hated to admit it, but he was knackered. Despite what Sarah believed, Drew often woke up in the night when Eva had a bad one. It was true, he tended not to get up like her, but that didn't mean he wasn't affected by the loss of sleep. However, last night, he decided that not getting up would be a massive faux pas.

When he got into Eva's room, her nappy was soaked through. Getting it off was easy enough; trying to get a dry one on afterwards, however, was a whole different matter. With her screaming and wriggling, Drew was sure she was going to wake George up. Taking Eva into their bedroom was no good either as she would wake Sarah up instead, at which point she would no doubt feel the need to intervene and point out all the things he was doing wrong. So, at a quarter to three, he was shut in the bathroom with his three-year-old, trying to get a clean nappy on to her without cracking her head against the tiles or the bathtub. When she was finally dressed, he brought her into bed with them the way Sarah always did. For the remainder of the night, Eva insisted on sleeping with her head shoved right up in Drew's armpit. He could have sworn he had barely closed his eyes when the alarm went off. Not wanting to seem like the rough night had put him out, he had forced himself out of bed before Sarah could, and raced downstairs to make George's snacks. Despite his tiredness, he actually felt good about helping out. That was until he got on the train, sat down, and went to check his phone.

'Bugger.' He tried all the pockets in his laptop bag, including the ones he didn't think he'd ever actually unzipped. The train was already pulling out of the station. He could, he thought, get off at the next stop, wait, and come back again, but that would put him over an hour behind. Better that he just managed a day without it. He would call Sarah from work when he got in. On the plus side, it meant no silly memes to distract him from his writing.

Calling Sarah from work proved more difficult than anticipated, given that he had no idea what her phone number was. Damn mobiles. The convenience of the whole world at your fingertips. Until it's not, and you're left on your own.

'Barry,' he said, calling out into the office area to where Barry was chewing on the inky end of a ballpoint pen. 'Can you come here a second?'

A moment later, Barry was standing in front of him, his whole face translucent with fear.

'I know what it's about.' Barry said, his eyes unable to meet Drew's as he moved to close the door. 'It's about the email, isn't it? I didn't mean to hit *send all*. I just get a bit confused sometimes. You know that. You know it wasn't deliberate.'

'Email? What email?' Drew asked. Then, with an inward

sigh, he rubbed his temples. Whatever Barry was about to throw at him, he was definitely too tired to handle before at least another two coffees. 'I haven't seen any emails. I was just about to log on.'

'I might have accidentally sent a photo of Aziraphale to the whole staff mailing list.'

'Aziraphale?'

'My cat.'

Sure enough, when Drew clicked on his email, there was the photo; a ginger and white moggy with its nose pressed up against the screen, it's rough tongue in perfect focus.

'Do you think I'll get fired for this?' Barry wrung his hands as he shifted his feet. 'I just wanted to send it to Alice, you see. And I typed AL, and then it automatically added *All staff,* and I'd hit send before I realised.'

Drew stared at the photo of Barry's cat. Several thoughts crossed his mind, including how he had never so directly seen up a cat's nostrils before, and how he could work in an office where a grown man was unable to tell the difference between emailing his wife and emailing the entire company, including the board of directors, and how another refused to use email at all.

'Maybe I should just get her to change her name?' Barry continued. 'I could suggest that, couldn't I; if they go to fire me? Tell them I'll change my wife's name, so I don't make the same mistake again. I think Casper would agree to that. He's a reasonable man. I'll tell him we'll get her name changed.'

'You don't need to tell them that.' Drew said. 'I'm sure it will be fine.'

'But if he calls me in—'

'Then I will vouch that it was a genuine mistake.'

Barry closed his eyes in relief.

'Thank you,' he said and moved to go.

He was part of the way out the door when Drew remembered the reason he had asked him into the room in the first place. 'I don't suppose you have Sarah's phone number, do you?'

'Sarah?'

'My wife.'

'Oh?' A confused expression crossed Barry's face. 'No, I don't think so.' He took out his phone and checked. Even if it was there, Drew wasn't entirely sure he'd know how to find it. 'Why do you need it?'

'I've left my phone at home,' Drew replied. 'I was hoping I could get a hold of her to let her know, but I have no idea what her number is.'

'How about ringing the house phone?'

The fairly sensible suggestion took Drew aback. Unfortunately, it didn't help.

'We unplugged,' Drew said. 'All we ever got were cold calls. Don't worry. I'll just send her a message online. Only, she doesn't always see those. It's not a problem. I'm sure she'll be just fine anyway.'

'No wonder he's been so horny lately.' Sarah shoved her nose into the wine glass and inhaled. 'Should I be worried? I feel like I should be worried about this.'

'You do not need to be worried about this.'

Sarah felt bad interrupting Nelly in the middle of the day,

but she needed someone to talk to. At home, she had been going around in circles. She picked up the glass of wine again and sniffed. It wasn't as good as drinking the stuff. But it was better than nothing.

'It's normal,' Nelly assured her. 'You guys have been married a long time. You said it yourself; you didn't really have time for him at the moment.'

'Still, *Naughty Nanny* books. I mean, maybe if I'd stumbled across a series of dirty magazines or a subscription to a porn link, I would understand. But I don't know when Drew last made an effort to read a book before this. And what does he do, hold his phone in one hand and, you know…beat his bishop with the other?' Sarah grimaced.

'To be fair, that's what I do.' Nelly replied.

'But you're a woman.'

'What's that got to do with it?'

'I don't know, but that's the unspoken rule, isn't it? Books for the women. And the videos for the men.'

Nelly raised an eyebrow. 'Really, you're telling me you've never watched a porn video?'

Sarah sniffed at the wine. 'That's not the point, is it?'

'That's exactly the point. Personally, I like the idea of a man using his imagination and reading books for once. It's got to be a little more romantic than someone sitting there whacking one off in front of a screen.'

A pause formed between the two. Sarah ran her finger around the edge of her glass before placing it back on the table. She sighed.

'I know it's stupid. I do. I just feel funny about it. He's never needed anything like that before.'

'That you know of. Besides, you've never been in a position like this before. Two kids, another on the way. I'm guessing your mum hasn't been down to help out at all recently?'

Sarah scoffed. 'Does she ever?'

'So you and Drew don't exactly have much time for each other?'

'More like no time at all.'

Nelly sat forward in her chair.

'Well, that's your problem. You need to make time. Believe me, speaking from someone who's been down that route.'

Sarah stared at the wine in the glass. Every range of emotion had flashed through her at some point in the last couple of hours, not in the least disappointment in herself as much as anything else. 'You really think it's that simple? Just put in a bit of effort?'

Picking up her glass of wine, Nelly chewed on her lip.

'You said your mother-in-law's got George and Eva now, right?'

'She's gonna bring them back for dinner,' Sarah glanced at her watch. 'Which means I should probably get to the shops so that I can get some food in.'

Nelly's eyes glinted.

'Why not see if they can keep them a bit longer? Bring them back before bedtime instead. I'm sure they'd agree.' It took Sarah a minute to decipher Nelly's thoughts.

'That's ridiculous. I can't just jump on him as soon as he gets home.'

'Really? Then when else are you going to do this?'

Sarah thought about it. Nelly was right about the lack of attention thing. She had never believed in all that wifely duty nonsense, but still, a fumble between the sheets now and again wouldn't go amiss. And even if they didn't get under the sheets, it might be nice to have dinner just the pair of them together for once.

'I could always ask,' Sarah said, after mulling the idea over.

A slanted grin coiled on Nelly's lips.

'Great, then I think it's time you took a bit of inspiration from some of those books.'

# CHAPTER 13

Sarah took a deep breath.

'You're being ridiculous,' she said, chastising herself yet again. 'Pull yourself together.' It was ridiculous that she felt as nervous as she did. She was a grown woman. A grown, married woman, waiting for her husband to come home so she could surprise him. They had children for goodness sake. And another one on the way. Doing something like this should not have been as nerve-wracking as it was. Perhaps the issue was with it being light outside. Yes, perhaps that was the problem.

Nelly had been right about Drew's parents.

'Oh yes, of course, we can keep them.' Amanda's voice had sounded uncharacteristically flustered. 'I mean, we'll have to go to the shops and pick up some food. Not that it's any trouble, of course. Had you told me earlier, we could have popped down to Waitrose and got something of a little better quality, but I'm sure the Tesco around the corner will have something suitable.'

'They can have beans on toast. Or just toast. They'll both be fine with that.'

'I'm sure I can do better than that,' her mother-in-law had replied.

So, with three extra child-free hours confirmed, all that was needed was for Sarah to find an outfit that could reflect Drew's apparently changing tastes in the bedroom.

Dressing up just wasn't something she and Drew did. Even on events like Halloween, or themed birthday parties, they were the couple searching through the back of the wardrobes, trying to find something that they could repurpose. The last 80s party Sarah went to, she had just worn one of her normal gym kits and crimped her hair; she'd been given so many comments on the authentic 80s trashiness that she'd considered giving the whole outfit to a charity shop.

That afternoon, crimped hair and legwarmers just weren't going to cut it. She needed something great, something special, something that would make Drew stop in his tracks and wonder why he needed any of those novels when he had a wife like that waiting at home for him. Yet, after twenty minutes of turning her wardrobe inside out, she flopped onto the bed.

At twenty-nine years old, Sarah's wardrobe contained nothing that even hinted at erotica. No leather whips or French maid's outfit. Not even a pair of crotchless knickers or elasticated stockings. All the underwear she owned that could have been considered even remotely sexy was now either ripped or stained or just so small that pulling them on was likely to cut off the circulation to somewhere. Casting her mind back to the various titles she had seen on his screen, one particular name stood out. A tiny spark flickered. *Naughty*

*Nanny, Book 5: Officer Oversized.* Perhaps there was something she had after all.

~

With what she considered an almost sexy outfit – black knickers and black bra with no obvious stains provided he didn't look too closely – cobbled together, Sarah waited upstairs. She had been pacing the house for the previous fifteen minutes, wondering if there had been a delay on the lines. Any second now, he would be walking through the front door.

George's plastic handcuffs pinched at her wrist, and the other end was clipped to the bed frame. She had gone for one of Drew's ties around her neck, along with one of his white shirts which did up nicely over her belly, and George's helmet propped between her legs at an angle she thought might have been sexy. However, she was beginning to regret the decision to shave as the red raw bumps were getting worse by the minute. Glancing at the time on her phone, she was still deliberating whether to unclip herself and rub in a bit of Eva's nappy rash cream when the door opened.

'Sah?'

The door slammed shut, and she heard the thud as Drew dropped his backpack at the bottom of the stairs. Two more short thuds indicated the removal of his shoes.

'I'm up here.'

'Where are the kids?'

'Your mum's still got them.'

'She has? Why? Is everything alright?'

The itching and pinching was becoming more uncomfortable by the second. What was it with her husband's ability to hold entire conversations on different floors?

'Perhaps if you could just come up here for a minute?' she called.

'I just need —'

'Upstairs. *Now!*'

~

Thirty minutes later and Sarah was lying stretched out on the bed while Drew fished around on the ground for his boxers. Her pulse was still high, and the backs of her arms ached from the stretch of being handcuffed to the bed.

'Not that I'm complaining,' Drew said, slipping back onto the bed beside her with his boxers now on. 'But where did that come from?'

She grinned. 'Did you enjoy it?'

'Maybe a little bit.'

She couldn't remember the last time they had sex like that. For the last couple of years, a quick fumble under the sheets before Eva started screaming and wanting to come into their bed was the best they could ever hope for. What they just did was definitely not a quick fumble.

'So,' Drew said, running his hand down the length of her neck. 'Do you want to tell me?'

'Tell you what?'

'Where your inspiration came from?'

Sarah paused before leaning down the side of her bed and picking up Drew's phone from the ground.

'You,' she said.

Drew's face crinkled at the screen, clearly confused by the dots Sarah was drawing for him to join.

'I don't get it. What do you mean?' His eyes glanced back down at the screen for just a second before widening to double their size.

'A fan of the *Naughty Nanny*, are we?' Sarah smirked as she spoke. 'I'm going to be honest. She's not what I'd have pegged as your type. But each to their own.'

Drew's eyes remained bulging from their sockets while his skin had paled to the colour of watery breastmilk.

'It is not what you think.'

'Of course not,' Sarah smirked at him.

'No,' he insisted. 'It's really not.'

The laptop was balanced on Sarah's knees, with Drew perched beside her on the edge of the sofa. He had been thinking about this moment for a while now; how he would tell Sarah what he had been doing. What her opinion would be when he finally did show her. He had looked forward to it, with just a mild sense of trepidation. But he'd expected to have more time. A few more edits. A thorough check through for any plot holes.

'I've been trying to edit as I go.' He twiddled his thumbs as he spoke, needing to break up the silence of his wife's reading. 'Obviously, there are still a few bits that need tweaking.' Sweat was slickening the back of his neck as he changed position and began drumming his fingers against his thighs.

'That doesn't make it any easier for me to read.'

'Sorry,' he said, stopping for less than a minute before starting up the drumming again.

'Well,' he said when he could no longer wait any longer. 'What do you think? You have to have read it by now. I know how fast you read.'

Sarah pressed her lips together and scanned her eyes down the page at an infuriatingly slow pace.

'Come on.' Drew pressed. 'What do you think? Is it any good?'

'I think…' Sarah paused and nodded. 'I think it's *not* terrible.'

A small smile lifted the corner of her lips. Drew's heart leapt.

'Really?'

'I've certainly read worse.'

'I told you,' he jumped off the sofa and turned to face her. 'I mean, I wanted to tell you. See, I knew it's not bad, is it? It's really not that bad. I mean, if we could manage to sell—'

'Hold on.' Sarah put the laptop down on the sofa. 'Don't get carried away. It's not exactly Hemingway.'

'I know, but it doesn't have to be. It wouldn't just be this book, obviously. There'll be a whole series of them. I was thinking about doing them in different countries, like Air Hostess hits Hawaii. Air Hostess hits Hong —'

'Okay, we need to back up a bit.' Sarah's eyes were back on the screen. Her lack of speech caused the sudden return of Drew's nerves.

'You've got a good base here. The story flows okay, but your editing is weak. Some of these sentences…' She paused.

Drew's stomach tightened further as the pause changed into a grimace. 'Like I said. Editing.'

Drew nodded his head repeatedly. 'I was doing some editing as I go,' he said, sitting back down next to her so he could get a better view of his toil. 'The posts I've read on writing these things say it's better to edit as you go.'

'That may be the case, but you need to get better at the basics if you want it to be taken seriously. Take this bit, for instance.' She used her mouse and highlighted part of a line. 'I don't like the way you've used *boobs*. Her boobs jangled. They're not keys. Keys jangle. Not boobs. And you can't use the word boobs, even in this type of book. Surely you can't.'

'I know,' Drew agreed. 'I didn't think it sounded right either. But I already used breasts too many times in this paragraph, see.' It was his turn to take over the touchpad and do some highlighting. 'I didn't want to use it again. Not so soon.' Sarah nodded thoughtfully.

'What about breastbone?' she said, deleting the current phrasing in place of her own.

Drew shrugged. 'It's a bit similar. Don't you think?'

'Maybe. How about below her clavicle, then? *He pressed his hand below her clavicle?*'

Drew ran the words over through his own mind. '*He pressed his hand below her clavicle,*' he repeated the words as Sarah typed. 'That would work,' he agreed. 'I like that.'

'And down here,' Sarah continued, her finger already on the delete button. 'Where you've talked about her heading to the shop in her six-inch heels.'

'That's when she meets the bartender. She needs to be dressed for the scene later.'

'But why? She takes him back to her place, doesn't she? Can't she just get dressed up at home? Wouldn't that be a bit more exciting too? You know, he goes back to her place, and she's dressed in her jeans and trainers, and when they get there—'

'She suddenly switches into the stiletto-wearing dominatrix. Yeah. I like it. I think that could work.'

'Okay,' said Sarah standing up and moving the laptop over to the dining room table. 'Let's take a look at the next bit.'

A mug of hot chocolate and a dozen pages later, Drew was sent to go and pick up the kids. Sarah's phone had rung twice, which they ignored both times. The third time, it sounded angry.

'You need to go,' Sarah said to Drew. 'She won't get mad at you. Just say your train was delayed or something, and that the sink backed up again. Maybe if we whinge about stuff long enough, they'll lend us the money we need.'

Drew pulled on his coat. He was in too good a mood to risk ruining it over an argument about money.

'Maybe I can pull the penniless writer line on them?' he said instead.

'It would be true,' she replied. 'I'll keep working on this if you don't mind? See how much more I can get done.'

Hovering with his keys in his hand, Drew stared at the wonder that was his wife.

'Thank you for this,' he said.

'For what?'

'For your support. I'm pretty sure most wives would have had some kind of breakdown had they discovered their husband had started writing erotic fiction on his commute.'

'Yeah,' Sarah said, a coy smile glinting in her eyes. 'Well, I'm not most wives, am I?'

Striding back to the table, he bent over and planted a kiss firmly on his wife's lips before moving back to go.

'Uh-um,' Sarah cleared her throat. 'Are you forgetting something?'

She nodded downwards to her belly. Drew grinned.

'My bad.' He crouched down by her chair and pressed his lips to her belly. 'See you later, little one,' he said. 'Daddy and Mummy are going to have some exciting stories to tell you when you come along.'

# CHAPTER 14

It was bizarre how quickly they fell into a rhythm, Sarah considered. Two weeks after the discovery of Drew's new secret hobby, and not only were they working nicely in tandem but, somehow, they managed to find the time for it. Obviously, it had taken a little bit of shifting around in terms of the children's schedules; waiting for Eva to go to sleep for her nap so Sarah could get another thirty minutes at the laptop was one of her biggest frustrations, but to counter that, she'd managed to wake up before the children twice that week and get half an hour done. These last few days, she really felt as though they were starting to get into their stride.

Drew was still writing on the train but had given up any attempt at editing.

'I don't mean to sound mean,' Sarah had said one week into the joint venture. 'You're just not particularly good at it. You don't see your own mistakes. Besides, I think it's better to have fresh eyes on it. A woman's eyes. You just get the story down, and I'll go over and edit it in the evening when the kids are in bed.'

He'd been sceptical. 'What about if they don't go to sleep? How are you going to manage to do it then?'

'Well then, you'll have to see to them. If you want me to do this, then I need to make sure I get at least an hour every night where I am not interrupted.'

'I guess if you think that's the best way…' Drew had conceded. 'The sooner we get it finished, the sooner we can start making money from it.'

That was the moment when she had subtly walked away and ended the conversation.

Sarah was actively avoiding any mention of money whatsoever when it came to the book. While it was great seeing Drew so excited, she couldn't help feeling he was getting a little ahead of himself. And that was putting it nicely. Obsessed was probably a more accurate term.

Every day, he was growing more and more convinced that this was the answer to all of their problems, and that they were somehow going to make their millions from this new idea in a matter of weeks.

'I read this blog post during lunch today,' he said one evening after he had got in from work. 'This guy makes eight grand a day self-publishing his books. Can you imagine that? Eight thousand pounds a day? We could pay off the mortgage in a month.'

'Most people don't make that sort of money,' Sarah tried to convince him. 'Most writers don't make any money at all.'

'I know that. But even if we could make 10% or just 1%. Imagine what that would do for us?'

And no matter how much she tried not to, she did imagine.

At toddler group, when the other mums strode around in their skinny jeans and tight tops, Sarah imagined how nice it would be to afford a gym membership again. Of course, it would have been nicer had she just been able to fit straight back into her size ten jeans without any amount of physical effort, discipline, or self-control on her part in any way, but second to that, a gym membership or personal trainer would come in a close second. She could stop buying budget food too; fresh salmon fillets and organic vegetables for the kids every night. And wine that wasn't on a three for ten pounds deal. A personal bodyguard wouldn't go amiss either, she thought, if only for the purpose of keeping unwanted mums – by which she meant Justine – away.

'I was reading a study about the effects of screen time on children,' Justine said, having suddenly appeared at Sarah's side twenty minutes into their Monday toddler group. Sarah cursed herself. She thought she had been keeping tabs on Justine's location in the hall, mainly to avoid being spotted stealing the children's biscuits from the buffet. Not only had she been literally caught with her hand in the cookie jar, but Justine's appearance was only moments after Sarah had given up trying to persuade Eva to play nicely with the other children and so had handed her daughter her phone to keep her quiet. She knew exactly what lecture was coming next.

'It's a necessity, of course, in this day and age. We all do it. But honestly, the more you read about it, the more terrifying it is. And it's not just their eyesight it affects, either.'

'No?' Sarah muttered, wondering exactly how long this passive-aggressive attack on her parenting was going to last and whether she should grab a handful of the biscuits and claim she was taking them as snacks for Eva on the walk home.

'Oh no, it's all sorts of things,' Justine continued. 'Hand-eye coordination, concentration levels. Not to mention the effects it has on their social skills. I mean, you only need to look at the children to see what it's doing to their brains.' She barely paused for breath before continuing her tirade. 'We try to limit the time ours spend on them, obviously, but some-times you just need that little break, don't you? Take last week. Philomena spent a full fifteen minutes on my phone. Fifteen minutes. In a row. Can you imagine? I felt absolutely ghastly afterwards. I made sure we had an extra-long yoga session together that evening.'

Sarah looked over at Eva, who had, at that minute, begun licking the screen.

'At least it's not affecting her eyesight now,' she said.

Back home, things were good. Better, in fact, than she could remember them being in years. And she knew the exact reason why.

Drew had been unsure at first; a man writing erotic fiction novels seemed like a recipe for disaster. Yet, the more he wrote, the more and more his preconceived notions were pushed further to the back of his mind. It helped that Sarah knew; he didn't feel quite so perverted when he went to look up a particular turn of phrase on Google and found himself face to face with a pair of double-f boobs and an unfeasibly large penis.

'Nope,' she would say when she read through his latest work each evening. 'You cannot say that about her backside. What backside have you ever seen that's the shape of a donut? And why is he all muscular and glistening? I thought he was an English teacher.'

'English teachers can get a sweat on too,' Drew protested.

'When he's writing reports?'

He wobbled his head contemplatively. 'Perhaps not then.'

'I think you need to tone it down a bit here,' she would say, highlighting yet another paragraph she was going to delete. 'Besides, didn't the guy in chapter three have *picture-perfect* abs? And the one in chapter five too?'

'I thought they had *pretty perfect* abs.'

'Whatever it is, it's too similar. How about perfectly chiselled? Or beautifully contoured? You have a thesaurus on the computer. It wouldn't hurt you to put it to use now and again. And there are more than two different body parts on each of the sexes you know.' At first, she had been delicate about taking a red pen to his work. Now she rarely waited for his approval before axing line after line of whatever he'd written and moving on. Yet somehow, even in its raw state, even with the whipping – metaphorical obviously – he received, it was cathartic. They had found their momentum. Together, they were a machine; not yet well-oiled, but definitely lightly lubricated, and getting better with every passing day.

Each evening, Sarah would tear his book to shreds, and each morning, he would get back on the train more excited and enthused about what the next chapter was going to hold. He was already at nearly 30,000 words; 30,000 words in a month. It was unbelievable when he thought about it. He could remember the time when writing a 2000-word essay felt like the biggest slog he was ever going to do. Now, if he didn't write 1000 words on the morning commute, he would arrive at work with a bee in his bonnet and have to shorten his lunch break until he reached the target.

He had even given up on the Monday fry up trips too, in favour of a half-hour silence at the office to get a few more words down, or at the very least, catch up on the latest podcasts. There were great things out there for people like him, he had discovered. Things that were going to make this a real career for him and Sarah. A whole new life. And people were starting to notice the difference.

'You're very busy again,' Polly said that morning as she passed his office. He had had a productive day so far - excluding the fifteen minutes spent on the phone to ICT on Barry's behalf as they would no longer deal with Barry directly.

'They're the unreasonable ones,' Barry had insisted. 'Thinking I spilled that cup of coffee on my laptop deliberately.'

'Wasn't that the second cup of coffee you've spilled on your laptop?'

'Exactly! Who would spill two cups deliberately?'

Drew wasn't entirely sure he saw the logic in his argument. 'Fine, just use my computer. But put your mug down on the window ledge first.'

'It's only tea,' Barry replied.

Drew scratched his temples. Some days it was even harder than managing Eva.

'Sorry,' Drew said, looking up from the computer to find

himself staring into a pair of perfectly made-up grey eyes. 'Did you say something?'

'Only that you looked busy,' Polly replied. 'And that we missed you today at lunch. Is it some kind of healthy eating regime? I thought you were almost as addicted to your black pudding as Barry.'

With a subtle swipe of the hand, Drew minimised the screen on which, only moments ago, he had been writing a highly explicit scene involving the air hostess, a hotel architect, and a bespoke mahogany bookshelf. Once his computer was clear, he leant back in his chair, in an overly exaggerated attempt at a casual, relaxed pose.

'Just trying to get everything sorted before the Christmas orders get finalised. Experience has taught me that any day now, your uncle's going to come through wanting the last six years' worth of figures on turkeys and cold cuts.'

Polly chuckled. 'Quite possibly, although I think he's currently too busy fretting over who put a dent in the side of his new car to worry about that right now.'

'They didn't?' Drew leaned forward in his seat.

'They did. Yesterday, while he was out at lunch. And he only drove it off the forecourt last week.' Drew winced. Polly didn't. 'Honestly, I don't get guys and the new car thing. Really, I don't. Is it that important what the piece of metal looks like that gets you to work each day? Surely there are more exciting things you could be spending your money on? Like holidays or nights out with friends?'

'Or bumper packs of nappies and burping cloths,' Drew finished for her.

'I'm not quite there yet,' she laughed. 'Besides, you're not exactly an old dad.'

'I'm not?' Drew questioned, shifting about so as not to aggravate his sciatica that had begun playing up again since he started all the writing. 'I bloody well feel like I am.'

Polly's smile broadened.

'Then you should come out with me. I'm sure I could make you feel young again.'

'I'm sure you could.'

It was meant as a simple response to her question, yet when the words came out of Drew's mouth, they went from being fun and polite to downright sleazy. An immediate flush of colour rose to his cheeks. 'Well, I, uhm…' A frog caught in his throat as he began to stutter. 'I should get back to this figure. Figures. These numbers. I have numbers to look at.'

She grinned. 'Maybe you could just save me a dance at the Christmas Party? Oh, and don't forget Stu will want the accounts drive before the end of the week,' she said, pivoting on the balls of her feet and walking out. As the door clicked closed, Drew threw himself back in his chair and groaned. At least Sarah never had to worry about him having an affair. He was about as good at speaking to women as he was at fixing the tumble drier. Not that he would ever consider having an affair, of course. Especially not with the way things were going between them at the minute. And then, for no other reason than he wanted to, he texted his wife to tell her he loved her. He was a lucky man, and he knew it.

## CHAPTER 15

'Don't you dare dump your bloody coat on the stairs,' Sarah shouted through from the kitchen while attempting to stop the stir fry from burning on the hob. 'And can you make sure George is not firing his archery set at the T.V. again? I swear, we are putting a ban on toys this Christmas. And sugar. And electronics. And things. They have too many things.'

Drew came into the kitchen, his coat over his arm, and planted a kiss on her neck.

'What exactly are people going to get them?' He hesitated and repeated the question with a substantially more concerned tone. 'Actually, what are we going to get them?'

Sarah paused, thinking it through.

'They can have books,' she said eventually. 'They're allowed books.'

'Didn't George almost give Eva a concussion with a book last week?'

'Paperbacks only.'

Disappearing from the kitchen, Drew reappeared a

second later without his coat. 'It's still a risk,' he goaded her. 'Paper cuts. Accidental arson. I think books might be pushing it.'

'Fine then.' Sarah scraped at the sticking vegetables. 'They can have oranges. Peeled ones, so they don't break the windows when they throw them in a tantrum at their rubbish Christmas. That's all any of us are getting for Christmas this year. Oranges.'

Drew's laugh lingered as he rested his chin on her shoulder.

'This all looks very healthy,' he said, sticking his nose above the frying pan only to withdraw it seconds later. 'Is there some reason?'

Sarah narrowed her eyes.

'I started with the *Loony Lamaze* classes today, remember?'

'That was today?'

'Yup. Twelve well-meaning hippies all telling me how my current diet is poisoning my unborn child.'

'It wasn't that bad, surely?' Drew asked, stepping back to rub her shoulders.

'Yes, it was. They're nutters, the lot of them.'

On the account of the fact that she had done it once before with George, and everything had gone just fine, Sarah had forgone birthing classes with Eva and just winged it. If that's what you could call it. The worst forty-six hours of her life. And Eva's too, of course. Still, even now, the thought of it made her woozy.

'Just do another course,' Nelly had encouraged her over the last few weeks. 'Get your confidence back.'

'But the cost of it…' Sarah's mind jumped straight to the

place it always jumped when someone mentioned doing something. 'And besides, when am I going to find the time?'

'If it's important, then you need to find the time. And I don't mind having the kids for a couple of hours in the evening if you need?' Nelly continued. 'Besides, you could always take a look at the Mind Birthing they're running at the village hall.'

'Mind Birthing?'

'Uh-huh.' Nelly drank her tea with her eyebrows raised. 'You know, it's one of those hippy things. *Birth isn't painful. It's just a manifestation of all the love we are squeezing out of our vagina* type mumbo-jumbo.'

'That does sound like nonsense.'

'But it's free.'

Sarah's head cocked with interest.

'And it's only four afternoons. I'll have Eva if that will help. One of my old work colleagues did it. She enjoyed it. It'll be nice company. And it's not like it can make you feel any more worried about it.'

Sucking her cheeks in, Sarah turned the thought over in her mind. There was no point asking Drew to join her, but free and short, that sounded like her type of deal. And if it helped relieve the constant knotting in her stomach by just a little bit, it would be worth it. Of course, it depended on exactly how much hippy nonsense she would have to endure. After her first session, she knew.

'First of all…' Sarah pulled two china plates down from the cupboard followed by two plastic ones. 'We were made to tell each other about all the toxins we are putting in our body.'

'As in… food?'

'You'd think.' Sarah chortled bitterly at the naïve simplicity of Drew's answer. 'But, no. Not just food. Makeup, pollution. Words.'

'Words?'

'Negative words. And technology. Social media. Even some colours are toxic, apparently.'

'Really?' Drew frowned, giving the impression that Sarah might not be recollecting the event fully.

'Seriously. Orange, that's a toxic colour apparently. And purple. Who knew?' She switched the hob off and reached for a ladle. 'I had no idea what was going on. After that, we spent twenty minutes watching women give birth in lakes surrounded by fish and mosquitos. Then crouched on the floor for half an hour trying to feel our nostrils move.'

'No.'

Sarah closed her eyes and inhaled deeply, trying to replicate the instructions offered in class. *See the flow of air. Let the energy fill you from within.* A couple of breaths in, and she remembered she was supposed to be dishing up dinner. 'That was the best bit. Hopefully, there'll be more of the deep breathing part next week. I'm pretty sure the woman next to me was asleep for the whole of it, so I might just use it as an afternoon nap time.'

'Then why bother going?' Drew helped himself to a piece of chicken straight from the pan. 'I know you're worried about it and everything, but honestly, it was all okay in the end, wasn't it? If you don't feel like you've got enough time, you might as well just skip it.'

Locking her jaw and avoiding his gaze, Sarah handed Drew the two filled plates. *Okay* was most definitely a subjective word. At this moment, more than ever. If there was one memory in her life she could keep eternally repressed, it would be that of Eva's birth. Even now, just thinking back, she could feel her pulse starting to race, the sweat building on her skin. Hours of excruciating pain and people offering endless words of encouragement. And then something changed. There'd been hushed whispers, furtive glances they thought she couldn't see. Doors swinging open and closed while everyone told her, *'Don't worry. Things like this happen. Just keep breathing.'* Like not breathing was even a possibility. That was when she discovered they'd lost Eva's heartbeat. Two doctors and the worst forty minutes of her life later, they found it again. Not that they made the birth itself any better. The epidural had been ineffective, her muscles had given up the will to live, and in the end, she had had two midwives and two doctors and a vacuum all racing to get Eva out, in case the lost heartbeat was something more than just an anomaly. She lost a lot of blood in the process too. Far more than with George. Thinking back to that time, the smell of blood would still strike as if it wafted right under her nose. All that time, Drew had been standing beside her, trying to make it look like he wasn't about to pass out, and acting like what she had gone through was entirely normal. And now, he was acting like pushing another one out was going to be as easy as pulling the lid off a Tesco's Finest ready meal.

'I will be there,' Drew said, apparently noting the change in atmosphere. 'I will be there, and the doctors will all be there, and nothing is going to go wrong.'

'Just make sure your bosses know all the dates.' Sarah spooned out more of the stir fry mixture onto plastic plates. 'The other two were late, so you might have to change the weeks around if that happens again.'

'I know.'

'And you're taking the holiday time and paternity. Don't forget that.'

'I'm not going to forget that, Sarah.' The two syllables' use of her name was quickly followed by a more amenable tone. 'Are the kids going to eat that too?' Drew asked.

'They better.' Sarah shook the memories of past labours and fears of the future one from her mind. 'Otherwise, I shall be projecting some seriously toxic vocabulary in their direction.'

Surprisingly, the children managed to eat enough broccoli and chicken stir fry that Sarah felt justified in serving them two oversized portions of ice cream. In fairness, Eva mainly mashed hers around her chair and into her hair, but the overall effect imitated eating closely enough that Sarah was satisfied.

While Drew bathed them and got down to bedtime stories, Sarah got to work on the editing.

'All done,' Drew said, downstairs before Sarah had even managed the first page.

'What do you mean done?' She momentarily lifted her eyes from the computer before lowering them back down and heading to the thesaurus in search of a non-mathematical synonym for *girth*. 'Have they brushed their teeth?'

'Top ones and bottom ones.'

'Stories?'

'Julia Donaldson times four.'

'And Eva —'

'Has knickers on *over* her nappy.'

Sarah straightened her back, mildly impressed, before

frowning in confusion. 'How did you get knickers to go over her nappy? Surely, they don't fit.'

'Well, we used yours, but she's fine with that.'

Sarah opened her mouth to respond, only to discover there wasn't a response to such a situation.

'Okay,' she said.

Her head was about to return to the task at hand when Drew squeezed down on the edge of the sofa and began to rub her feet.

'I'm sorry,' he said, digging his thumbs in below her big toe and distracting her entirely from the metaphor she had previously had on the tip of her tongue.

'What for?'

'For the birthing class. I'll get the train back earlier next week. I'll come with you. Maybe I could just wear a blindfold for the… you know…'

'The vaginas?'

He nodded in a minuscule motion. Sighing, Sarah placed the laptop on the floor beside her.

'It's fine,' she assured him. 'It's a nice group. I mean, it's weird, but they're nice. There are all sorts there. Several single people. Besides, I like the enigma that comes with being on my own.'

'Enigma?'

'You know…'

She shuffled up closer and wrapped her arms around his neck. 'Have I walked out on my husband to do this by myself, or am I part of a polyamorous relationship and don't want people to know? Is there no father at all?'

'Isn't the class run by one of the teachers at George's school?'

Sarah dropped her arms. 'Okay, so I'm not that much of an enigma, but it's fine, honestly. It wasn't as bad as I thought.' Drew's jaw remained tight. She lifted a hand to touch it. 'Honestly,' she said again.

With a heavy sigh, his eyes moved down to her laptop, only to jump straight back to meet her.

'I keep forgetting to tell you. The Christmas Party is on the fourteenth this year.'

'The party where Barry gets drunk every year and spends half the time telling me you're the best boss he's ever had and the other half in tears telling me he's convinced he's going to get fired?'

'That's the one.'

'Okay.'

'It's a Friday night.'

'Alright.'

Sarah's eyes went back to the laptop, another pair of *perfect abs* to try and deal with. Seriously? Highlighting the area, she clicked delete. She was just about to deal with the woman's *heaving bosom* when she realised Drew was still looking at her.

'Everything okay?' she asked, noting the twitch to his lower lip.

'What? Oh, yes, everything's fine. But, well… I wondered…'

Recognising the signs as an indication that this was not going to be a short conversation, Sarah hit save on the top of the screen and placed her laptop down on the sofa beside her. 'You were just wondering what?'

'Well, did you want me to see if I could get mum to babysit?'

'Babysit? What for?'

'For the Christmas Party?'

'I assumed we would.' Sarah's hand went back to the computer.

'I meant *babysit*, babysit.'

Sarah frowned.

'What's *babysit*, babysit?'

'You know. Overnight. It's at a hotel this year. One in town. I thought I could book us a room. We get a discount with work. And it would probably be the last chance we would get to have a bit of time to ourselves before the baby arrives? And before you mention money, don't forget, it'll be December. I'll get my Christmas bonus. I can reserve the room now and pay for it then. I've already checked.'

Pursing her lips, Sarah ran her tongue along the top of her teeth. As nice as it sounded, a bit of time to themselves would come with hours of preparation. Eva had never spent a night at her grandparents' before, meaning it would probably be a disaster. George was always so grumpy and tired at the end of term that he probably wouldn't want to stay either. All the excuses tumbled their way to the front of her mind. Not to mention the fact that they would be pushing it dangerously close to her due date. It was highly unlikely that she'd be up for anything other than an early night and a breakfast buffet. There were tens of reasons as to why it was definitely not a great idea.

'That sounds nice,' she said.

Every third line, her mind drifted from editing. One minute she was thinking about Christmas – what they were going to cook and whether it was really worth pulling the dining room table out into the centre for just the four of them – and the next moment, she was pondering the chances of Drew's parents surprising them with a massive wad of cash for the holiday season, and then her thoughts were off again, this time wondering what the hell she was going to wear to the Home Crew Christmas Party. For over forty minutes, she stared at the same paragraph, getting exactly nowhere. Worse still was that it had been the same paragraph she had been staring at that morning while Drew got the kids ready for school too. Last week, it hadn't been like that at all.

Tiredness would have been her normal excuse, only she wasn't any more tired than she had been for the last five years, and she had just got her bloodwork back from the doctors, showing she was actually in pretty good shape. It had to be the writing, she decided. Something was stopping the words from moving properly. If only she could place her finger on the problem. There was nothing wrong with the syntax, and the dialogue appeared natural enough, but something about it just wasn't sitting right.

As such, by the end of her afternoon editing session, Sarah was nearly two chapters behind where she had hoped to get up to that day. Add to that the fact that she hadn't even managed to wash up the breakfast bowls from that morning or run the vacuum through the house. Oh well. If Drew wanted a full, cooked meal when he got in from work, he was going to have to be the one to make it. She was an editor now. She had deadlines to meet.

# CHAPTER 16

Drew thumped his hands against the plastic table.

On his morning train ride, it had been fine; words spilling from his mind quicker than his fingers could keep up with. He had been on a roll. He had been on fire. And then, on the way back, nothing.

'Come on,' he said to himself as he attempted to put down a single sentence, only to delete it thirty seconds later. 'What is wrong with you?' The man in the opposite seat lifted his head from his paper to offer Drew a glare, but he didn't care. There were bigger things to deal with than funny looks from other commuters. Like what the hell was going on with his writing.

For a further twenty minutes, he continued to battle away, writing and deleting, writing and deleting, until he gave up altogether and spent the last fifteen minutes of the journey playing Scrabble on his phone. He told himself it had been a long day at work as he ambled back home from the station. He would be back on form the next morning.

To Drew's distress, the next morning was just as bad, as

was the following afternoon. He got on with other jobs. There was plenty of Home Crew work to keep him occupied, and he booked the hotel for Sarah and him to stay at for the Christmas Party before she could change her mind, but for three full days, he managed no more than four badly-formed paragraphs. Fortunately, Sarah was behind in the editing, meaning she was oblivious to his sudden case of writer's block. However, despite her obliviousness to the current situation, surprisingly, she was the one who found the solution.

Sitting at the dining room table with her reading glasses moved down to the end of her nose, she flicked her line of sight from the screen to Drew. 'I don't want you to take this the wrong way…' She looked somewhat apologetic as she spoke. 'But I'm finding it a bit boring.'

'What? The editing? I thought you were enjoying it,' Drew said.

'Oh no, I love the editing part. And I'm getting rather good at it. I mean your story. I'm finding the story a bit boring.'

Drew stiffened. 'What do you mean, boring? How can it be boring? It's full of sex. Sex isn't boring.'

'Well, it kind of is. At least, what you've written is.'

With a strong sense of purpose, Drew moved across the room and pointed at the screen from over her shoulder.

'What are you on about? She's just been rescued by a fireman who swept her off her feet during a house fire and ravaged her against his pole. That's exciting.'

'I know. But in the previous chapter, she was rescued by a handsome doctor, who just happened to pass when she was feeling faint, then he took her back to his surgery to ravage her on his hospital bed.'

'She was suffering from a lack of iron —'

'And in the chapter before that, she was rescued by a sailor when she got into trouble on her dingy, and he took her back to his cabin and r—.'

'Okay, okay. I can see there's a little bit of a theme going on here.'

'It's the only thing going on. There's just a lot of rescuing and ravaging.'

Drew stepped back away from the computer.

'It is erotic fiction, Sarah. That's what erotic fiction is. There's meant to be sex going on.'

'I get that, but there's meant to be other stuff going on as well,' she protested. 'And the sex. It's all the same. Honestly, if I have to read about a hot tub one more time, I'm going to give up editing this thing altogether. Why did the doctor even have a hot tub in his surgery?'

'It's called artistic license,' Drew protested.

'No, it's called a weak storyline. And it's showing.'

With his jaw jutting out in a remarkably similar manner to Eva's, Drew stared at the screen. There was no point denying it; she was right. That was probably why he'd been struggling so much for the last chapter and a half. Still frowning, he let out a low hiss. As a young man and now as a married older one, he'd always been perfectly happy with the standard of his and Sarah's sex life and, to be brutally honest, when he'd needed that little extra, he'd never been one to shy away from porn. But normal porn. Married man porn. Looking at it now, there was no point in pretending they were anything other than what they actually were; traditional. If statistics were to come into it, he'd estimate around eighty-five percent missionary, ten percent doggy, and an additional five percent left for late-night fumbles in the dark where either hc or Sarah didn't fully appreciate the position of one another's legs and therefore put things in very unexpected places. At least 98 percent of all encounters happened in the bedroom, on the bed, and under the covers, and that was fine for him. Just apparently not for his new-found career.

'You just need to find some ways of spicing it up,' Sarah said, breaking his stream of thought. 'The bulk of it is fine. You just need to change the pace now and again.'

'What do you suggest we do?'

Sarah wasn't entirely sure she had made the suggestion to open up six tabs' worth of different porn sites, but fifteen minutes later, she and Drew were sitting together on the sofa with the laptop open and a screen full of flashing logos and X-rated images.

'Nope,' she said, as a pair of legs opened wide onto the screen in front of her. 'This is not what we're after.'

'What about this one then?'

'With the piercings? No, definitely not.'

Drew went back to the search bar and tried again.

'This site says it's good for women.'

'Let's give it a go.' Sarah said, looking at the pages of whips and handcuffs, along with a variety of hairstyles. She couldn't help but wonder how people designed such features, let alone coiffed them. The sight of them was enough to make her itch.

'Inspiring?' Sarah asked.

Drew's eyes bulged as he scrolled the screen down from one video to another.

'I think *intimidating* may be the better word. That's not natural, is it?'

Closing her eyes, she sucked in a lungful of air and clenched her fists. She wasn't going to be a prude about this. She just wasn't. She was young and in her prime. Besides, they were looking for work. *Inspiration,* she reminded herself again.

'What about that?' Drew pointed to a five-second clip on rotation. 'That could have a story to it.' He clicked on the photo. A pair of shaved testicles bounced onto the screen in front of them.

'Nope. No. No inspiration there!' Sarah leaned across Drew and clicked the back arrow on the computer. 'Maybe this was a bad idea,' she said. 'Maybe we should just be looking at more books.'

'Do you have time to read them?' Drew asked in earnest. 'Come on. This can work. We just need to find the right site. Please. I want you onside with this.'

Sarah inhaled. It was necessary market research, she told herself. It was for the benefit of the book. She cast her gaze at her husband. Drew was so happy at the minute, and the pair of them, as a couple, it was helping. Besides, she liked the editing. Really liked it. It was the first time in years that she felt like a person, not just a mum or a housewife. Just walking to the shops, she could feel the spring returning to her step. And it took her mind off the impending birth. With that in mind, she reached across the sideboard and grabbed a notepad and pen. She wasn't going to write full sentences, just a few key terms or words to make sure they didn't forget anything.

'What are you doing?' Drew's hand moved away from the laptop to lock with Sarah's, a quizzical look on his face.

'What do you mean? I'm making notes.'

'What for?'

'For you to use. You know, if any plot ideas jump out at you.'

The quizzical look deepened.

'You're turning this into a work activity?'

'Well, that's what it is, isn't it?'

The corner of his lips curled upwards. 'Sarah, my love.' He shifted the computer from his lap to the floor. His eyes narrowed as his hand lay flat against her thigh. 'Sometimes, work can be fun too.'

The next evening, when the children were in bed, and Sarah sat down with the computer at the dining room table, Drew drummed his thumb against his thigh, trying to figure out the best way to broach the subject. While the porn-induced fumble had been nice, it hadn't helped him in quite the way he had hoped. Sure, he'd managed half a chapter that day, if you combined his commute there and back, but it had still been a slog. Things just weren't flowing as naturally as they were.

'I've been thinking,' he told Sarah, stopping his thumbs from drumming just long enough to start to twiddle them together.

'Uh-huh,' Sarah's eyes stayed focused on the screen.

'Well...' His throat constricted. 'I had a couple of ideas. A couple of things I think might work.'

'Sounds good.'

'Just that I want to run them by you.'

'Uh-huh—'

'Will you just look up for one minute?' Drew's nerves got the better of him. 'I want to talk to you.'

With a look of moderate surprise, Sarah lifted her gaze and placed her hand to the side of the keyboard. Drew filled his lungs with a deep breath of air.

'Okay,' he said, his head nodding as his internal dialogue continued to convince him this was a wise thing to suggest. 'I was thinking that perhaps we should invest in some, you know, toys.'

'Toys?' Sarah frowned. 'What toys? The kids already have more toys than we can fit in the house.'

'Not kid's toys. You know, toys. Like the ones they had advertised on the websites.'

Sarah's eyes widened. 'Oh. You mean sex toys?'

Drew could feel the colour draining from his cheeks. He was sure it wasn't meant to be as difficult as this to discuss vibrators with his wife. After all, weren't they all designed for women anyway?

'There were lots of interesting packages online. And I thought it would be good. You know, for us and the book.'

'You realise we're having a baby? I'm not letting down there for at least six months after this thing's born.'

'I know that. But we've still got a few weeks before then. It could be fun.'

A thick crease formed between Sarah's eyebrows, one that Drew recognised perfectly well. In fact, it was the one response he was a hundred percent certain she was going to give, and therefore, he was fully prepared for it.

'Drew,' she said with a sigh, confirming exactly what comment was coming next. 'Do you really think we have the—'

'I know. We don't have the money. But what about if it's our Christmas present to each other? What about if this is all we get each other? No silly stocking presents. No novelty socks that neither of us need, just—'

'Sex toys?'

'Exactly.'

With his chest pounding, Drew watched as her lips disappeared into a thin line. Her pondering pose.

'And I suppose you're going to order these?'

'I could,' he said, his pulse quickening with the knowledge that he had almost got her on board. 'Or we could order them together. Or you could go into a shop and choose what you think you'd —'

'I am *not* going into a shop,' Sarah said, with absolute certainty.

'Fine, then. We can order online. As long as you're sure that's okay for your Christmas present.'

With a withering look, Sarah raised her eyebrows. 'To be honest, it's probably a step up from The Best of Coldplay DVD you got me last year.'

'There you go then,' Drew smiled. 'Everyone wins.'

'But they are not going under the bloody tree. The last thing we need is Eva unwrapping a rampant rabbit in front of your mother on Christmas morning.'

～

～

Why she had agreed to spend the whole of their Christmas budget on kinky sex toys, Sarah didn't know, other than it made Drew happy, and she had wanted to get on with her editing. She hadn't been joking about him not going down there for six months after the baby was born, though. That was the thing about all the films and television shows about childbirth; they were more than happy to show images of women squeezing the bars of their beds as they screamed out in pain, but what they didn't show you was what came next. The disgustingness of never really knowing what was going to fall out of your nether regions. And the stitches that made it more than a tad uncomfortable to do pretty much anything. And a bladder that may or may not be able to withstand a tablespoon of anything before letting you down at the most inappropriate times. For some reason, Hollywood didn't like to talk about those things. When was the last time you saw a woman's pelvic floor fail them in a blockbuster movie? Never, that was when. Still, if that was what he wanted to do, that was what they would do.

The next morning, after a text reminding her, she went online to make her purchases. By force of habit, Sarah went straight for the reduced section of the first website, only to flinch at what greeted her. Veins and flaps made her simultaneously scrunch up her eyes and gag. How could these things possibly be a turn on? Each to their own and all that, but really. She shuddered and forced her eyes back open. And there were so many things on there. How was she meant to know what Drew would like? Or what she would like for that matter. What she really needed was some kind of selection pack. A sex-toy selection pack.

Being unable to think of a better course of action, she typed *ultimate sex toy selection pack* into her browser. A second later, her screen filled.

Sarah read the first search result, *The ultimate sex-toy set*. She clicked on it and read through the contents. There was certainly a lot in it, and while it cost the same price as a weekly food shop, it did say the total package saved over 30% compared to purchasing the items separately. Still, it was a lot of money. Too much. And there was no guarantee they'd like using everything in it. She went back to the previous page and removed the last word. *The ultimate sex-toy*. After taking a second to load, a series of images and adverts filled the page. Of them, one caught her eye. With nearly 1000 reviews, all of which were four or five stars, it looked like as safe a bet as she was going to get in such a situation. Determined not to spend the rest of the morning messing up her cookies, resulting in her computer never showing her anything other than ads for vibrators again, she pulled out the only credit card she knew for certain worked and typed the number in. A receipt appeared on the screen. Delivery in two days. Perfect.

# CHAPTER 17

At the office, the strain of the impending Christmas season was starting to cause tension among the staff.

'We've got another three warehouses on short-term leases for this period,' Casper told them at the morning briefing. 'And we're just finishing off the recruiting for December. Our hope is to employ another 200 pickers in the warehouses for over that Christmas week, but we've only got four weeks to go.'

'What about the turkey issue?' someone asked. 'Have we managed to sort the turkey issue?'

'We've put a cap on the limit people can order. That's all we can do.'

'And the drivers?'

'We should have a new fleet arriving next week.'

Drew jotted down what he felt he should while trying not to let his mind drift too far away from the job he was actually paid to do. Maybe it was because he was a man, he thought, as someone pointed to a PowerPoint slide. Perhaps that's why he was struggling to keep the book engaging.

That morning's commute had been a little more productive; he had managed to get a solid thousand words down involving a farmer and a hay barn, but Sarah was right. It was more of the same with his impeccably dressed heroine rescued by the farmer. Perhaps there were a few more twists and turns – both metaphorically and physically – than in previous chapters, but was that enough? Did he really just want to produce another run of the mill book to be flicked over and then discarded? He was hoping he would manage something more than that. Something with a little panache.

Noticing that a couple of eyes were on him and aware that he had probably missed a question, Drew straightened in his seat. Clearing his throat and nodding, he emitted a glottal hum.

'I agree. I fully agree,' he said, praying they hadn't just asked him for his opinion on child trafficking or deforestation. A few satisfied smiles confirmed that he had responded correctly, although as he sank back into his chair, he caught Polly's eye, a suppressed smirk twitching on her lips.

For the rest of the briefing, Drew tried to pay more attention, although the moment he returned to his office, his mind was already back on the issues with the book. Time and time again, he came back to the same overriding thought; it was because he was a man. It had to be. Weren't most of these things written by women? At least the big ones were. Maybe his male perspective on the matter was why he was having such difficulty. If he wanted to appeal to a female audience, there was only one thing for it; he needed more female input.

'No,' Sarah answered before Drew had even finished asking the question. 'I'm not doing it.'

'But just hear me out.'

'You don't think I've got enough to do? I already spend all my spare time editing your parts. When am I supposed to do that if I'm writing too? We have a baby due in two months, remember?'

'You wouldn't be writing all of it. Just a chapter here and there. You know, to add a bit of a different voice. Just to break things up.'

'I thought the whole point of writers was that you had your own voice? That you didn't switch and change.'

'Says who?'

Squeezing past him to get into the hallway, Sarah bent down and began picking up severed LEGO heads.

'Please.' Drew followed her, picking the pieces straight out of her hand and dropping them into the toy box. 'Just do one, then. One chapter. And then, if you don't want to write anymore, I'll leave you alone.'

'Drew, I—'

'Please.' He dropped onto his knees and helped her fish a piece out from beneath the radiator. 'From what I remember, you're pretty good at the dirty talk. Just bring a bit of that. And I'm not going to stop pestering you until you do. So, unless you want our baby to arrive to the sound of me begging, I'd just get on with it.'

Her lips tightened and twitched, but there was a glint in her eye. A glint Drew recognised to mean she was almost there onside, finally succumbing to his irrefutable charm.

'If I do this, then I'm just doing one, you understand that? One chapter. I'm not doing any more than that. And I don't even know if I want it to go in the book.'

'That's your choice.'

'Our writing styles are probably completely different.'

'I understand.'

'And I'll do it on my own time. You're not allowed to nag me.'

'No nagging. No nagging at all.' He pushed himself up to his feet before reaching down and helping Sarah up.

'So, you will then? You'll do it?'

'That sounds like nagging to me,' Sarah replied.

To give Drew his due, it was substantially harder to start writing her chapter than Sarah had anticipated. The truth was, she had been toying with the idea herself long before Drew suggested it. Lately, she had taken her role as editor to be *rewriter* and was removing more and more of Drew's clichés in favour of her own turns of phrase. All the same, that had been easy in comparison. Just starting the first sentence was proving impossible.

*The wind howled,* Sarah began before pressing delete multiple times in rapid succession. It sounded like a horror book in the making.

*The sun shone brightly through the window.* Delete again. *The air smelled of cut grass and fresh laundry* – she hit delete before she even finished the sentence; who on earth would start with a sentence like that?

Singing away to herself, Eva was threading pasta onto

string. The activity had already been going for a record fifteen minutes, and it felt unlikely that she would keep at it for much longer without throwing the whole thing across the room or else getting a piece stuck up her nose, but still, Sarah was determined to make the most of the peace and quiet.

*The music in the bar thumped loudly from the speakers as people pressed up against one another on the dance floor.* She re-read the sentence and cocked her head to the side. She didn't hate it. That was something. And it certainly offered a place to start. A dance floor, bodies, what more was needed?

On the ground, Eva smashed a piece of pasta into the carpet. Sarah pulled a shard of raw pasta out of her daughter's hand and got back to typing. After all, if Drew could manage this, how hard could it be?

She had just about got into the swing of things when it was time to go and pick George up. Autumn had very much gone. With December only five days away, she really should have headed into the loft and fished out all of George's old winter clothes for Eva to wear. For now, she just double-layered all their jumpers. Clutching a shivering Eva, she waited in the playground for George to appear.

'We will be two minutes,' she said to her writhing daughter, having no intention of spending a second longer at the school gates than she needed to. 'Georgie will be out any second.' As would be typical on the coldest day of the year so far, George was the last child to emerge from the school. When he did finally make his way into the courtyard, he was standing at the side of Miss Jenkins. Sarah's stomach dropped. George's teacher never came outside unless she wanted something. And the way she was grinning and looking directly at Sarah in that annoyingly perky manner of hers meant she was almost certainly about to be accosted.

'Sarah, do you have a minute?' For some unfathomable reason, it irked Sarah that teachers now thought it was fine to call parents by their first name. Not that she liked being called Mrs. Morgan either. That made her feel like her mother-in-law. Basically, it was a lose-lose situation. 'I just wanted to check that you're okay to bring in your prizes for the Winter Fair this week?'

'Prizes?' Sarah's words betrayed her before she could stop them. The teacher was looking at her expectantly. No doubt there had been a notice in one of the dozens of emails and letters that were sent home, most of which went straight into her deleted inbox or, if they were of a physical variety, stayed at the bottom of George's school bag until they had formed a cement-like paste with all the spilled drinks, dropped grapes, and moulding apple slices. 'Oh, yes, of course, the prizes.' Sarah nodded and smiled as she tried to hide the fact that she had absolutely no idea what the teacher was on about.

'It doesn't have to be much,' the teacher continued 'Half a dozen small gifts for the tombola would be perfect. Or perhaps one larger gift for the raffle? We've had everything from gift vouchers to an iPad this year.'

'An iPad?'

'Yes, some of our parents have been exceptionally generous.' Her eyes skirted past Sarah to the playground, where with a broad smile, she lifted her hand in a wave. Sarah twisted her neck around. Justine. Of course, it would be Justine. That would be right up her street; make sure that everyone else's child had a screen to glue their face to, just so she could laud it superior over them when their kid went blind from too much screen time.

'Of course, we don't want to put you under any pressure,' the teacher continued, her attention back on Sarah. 'Any little thing will do. Obviously, it is a no-sugar policy, so sweets won't be allowed, and second-hand goods must have gone through the required safety ch—'

'I've got it,' Sarah said, taking George's hand. 'Don't worry. It's all sorted. I've got them at home. I just keep forgetting to bring them in.'

'Brilliant. Tomorrow?' Miss Jenkins asked, raising her eyebrows. 'Only the members of the PTA are planning on using this week to do some sorting. You're not a member, are you?'

'Tomorrow should be fine,' Sarah smiled back sweetly. She was eighty percent sure the PTA comment was meant as a dig, but even if it was, it wasn't like there was much she could do. 'I've got a little too much on my plate for the PTA at the minute,' she said, patting her bump.

'Of course, how silly. Well, have a lovely afternoon. And honestly, don't stress about the prizes. They don't have to be anything big. Every little bit helps.

Three minutes later, and Sarah was sitting in the car wondering what the hell just happened, and why the hell she had not just said the end of the week. Screw it, then, that was just another thing to add to the to-do list. Thank god Amazon did next day delivery.

That evening, when she had hoped she would be able to continue with editing Drew's latest work – or perhaps carry on with her own dalliance into writing – Sarah sat at her computer, trawling through the internet for school-worthy tombola prizes. Sodding Justine and her pissing iPad. It was bound to be the latest model too. Probably with the cellophane on. It was probably a gift. Rich people always got expensive gifts, which was ridiculous when you thought about it. They were the ones who could afford to buy stuff in the first place. They didn't even need any gifts.

'What are you doing?' Drew asked.

'George's Winter Fair. We've got to buy some prizes.'

'Winter as in Christmas? Are they not having a Christmas Fair now?'

'Oh no, they're having both. That school's all about finding as many ways as possible to bleed us dry. What do you think about glow sticks?'

'Glow sticks? What for?'

'For the tombola.'

Drew's scrunched up face was all the answer she needed. 'Don't they contain some weird chemicals? Aren't they poisonous or something?'

'Maybe.' She continued her browsing. 'What about paints?'

'What type of paints.'

'Just *paint* paints. Children's' paints. In little plastic boxes.'

'They sound okay.'

Sarah clicked on the links. Thirty-two boxes for ten quid. That would do. Certainly better than half a dozen packets of fruit roll-ups. 'Holy crap,' she said as she went through to pay. 'Seven quid for next day delivery. That's almost the same price as the bloody things cost.'

'Then get them to come snail mail. They don't have to come tomorrow, do they?'

*Do they?* Sarah thought to herself. They wouldn't have had to, had she managed to keep her mouth shut. But now she had told the Miss 'Perky' Jenkins that she would have them, and no doubt, she'd be pounced on the minute she arrived at school. She could probably manage to think up a viable excuse for the morning drop off, but she'd be hard pushed to manage the afternoon one too, without it being blatantly obvious she'd lied. Still, guaranteed two to three days delivery was free. She was sure she could make up enough excuses to see her through until then.

# CHAPTER 18

Drew's email pinged through. His normal response was to ignore at least forty percent of emails until his dedicated *email answering* time, but it was the end of the day, and all productive work had near enough stopped. Besides, it was the sender that had caused him to do a double-take. Sarah never sent emails, especially not to his work address. She sent text messages, instant messages. Things she could check and see whether he had actually read or not. The fact that she would send it through to him so close to home time obviously meant she wanted him to see what she had written.

His eyes darted quickly through his interior window and out into the cubical area. Polly was there, nodding her head repetitively to a stressed looking Barry. Whatever it was, Drew hoped that somehow, she would be able to deal with it. He really didn't fancy handling another Barry crisis now. His attention went back down to the email and its attached file. There was no way Sarah could have finished her chapter already, he thought to himself. He had only asked her a couple of days ago, and each of the evenings had been filled with editing his work. Chances were, it was just a single paragraph that she wanted him to have a look over. A minute later, he found himself looking at the first page of a six-page document; at least she wasn't lying when she said she typed fast.

It was difficult to maintain a look of complete and nonchalant professionalism when reading words Drew didn't realise his wife knew, let alone was able to describe. His eyes bulged as he scrolled down the page. It would certainly spice things up, that was for sure. A delayed flight, our good old air hostess, the female pilot, and a male trainee pilot. It was definitely not a simple case of ravaging her again in the cockpit. In fact, there was so much more than ravaging going on that Drew was having a hard time keeping on top of it all.

'Sorry to interrupt, boss.'

Jumping from his seat, Drew minimised the document on his screen.

'Barry!' he said, with far more force than intended. 'What is it? I thought you were going home. Why haven't you gone home yet?'

Barry puffed out his cheeks as he sighed. 'That was the plan,' he said. 'That was definitely the plan. Only she…' he paused to wave through the window at Polly, who was peering at them, clearly within listening range '…has found an error in the datasheet I sent through yesterday. I tried to explain to her that I can't redo it now, as my computer is with the IT guys. Well, I left it outside their door as they refused to open it, but anyway, I haven't got it. And she's telling me that if I haven't got it completed by tomorrow, she's going to have me up for a formal review? Can you believe it? I mean, I tried to explain, but would she listen? Formal review. Because IT has my computer. Do you think I want them to? Of course I don't. And you'd think I'd be given a little bit of credit after how long I've been here? You know I have a good mind to —'

'Just use my computer,' Drew stood up, the endless diatribe having brought on an almost immediate migraine. The man had a gift. How one person could change the mood of another so completely in such a short space of time was probably worth some serious research. Just as long as he didn't have to be part of it. Stepping to the side, Drew stretched out his hand towards the desk. 'Honestly. I was about to head home anyway.'

'You were?'

'I was. Just make sure you log everything off before you go.'

Sighing with relief, Barry flopped down into Drew's chair. 'What would I do without you?' he asked.

Sarah had mulled over the decision of whether or not she should have sent her first draft to Drew's work email. In the end, she decided to go for it. It was far easier that way; he would read it away from her, and she wouldn't feel the need to analyse his every single expression. Already, only seconds after sending it, her stomach was doing backflips, wanting to know what he thought. Two days. She was impressed. With all the things that had been going on, she was amazed she had managed to get her first chapter done in two days. Now she just needed to find out if it was any good.

Nervous trepidation roiled through her. She felt like it was good. At least good in the sense of what these things were meant to be like. It was rude, that was for sure. Far ruder than she'd even thought she was capable of. And funny in places too. Even now, she blushed, thinking about some of the things she had described.

Stirring the children's pasta sauce – which she was certain contained a thousand toxins that her hippy birthing group would disapprove of – she glanced again at the clock on the wall. Five forty-five. Drew would be home soon, assuming there were no delays.

Sarah was upstairs in the bathroom when the front door finally clicked open.

'Sah?'

'Upstairs,' she called. Any hope of speaking to Drew immediately had been abandoned. Only minutes after she served the children dinner, having discovered that the pasta sauce she bought on offer appeared to be made of indelible ink, Eva had grabbed handfuls of the stuff and smeared it into every orifice she could. By the time Sarah had returned to the dining table from fetching the children their water, Eva's entire body, from her belly button to her ears, was glowing red.

'Pretty, pretty pink.' She chirped excitedly. 'Eva's pink. Eva's all pink!'

'Why didn't you stop her?' Sarah snapped at George immediately, knowing it was an unfair comment.

'She just looked so happy,' George replied before his eyes

began to well with tears. 'I'm sorry. I'm sorry, Mummy.' The rest of the dinner involved trying to stop George from crying and trying to get some of the remaining food into Eva. Forty minutes later, and Eva was in the bath while George was enjoying a chocolate biscuit – by way of an apology – in his room. Sarah had tried every type of soap and shower gel they had. Short of going for the bleach, she was stuck.

'Well, I wasn't expecting —,' Drew stopped the moment he appeared in the doorway. 'What happened?'

'She had pasta sauce for tea,' Sarah replied. 'Toxic pasta sauce.'

He nodded, although a large V had formed on his forehead, as though he didn't quite believe that one simple meal could have transformed his daughter quite so much. 'Anything I can do?' he asked, pulling his eyes away from Eva.

'You can read George a story,' Sarah replied, now scrubbing in a circular motion and unsure as to whether the redness of Eva's cheeks was from the sauce or the fact that Sarah had removed the top layer of her skin. 'Make sure he cleans his teeth first. And can you check under his bed for food?'

'Why would there be food under his bed?'

'I don't know. He seems to be squirrelling it away. I found half a packet of Cheddar biscuits in the dishwasher earlier. And two Oreos under his pillow.'

'I'll check,' Drew said, then leaned in and kissed Sarah, Eva, and the bump before disappearing into George's room.

Finally, after finding one-quarter of a cheese sandwich in George's dirty washing pile and trying not to appear too concerned over his daughter's fuchsia skin, Drew was able to sit down and have a proper conversation with his wife. The conversation he'd been wanting to have since he got home.

'I can't believe it. Honestly. It was brilliant. Better than brilliant. I don't even know what's better than brilliant. What word can I use that's better than brilliant?'

A bashful pink tinged Sarah's cheeks.

'Well, you can say it was phenomenal, outstanding —'

'That's it, exactly. It was phenomenal.'

Sarah shook her head and laughed. 'You're just saying that. You have to say that.'

'No, I don't. I don't.' Drew reached over and took her by the hands. 'Don't get me wrong. I knew you'd be good and everything. I really did, but seriously. Wow. It was certainly the best email I received all day.'

She winced. 'Yeah, sorry about that, I just wanted you to read it away from me. I'd have been too embarrassed to have you read it in front of me.'

'Do I even want to know where those ideas come from? Should I be worried? The two women...' He let out a long-drawn whistle and watched her colour deepen. His wide grin dipped slightly. As proud as he was of his wife, it did raise one big question. One that he really didn't want to admit. Trying to maintain an upbeat tone, he forced the words out of his mouth. 'Sah, I think maybe it should be you writing this thing and not me. I mean. You're clearly the one with the better writing skills and the better imagination.' His pulse ticked a little faster as he recalled exactly what went on in the cockpit of Sarah's world. 'Maybe we should swap roles. You do the writing, and I'll take over on the editing front. I could still do it on the commute?'

A moment's pause infiltrated the room for the first time since they had sat down together, causing Drew's heartbeat to hasten even further. If they wanted to make this a career or at least make a little money back after all the hours they had spent working on it, then they needed to give the story the best chance possible, and from where he was standing, that looked like handing the reins over to Sarah. A sad tug twisted somewhere around his stomach. It was a shame, though. He'd really started to enjoy it, at least for the most part.

'You know what…' Sarah hoisted her bump and body back onto the sofa, almost as if they were two separate entities. 'I actually think I like the editing part best.'

'You do?' Drew felt the spark igniting his eyes. 'But why? You're so good.'

Sarah shrugged nonchalantly. 'I don't know. I like the wordplay. I like reading through your work and figuring out ways to make it better. It's like a puzzle, and I enjoy that.'

'So, what? We just keep doing it like we are?'

'I think so. I'll just add a chapter or so in now and again if it feels like it's getting stale again. As long as you don't mind. How does that sound to you?'

With his stomach having shifted from feeling like he was about to get fired to where it felt like he was about to get promoted, Drew leaned in and kissed his wife on the lips. 'I think you ought to tell me how on earth you came up with those ideas for the hostess and the female pilot,' he replied.

∾

*It was worth it,* Sarah thought, as she curled up in bed and rested her head in the crook of Drew's arm. Just seeing the way his eyes lit up when she said she thought he should keep on doing the writing was totally worth it, although, even now, she had mixed emotions on the matter. There was no denying how much fun it had been, and how easily it seemed to come to her. Twisting together the storyline and plucking the perfect words for each bit of dialogue. She had loved it. But this project was Drew's baby. Drew's idea. Drew's drive. And from his expression when he suggested she take over the writing, it was blatantly clear there was only one answer he wanted to hear. It would be fine, she thought, manoeuvring herself onto the other side of the bed where it was just a fraction cooler. Maybe if this did take off, she'd be able to write a series of her own. Or if it didn't, then perhaps she could work on something different. She'd always been a fan of regency romance. Perhaps she could try her hand at one of those.

With a snort and a snuffle, Drew shuffled around in the sheets, only to flop into the perfect spoon. No matter how comfy the movies made spooning look, it was an impossible position for her to sleep in, what with his snoring in one ear, spare arm syndrome, and the added fact that she was already so hot, she had secretly turned the radiator off. Being pregnant at least cut down on the heating bill, if nothing else. But she would leave him there curled up with her for a little while longer, she thought, interlinking her fingers with his. It was nice for a little while.

Drew was back on form. From the moment he opened his laptop and started to write, he knew it was going to be a good one. The words flowed. Good words. Not just the normal ones; breast, boobs, bottom. No, Sarah had shown him the error of his ways. He was all about the details now. The base of her spine, the skin stretched taut across her stomach. He was on fire. Even when he reached the station and headed toward the office, his mind was a whir with what he was going to write next. Three more chapters, he figured. Three more chapters would be enough to finish the book off. And what a phenomenal three chapters he was going to make them.

Half skipping, he hummed to himself as he walked out of the elevator and into the office. From one of the cubicles, a pair of eyes lifted and caught his.

'Morning, Drew,' the owner of the eyes said, a bizarre grin on his face.

'Morning, Andy,' Drew replied.

'Drew.' A greeting in the form of a nod came from the next cubicle, too. Once again, accompanied by the bizarre, tight-lipped smirk.

'Heidi,' Drew replied, wondering if there was something going on that he had missed. When the third person on his team, Arnold – who had been at the company for four years and probably only said good morning to Drew a total of three times during that period – lifted his gaze up from his computer and offered him a morning salute with his coffee mug, Drew knew something had to be up. His immediate instinct led him to Barry, and he wondered what mess the fool had made that he needed to clear up now. He didn't need to wait long to find out.

'I'm so sorry, boss,' Barry said, leaping out from his desk and hissing in Drew's ear. 'I didn't realise I'd sent it to everyone. I thought I'd just shut it down. Closed it you see, so no one else could see it. I didn't realise I'd forwarded it to everyone.'

'Forwarded what?' Whatever he'd done this time had clearly got Barry into a state. Beads of sweat were already coalescing and running in streams down his temples as he wrung his hands together, barely able to look Drew in the eye.

'What is it you've done?' Drew repeated. 'What is it you've sent?'

And then just like that, he knew.

'Oh, shit no, Barry.'

## CHAPTER 19

Drew shoved Barry into his office and pulled down the blinds.

It was as though he had been simultaneously kicked in the balls and taken a baseball bat to the stomach. Air rushed from Drew's lungs, his legs quivering beneath him.

'Barry,' Drew hissed, barely able to make the two syllables. 'Tell me you're not talking about what I think you're talking about?' A tightening around his guts combined with a sudden chill. Barry wasn't the only one who was wringing his hands out or sweating. From feeling like he had been standing in an icebox only seconds ago, Drew now felt like he had been locked in a sauna on full heat.

'I don't understand. What did you send? Exactly what did you send? And to who?'

Barry had paled even more than usual. 'I got confused. Sometimes the arrow button means close.'

'When? When does the arrow button ever mean close Barry? The cross is close, Barry. The cross has always been close. Since the beginning of freaking computers. The cross has meant close. *When has the arrow ever meant close?*'

He switched on his computer and waited for it to start up. Of course, it was taking forever. Why wouldn't it? The whirr of the fan barely made a dent in the sound his heart was making as it used his rib cage as a percussion kit. Finally, the start screen flashed open. He pulled open his emails and clicked on the *sent* file.

'Bloody hell, Barry.'

Dragging his hands down the side of his face, Drew's stared at the nuclear meltdown that was now his life. Barry had sent it to everyone. Everyone. Sarah's attachment was now in the work inbox of every person in the company, from the pickers in the warehouses, to the chair of the board. Every one of them had Sarah's chapter on their computer. Their personal exchange out in the open.

'I'll tell them. I'll say it was all me.' Barry's swallowing reflex had now reached the extent that his Adam's apple looked like it was attached to the end of a miniature bungee cord. 'They'll believe it. I always mess up like this. They'll believe it was me.'

Unable to stay seated any longer, Drew moved to the window. Using a finger, he pulled down one of the slats on the blind. Heidi and Andy were now out of their seats, with all eyes directed towards him. He recoiled back towards the desk. Maybe the important people wouldn't see it. Maybe people like Casper Horton got too many emails each day to bother reading something that came from a lowly junior supervisor. Maybe the worst he'd get was Trisha, the junior director having a brief gander. And she had a sense of humour; she had to, the way she made everyone suffer through her karaoke renditions at every staff night out. Maybe if he just got to her first, it would all be okay.

Still considering which way, if any to move, the shrill sound of his desk phone caused Drew to jump back and smack his knee against the desk.

'Crap!' he shouted.

The single word faded into the continued ting of the phone. 'Who rings the desk phone?' Barry said in a whisper, his voice quivering 'I didn't think anyone rang the desk phones apart from the big bosses.'

'They don't.'

On average, Drew visited Casper Horton's office twice a year. Once to discuss professional development, and once after Christmas to receive a pat on the back for such a sterling job. Some years, when he had had interviews and promotions, he had been up there more. Never had he been called to the twelfth floor unexpectedly.

'I'll come with you.' Barry continued to wheeze as Drew took in a steadying breath and clasped his hand around the door handle. 'I'll explain. I will.'

Twisting the handle, Drew prepared himself a little more.

'Barry, it's fine. Let me deal with this.'

'But what are you going to say? Are you going to say it was me?'

'Just let me think for a minute, Barry.'

Lowering his head and pinching the bridge of his nose, Drew stepped out onto the floor. Then, keeping his head down – and refusing to acknowledge the dozens of eyes he knew would be boring into him – he hot-footed his way to the elevator.

The fact was, he didn't know what he was going to say. Barry was right. Drew probably could pass the blame easily enough; it wasn't like Barry had an outstanding reputation, after all. The cat photo was all the evidence Drew needed that he'd done something like this before. But could he really do that? Dump his friend in a position where he would almost certainly get fired? Besides, it wasn't even that clear cut. Barry was in admin. If it came out that Drew had been letting him use his computer unsupervised, it would lead to all sorts of questions. Either way, the outcome would probably be the same.

'Damn it.' He thumped a closed fist against his head. Four weeks before Christmas. Four weeks. How the hell was he going to explain this to Sarah? Maybe they would accept a demotion instead of outright firing him. Maybe he could offer to work as a picker in one of the warehouses. They were almost certainly still short-staffed. At least that would get them through the holidays. Through the next arrival and one more mortgage payment. After that, he would have to work something out. He had a baby on the way, for crying out loud.

With his fist still closed, he repeated the thumping movement, this time against his knee.

'Drew, are —'

'For God's sake, Barry. Haven't you done enough?'

He spun around. A momentary vision of grabbing Barry by the throat and slamming him into the wall flashed through him. But even if Drew had been the type of person to slam someone against the wall, there would have been zero point

154

to him seeing through his vision, given it wasn't Barry currently facing him. It was Polly.

'Polly?' He shrank back, shaking his head. He hadn't even noticed she was in the elevator. 'Look, I'm… sorry… I, I —'

'Drew?' Polly's forehead crinkled with concern. 'Are you okay? Is everything okay?'

His temperature was now up past a sauna and onto a furnace as the collar of his shirt struggled to soak up the rapid excess of sweat. His eyes went from Polly to the floor indicator. Floor twelve. The elevator door pinged open. With one last deep breath, he turned around from his colleague and stepped out of the lift. This was it then. It was all going to end right here.

For a pleasant change to the boring old humdrum routine, George had been the source of all the morning's mayhem. It had started with him squeezing toothpaste all down his school uniform while Sarah was changing Eva's nappy. Then, in an attempt to be helpful, he had pulled the T-shirt off himself and managed to coat his head in bright blue, fluoride-free, strawberry flavoured toothpaste. It was in trying to remove said toothpaste from his hair that Sarah noticed the little flecks of brown scuttling across his scalp.

'Nits? Really?' She rolled her eyes and sighed. 'This is just what I needed.'

Banishing him onto the landing, she got to work on Eva. After thoroughly scouring every inch of her daughter's head and finding nothing, Sarah wasn't taking any risks. Shampooing George would be bad enough. Trying the lotion on Eva was likely to induce an early labour.

'Sit there,' she said to George, plonking him in front of the television. 'And do not go near your sister. Do you understand?' She shifted him a little farther down the edge of the sofa and headed back upstairs. Digging around in the back of the bathroom cupboard, she finally found what she was looking for between a box of old tampons she didn't know she had and an old eyeliner brush that had started to grow mould. Throwing the brush in the bin and leaving the tampons where they were – they weren't going to be needed for a good few months, she reminded herself – she pulled the item out of the dust encrusted box and gave it a quick once over. The thing had to be at least six years old – dating back from a time when she and Drew could still afford to do exciting things like stay at cheap hotels that gave you such luxury items. But it looked like it would still be in working order.

There was no denying that Sarah was impressed with her own ingenuity as she pushed Eva's pushchair into the chemist. Beside her, George held her hand and scowled, the plastic shower cap covering every last strand of his hair. It was pretty gross, Sarah had thought as she pushed his ears and stray fringe pieces under the plastic lip. Like she had created some kind of bio-dome for head lice. Still, if it meant that he wasn't going to pass them on to the rest of the family, that was fine. She had rung the school and informed them that he was going to be late. He would still be going to school, though. All she needed was long enough to grab the shampoo, stink the house out with its toxic fumes, and rinse the little buggers down the plughole. Then George would need to go to school so she could get on with changing the sheets and washing all his hats and scarves. Goddamn kids.

Like always, the pharmacy was busy, and while Sarah had never been opposed to queuing – as long as it happened in an ordered and structured way and woe betide anyone who tried to queue jump on her watch – today, she wasn't in the mood.

All morning, the bump had been performing pirouettes in her belly, with each perfectly timed turn landing squarely on her bladder. With George, those issues had been fine. With Eva, she had managed to maintain some control, but at this stage, with bump number three, she could have replaced her pelvic floor muscles for two of Eva's broken hair ties for all the good they did. If she didn't get out of there fast, she was going to be in hot water. So to speak.

'Sarah, how funny seeing you here.'

She felt her whole being sink. Slowing turning around, Sarah's cheekbones resisted as she tried to force them up into a smile.

'Justine,' she said.

Today, the colour scheme was mustard yellow. A long-sleeved dress and simple pumps that would have looked like vomit if worn against Sarah's complexion, but somehow made Justine glow like some long-legged sunflower. This was humiliation at its absolute optimum.

'Oh…' Justine's lips formed the perfect letter O as her eyes lowered to the shower cap on George's head. 'Ouch, that's never fun. Not from what I've heard. We've been lucky with ours. Have you informed the school?' she said.

'Sorry?'

'The school. You know you have to inform them if your child, you know? You have to inform them in your child gets…you know… infested.' She said the last word in a strange imitation of a horror movie trailer voiceover. George looked at his mother with a look of genuine concern. 'Oh, Georgie, it's fine, I'm kidding. I'm just kidding.' Then back to Sarah. 'But seriously, have you told the school?'

The less-than-subtle criticism turned to bile in Sarah's throat. There was no way Justine was going to manage to twist this one around on her. She was the victim here. She was the one who would have to suffer the asthma-inducing fumes and wrestle as she tried to drag the nit comb through her son's hair, despite the fact that every sane adult on the planet knew it was impossible to get a nit comb through hair no matter how much conditioner you covered it in.

'Told them what?' she said innocently.

Justine's unfeasibly smooth forehead crinkled. 'Have you told them about George? It is… I mean, is it, has he got —'

'Psoriasis,' Sarah finished for her.

Justine's eyes pinged open even wider.

'Psoriasis?'

'Of the scalp. Yes. Poor thing.' Sarah moved her hand to her son's shoulder. 'He suffers with it quite a bit.'

'I… I didn't know that.'

'No,' Sarah proffered her best smile. 'Usually, you can't tell, the creams do such a marvellous job of keeping it under control, but we've just had a bit of a flare-up, that's all. Haven't we, dear?' She looked to George before turning to Justine and lifting her hand up to her mouth in mock surprise. 'Oh, you didn't think… nits?' Sarah shook her head and laughed. 'Oh, no. I mean, we use this wonderful organic shampoo. Works like a dream. We've never had a case actually. Anyway, it turns out they're out of stock of the psoriasis cream that we need, so we're just going to have to get daddy to pick some up, aren't we, darling?' And then, without waiting for any further response from Justine, she swivelled the pushchair back towards the door.

'Toodle-oo,' she called back to Justine with a grin.

Later on, after she had finished laughing at Justine's face, combined with the fact that she had actually used toodle-oo as a way to bid a grown adult farewell, Sarah began to regret her decision not to at least head back to the pharmacy and get some nit lotion. At least that way, she could have sent George to school. As it was at six p.m., he was still wearing the shower cap, sitting at the end of the sofa watching cartoons, the same position he had been in for most of the day. But it was worth it, just to see Justine's face. Really, why should she have to ring the school? School was obviously where he got it. They should be the one ringing her and explaining where it had come from.

With the kids merrily munching away at their TV dinners, Sarah swiped across the screen of her phone. It had been almost four hours since she had sent Drew a message asking him to pick up a bottle of nit lotion before he came home. He never usually went that long without replying. Something niggled inside her. With the little one's arrival getting closer each day, immediate replying was something she insisted on. Even now, with a month to spare, the thought of not being able to get hold of Drew when the time came caused her stomach to coil and constrict. She just hoped everything was all right.

# CHAPTER 20

Drew put his hand on the purse in front of him.

'I am paying for this one. I insist.'

'You paid for the last one. Let me get this round.'

'You just stopped me getting fired. I think I owe you a little more than one drink.'

'Well, when you put it like that…' Polly grinned.

Even now, Drew was having a hard time shaking the queasiness that had gripped his intestines as he rode the elevator up to the top floor and knocked on Casper Horton's door. It had been a superfluous knock. His employer was already out from behind his desk, pacing the room in much the same way Drew had been doing downstairs.

'I haven't opened it,' Casper said as he took a seat in his custom-built swivel chair. 'But I'm guessing everyone else in the company has by now.'

Drew's cheeks went from ashen to fuchsia and back again as he stared at his feet. It was worse than being called into the head teacher's office. At least there you could claim childish ignorance and promise to try better in the future.

'It was my assistant, Hilary, who read it this morning,' Casper continued. 'She said it contained some kind of…' he emitted a stuttering sound from the base of his throat. 'Pornography?'

The gut-wrenching contortions of Drew's stomach had only increased.

'I wouldn't call it porn,' he said, feeling that Sarah's hard work deserved a little more credit than being thrown into the mix with a badly shot home video.

'But it is of a sexual nature?'

'Well… I…' There was no way out of that one, he could tell. It was just a matter of phrasing it, so he didn't sound like he was some kind of pervert. 'The thing is —'

'Sorry.' A rap on the door and the apology came at the exact same time, causing Drew to swallow back his words before he'd even figured out what they were.

'Polly?' Casper's eyes narrowed at the figure in the doorway.

'What is it? This really isn't a convenient time.'

'I know, I'm sorry.' She cocked her head to the side as she bit down on the corner of her lip. 'But it is rather urgent.' The flare of Casper's nostrils was accompanied by a loud inhale. 'It's about the email I sent,' Polly pressed. 'From Drew's account.'

'The email —' Casper's eyes went from overly narrow to bulging from their sockets in a matter of seconds. 'You mean?'

'Uh-huh.' Polly nodded slowly, throwing the smallest of glances Drew's way as she did. If Casper was confused, it was nothing compared to how Drew was feeling. He wasn't sure if he was supposed to interject, but something about the way that Polly remained so poised told him it was probably best if he stayed silent. At least until he'd figured out what on earth was going on. 'Look.' Polly inched into the room, partially shutting the door behind her. 'Would you mind if I talked to you about this privately?' she said, her eyes on her uncle, whose nostrils were now doing a repeated flair and flatten performance. 'Please?' After one more round of inhale and exhale, he rolled his eyes.

'Fine. Come in and shut the door.' She made a face, somewhere between a grimace and a frown.

'Actually, can I talk to you *alone* alone?' She tipped her head towards Drew. Now he was even more confused as he shrank back into his seat. What the hell, he thought. It wasn't like it could get any worse.

'Fine.' Casper snorted as he spoke. 'I'll give you two minutes. Drew, you wait outside. Do not go anywhere, you understand? Do not leave this floor.'

Drew nodded, not really understanding anything that was going on at all, but swiftly getting up and out of the chair all the same. On the way through the door, Polly caught his eye and winked. Whatever she had planned, she, at least, looked confident.

He had waited a lot longer than two minutes, and each one dragged out more than the previous. He drummed his fingers on the wooden arm of the chair, checking both his watch and his phone. For a full ten minutes, he remained shut outside with exactly zero idea what was happening. A ping from his phone caught his attention. Drew lifted it from his pocket, saw Sarah's name, and promptly thrust the phone away and out of sight. Whatever it was, he couldn't deal with it right now. He couldn't deal with anything. Sixteen minutes after being sent outside, the door to Casper Horton's office sprang back open, and out of it walked a sheepish looking Polly.

She had made a subtle OK sign with her hand as she passed him. A second later, Casper's voice had bellowed from within.

'Drew, get in here.'

Leaping to his feet, Drew scuttled back into the office.

'Well.' Casper paused after only one word and scratched the bridge of his nose. The silence elongated around them. 'Polly just explained the situation,' Casper said eventually said with a sigh.

'She did?' Drew wondered if they were even talking about the same situation, and if they were, how the heck Polly would have been able to say anything. Unless she had mentioned Barry, of course. A sinking feeling of dread corkscrewed in Drew's stomach. That must be it. That must be what she had done. God. The corkscrewing continued. It was Barry's fault, of course, there was no denying that, but to just throw him under the bus like that… that wasn't what a team did. And Barry was bound to think it was Drew who'd dobbed him in. He was bound to think Drew had passed the buck just to save his own skin.

'I have to say, I feel a little embarrassed for you if I'm honest,' Casper continued. 'I went through a similar thing myself, not so long ago actually.'

'You did?'

'It's our positions of power, you see. Women like that. And not just women, other men too.'

'They do?' Drew had no idea where the conversation was going, or even where it had come from.

'I'm just sorry it had to get this far.' A heavy sigh reverberated in the air between them. 'I know it's a lot to ask, but try not to think too badly of Polly, even after all of this.'

Now Drew was sure he was part of a different conversation. Polly? Didn't he mean Barry?

'I, well, I'm not —'

'I know it's difficult. I do. But she's only young. And it's different for young people today, you know. In my day, we knew about boundaries. We had limits. But young people, it seems like nothing's off-limits to them. I have to say though, I'm surprised. And disappointed. I would never have expected anything like this from her. I guess she gets it from her father's side.' After one more contemplative sigh, Casper pushed himself up to standing and stretched out his hand. 'My apologies,' he said. 'And good work on all the Christmas load allocations. It's going to be a good year. I can feel it. Oh, and Drew?'

'Yes?' A sudden soar in pulse caused Drew to feel that maybe he had not escaped quite as easily as he had thought.

'Perhaps put a better password on your computer.'

Swallowing, Drew nodded rapidly. 'I will do that,' he said.

With that, Drew could tell, he had been dismissed. He was not quite sure what he was feeling. It was a bit like when you miss an episode of a series you are watching without realising, and the one you are now watching doesn't seem to quite make sense. When he returned downstairs, he found Polly waiting outside the elevator, grinning.

'Do you want to fill me in on what just happened there?' Drew had asked.

'How about I fill you in after work with a drink? You're probably going to need it,' she said.

'Just explain it to me again?' Drew said. 'You told him what?'

'I told him I had a major crush on you.' Polly lifted the wine glass her to lips, utterly unfazed as she spoke. 'I told him that after you left, I logged onto your computer because I wanted to leave some naughty photographs of myself.'

Drew choked on his beer, causing a bit of froth to come foaming from his mouth.

'You did not?'

She shrugged.

'Believe me. I have a whole laundry list of things my uncle has done. And he knows it.'

'So you threatened him?'

The same shrug.

'There was no need to. He knows why my aunt insisted I got a job here to help curb my wild ways.'

Having wiped the coughed-up beer from around his mouth, Drew went back in for another gulp. 'But that still doesn't make any sense. What about the email?'

'Ahh, yes.' Polly sat back on her swivel stool and twisted from side to side. 'Well, I told him I was just having a nose around when I saw the email from your wife and went mad with passionate rage. I forwarded it before I could even stop myself.'

'You did not?'

'I did. It's just the type of thing some crazy lovestruck intern would do.'

Drew was dumbstruck. His hand gripped the glass as he shook his head from side to side.

'But why? I mean, why would you do that?'

He could probably have guessed that the question was going to be met with the same nonchalant shrug she had used to answer most of his questions. Maybe it came from having lots of money, he thought. Maybe when your family was rich enough, then shrugging was what you did when someone was about to become unemployed.

'It was Barry, right? Barry was the one who forwarded the email by mistake?'

'Well —'

'See, even now you feel bad about it. About letting him take the blame. Even though he told me himself. Even though you were going to lose your job over it. You didn't deserve to be in that room, Drew. Not for a second.'

'But that still doesn't mean you had to lie.'

'Who said it was all a lie? Everyone needs a workplace crush now and again.' The statement took a second to digest. When it did, a nervous squirming began to coil its way around Drew's insides. Unsure whether he should look away or continue looking at her suddenly glinting eyes, he reached for his glass and took a very big gulp. It was starting to get very hot.

# CHAPTER 21

'You're home late?' Sarah said as she heard the front door shut. It wasn't a bad thing. The kids had gone down easily enough – George still with the shower cap on his head. Sarah had allowed him a half-hour respite while he was in the bath. When he was all dried off, and she placed the cap back on, she had coated the edge in Vaseline, partially to stop any nits escaping, partially to try and lessen the red mark around his head that would surely be a red flag for social services. After that, she had got onto the editing. Drew sauntered in, dropping his coat on the back on the sofa.

'Everything okay?' she asked.

He nodded, closing his eyes.

'Yeah. Strange day.'

'Strange how?'

'Just strange,' he said. She waited to see if any more details were going to be given to expand his answer, but when none came, she got back to the computer.

'Oh crap,' she said, lifting her head back up only seconds after it had gone down. 'Did you get the nit lotion?'

'Nit lotion?' His wide-eyed confusion, followed by the fumbling for his phone, told her all she needed to know. 'Sorry, I didn't see the message.'

Sarah groaned and looked at the clock. There was no point going now. The pharmacy part of the supermarket closed at seven-thirty. Trust Drew to pick today of all days to be late.

'Fine then,' she said, eyes going back to the computer. 'But you're going to have to get Eva ready before you go tomorrow. I'll need to leave by seven if I'm going to get George de-loused before school.'

'George has got lice?'

Dropping her hands down to her sides, Sarah studied her husband with an increasing tilt to her head.

'Have you been drinking?' she said.

'What? Oh, yes, just a couple after work, that's all. Nothing special.'

Sarah's normal reaction to Drew informing her that he had been at the pub spending copious amounts of money on overpriced draught ales would be to remind him exactly how much their weekly shop was, how close to the limit of their overdraft they were, and exactly how much nappies cost. But things had been so good between them lately. Besides, he looked happy, sitting there on the sofa. Like a huge weight had been lifted. So instead of berating him, she said, 'You haven't done that in ages. Who did you go with?'

He felt like crap. Worse than crap. Like crap that had got stuck on the bottom of his shoe, clinging to the sole, so he hadn't noticed until he had trodden it all the way through the house. What a prick.

He hadn't meant to say that he had gone for a drink with Barry. He hadn't meant to say anything at all. But then Barry's name came out, and the lies just came tumbling with it.

'He's going through a bit of a rough time,' Drew said, his mouth elaborating on the first lie before he could stop it. 'Divorce,' he added.

Sarah frowned. 'Didn't he get married last year?' she said. 'Alice, wasn't it?'

A lump wedged itself into Drew's throat. 'Yes, well, erm. I think maybe it was a bit of a quick decision.'

'Hadn't they been together since school?'

'I'm not too sure…'

The lump was now causing a violent case of sweating and a rapid increase in heart rate. Any second, and his eyes would start twitching, he realised. His eyes always twitched when he lied. And Sarah would spot it in an instant.'

'I think I'm going to have a bath,' he said, standing up and angling himself away from his wife. 'You don't mind, do you? Just that the train was really packed tonight.' Another lie, what was wrong with him?

'No, you go. Then maybe afterwards you can have a look at the corrections I've made in this last chapter. Check if you're okay with them?'

'It's fine,' Drew insisted, now racing up the stairs. 'I trust you. Change what you want. Change everything. It's fine.'

In the bath, he dunked his head under the water, letting the soap suds settle before thrusting his face back out. He tried to convince himself that it was better this way as he fished around for the soap that was now sliding around beneath his calves. If he'd said he was out with Polly, Sarah would have been bound to ask him why, and if he said why, then he'd have to tell her. At that point, she'd have found out that his entire company had seen the chapter she wrote for their book. She'd have been mortified. Beyond mortified. And the last thing she needed this late on in her pregnancy was stress. No, he had done the right thing in protecting Sarah and the baby from stress, he told himself. He had definitely done the right thing.

Nothing good was going to come of today, Sarah could tell. It started with running out of milk. There was a bit in the bottom of the bottle, enough for one child but not two. Struck by an inspirational idea, Sarah decided to add a bit of water to it, just to make it go a little further. She turned on the kitchen tap the exact second George had bolted into the kitchen and ran headlong into her leg.

'Shit,' she said as the bottle dropped from her hand, spilling what little there was down the sink.

'We're not supposed to say, shit.' George scowled. 'You tell daddy off when he says that word.'

'And we're not supposed to be running in the kitchen either. And why haven't you got your clothes on? I told you to put your clothes on.'

'But I couldn't get them on over this.' He pointed to the shower-cap that had slipped down the side of his face, while the Vaseline had glued his hair to his skin at peculiar angles like a hedgehog that had got itself caught in a hedge.

'Okay, well, I'll deal with that. How does bread and ketchup sound for breakfast?' she asked. George crinkled up his nose.

'Well, it's all we've got, so you're having it.' She'd run out patience. The plan was to leave in five minutes, and she hadn't even brushed her teeth yet. 'Where is your dad?' Sarah handed George an uncut slice of bread on a plate and squeezed a dollop of tomato sauce on the side. He was meant to have Eva down by now. 'Drew? What are you doing?' She hollered up the stairs. 'Do you not remember me saying I needed you to help this morning? *Help*,' she reinforced. Five minutes later, and he appeared downstairs, Eva dressed in a tutu with a Paw Patrol T-shirt and a pair of George's old wellington boots that were at least three sizes too big.

'It's what she wanted to wear,' Drew said.

'It's so pretty.' Eva responded, tugging at her skirt.

Resisting the urge to roll her eyes at her husband, Sarah took their daughter from his arms and slipped off the boots. 'If this is what happens when you go drinking with Barry, then I'm putting an end to it now,' she said. 'And you'll have to drive me to the pharmacy and park the car in the station today.'

'That means we'll have to pay for parking for the day.'

'Would you rather we get a letter about George's unauthorised absences?' She took his silence as acceptance.

While they had managed to get to the pharmacy only ten minutes later than planned, the delousing experience was every bit as horrific as Sarah had anticipated.

'It's in my eyes. It's in my eyes!' George thrashed around in the bath.

'You're wearing your swimming goggles. It is not in your eyes.'

'It's in my nose. It's in my nose! Argh! That hurts!'

Sarah inhaled deeply, only to fill her lungs with the acrid fumes of the lotion.

'When you get to school today, you are to play with no one, do you hear me? No one. Because if you get these things again, I will throttle someone.'

George's bottom lip began to wobble. 'But I like playing with people,' he said. His eyes, magnified by the goggles, started to fill with tears.

'Fine,' Sarah said. 'But you have to sit at least two feet away from them.'

'How far is two feet?'

Eva, meanwhile, had a mini-meltdown about the fact that Sarah wouldn't let her eat the tiny round pieces of George's LEGO set and was sent to her bedroom, screaming away. She was still screaming when Sarah bundled them into the car.

In the classroom, she was met by Miss Jenkins.

'Sorry, we're late,' she said, taking George's coat from him as he went.

'No, it's quite all right. Mrs. Fairwright explained.'

*Mrs Fairwright.* It took Sarah a second. Justine. Of course, she would have had to get in there and say something.

'It's better now though, the psoriasis?' The teacher asked, causing a pink hue to rise to Sarah's cheeks.

'Yes, thank you. It's much, much —'

'The only thing is, it isn't on his record. We have to have any conditions on his record.'

'Oh, is it not?' Sarah feigned surprise while simultaneously wanting to slap Justine silly and cursing herself for such a ridiculous lie. Bloody Justine. Next time George got nits, Sarah was going to insist he only played with Philomena for a week before she did that lotion. That'd wipe the smile off her face. 'I'll send an email through with the details when I get home.' She was about to move to leave when she noticed that the teacher's smile was still fixed on her, just a fraction too broad to be casual.

'About those Winter Fair prizes...'

'Oh, shi-oot.' Sarah tried and failed to hide her expletive. 'Yes. I know. I'm so sorry. They're are on their way. They really are. I thought I'd got them at home. The thing is…' she could feel herself starting to babble under pressure and clammed her mouth shut.

'Hopefully by the end of the week?'

'Hopefully,' Sarah said. Then, before she could dig herself into an even bigger hole, she grabbed hold of Eva's pushchair and swivelled out the door.

A small, red slip was poking out of the letterbox when Sarah arrived back home. She pulled it free.

*We tried to deliver your package, but you were out.*

'Great,' she said, rifling around in her bag for her keys. She had only just found them when her eyes fell on the other sentence at the bottom of the card.

*Your item will be kept at Wokingham post office for twelve hours. After that, it will be returned to the sender.*

'Twelve hours?' Sarah said out loud. What happened to keeping things for a week? Or three days at the least. Bloody companies, she could see their plan. They'd probably timed it exactly so she wouldn't be in when they delivered it, then she'd have to pay another fifteen quid to get it re-delivered. It was a scam, the whole lot of it.

With a despairing moan, she turned Eva's pushchair back around. Off to the post office it was, then.

The niggling sensation that had been present in Drew's stomach the night before was still unsettling him as he made his way off the train and into the office. It wasn't like he had done anything wrong. If anyone was to blame, it was Sarah. She was the one who'd sent the damn thing to his work email in the first place. And yes, there was the teeny weenie lie he had told her about going to the pub with Barry. But was that the cause of this new anxiety? He didn't think it was. The fact remained that Polly was only doing what she thought was best to keep him out of trouble. Yet, for some reason, that made him feel uncomfortable.

Several eyes turned to him as he entered the office building. Smirking eyes accompanied by smirking lips. Of course, they would have all read the email by now. All it would have taken was for one busybody to open the attachment, and the whole place would have known in a matter of minutes. Still, he thought to himself as he made his way past the cubicles and to his office, that was yesterday, and Casper had even sent him a personal email, apologising once again for Polly's behaviour, and reminding him that their work emails should be used for work only. Trying to ignore the myriad of whispers he knew were occurring outside his door, Drew buried himself away behind his computer and got started on his never-ending mountain of tasks.

At ten to ten, a knock on the door pulled his eyes away from the computer screen for the first time all morning.

'Have you got a minute?' Today, she was dressed all in cream, like one of those mini-milk ice lollies Eva liked so much. Drew shook that particular thought from his head. Where had it come from? When on earth did he become the type of person who thought about his work colleagues in terms of ice lollies? Feeling an increasingly common sweat budding on the back of his neck, he cleared his throat.

'Polly? Is everything okay?' His voice came out as a coarse croaking.

'Do you have a minute?' She gestured to the chair in front of his desk. 'It won't take long.'

'Eh. Well, yes, I suppose.' Not only was his shirt collar growing more stifling by the second, it was now causing a strange constricting sensation around his throat. 'Sorry, I mean, of course, take a seat.'

With a quick glance behind, Polly slipped into the room, closing the door behind her.

'I'm sorry,' she said, taking a seat and shuffling it towards the front of the desk. 'I realised after you left, I probably made you feel uncomfortable.'

'Uncomfortable?'

'What I said about my little workplace crush.'

'Ahh.' That was the cause of the gastric bubbling. Polly admitting to having a crush on him. Deep down, he had already known that but had been doing a damn good job of denying it to himself. However, now that it was out in the open, denying it, even to himself, became a lot harder. That didn't mean he wasn't going to try. 'To be honest, I didn't really think anything of it.' He tried to sound as casual as possible when he spoke. 'I assumed it was a joke.'

'Phew.' Polly used the back of her hand to exaggeratedly wipe her forehead, accompanied by a distinctly coquettish grin. 'It was. It really was. If I'm going to be honest, I do have a small crush, but not on you. On Phil.' She nodded out the window to where Phil, the resident body-builder, was leaning over a cubicle. 'Did you know he works with rescue dogs on the weekend?'

'I didn't,' Drew said, his pulse rate slowing back to an almost normal pace for the first time since Polly had entered the room. Of course, she would go for a man like Phil. Even without the puppies. 'Muscles and a soft side. Sounds like he's a keeper.'

Polly pulled a face. 'Well, I'm not sure about that.' Her coquettish grin deepened before being replaced by a far more business-like expression. 'Okay, now that I've got that off my chest, I have to ask you something.'

'Fire away.' A wave of relief washed over him. Questions about databases. Warehouse facts. He didn't care. He would even answer questions about standard deviation analysis on global tax rates to avoid going back to the conversation about men and crushes.

'Your wife,' Polly said, leaning in and resting her elbows on his desk and causing the contortions in his stomach to immediately recommence. 'Did she actually write that? I mean, it came from her account.'

'Well —'

'Because if she did, that woman has a talent. I'm not joking. I read a lot of things like that. You know, single girl and everything, and that one…' Her eyes shone as she let out a slow breath from between her lips. 'Well, just imagine. It was hot. That's what I'm trying to say. Seriously. If I could write like that, well, I wouldn't be here. I would be writing those types of books as a living.'

Trying desperately not to use his imagination the way she had asked him to, Drew focused instead on the end of her sentence.

'You think so? You think it's that good?'

'So, she did write it?' Polly's eyes glinted. The gut-churning Drew had been feeling was replaced by something a little more fluttery. Maybe… pride.

'We're actually writing a book together.' He lowered his voice as he spoke. 'Sarah's mainly been doing the editing part, but I asked her to have a go at a chapter by herself. I knew it was good. I told her it was good.'

'You're doing it together?' Polly's eyebrows arched in a way that indicated she was impressed. 'Wow, that is hot stuff. And you're doing it as a proper book? You're going to get it published and everything?'

'That's the plan. We're hoping to get it online before the baby arrives in January.'

The eyebrows remained arched, the look of awe only increasing. 'That's amazing. And all while working here? And she has the kids at home too, right?'

'She does.'

'She sounds like a wonder woman.'

A comforting warmth fanned out through Drew's previously contorted insides.

'Yeah,' he said. 'She is pretty amazing.' Sitting back in his chair, he took a moment to consider the fact. Sarah was amazing. He had married an amazing woman.

'Well, I've taken enough of your time anyway,' Polly said, rising to her feet. 'I'd better be on my best behaviour. The last thing I want is for Casper to come down and see me bothering you. He'd probably order a restraining order on your behalf.'

Drew chuckled.

'Oh, and are you okay to drop your figures down to Stu? I can run them down later if you want. I've only got to run some numbers for the marketing group.'

'Of course, that's no problem.' Then realising that Stu was the only person in the office that wasn't going to have to suppress a smirk when they spoke, Drew added, 'Maybe I might choose to be like Stu now too. Stay off all forms of the internet for the rest of my life.'

Polly chuckled in her normal light-hearted way.

'Great. And like I said, you need to hold onto that wife of yours. She's a keeper. And don't forget to tell me when the book comes out. I am definitely pre-ordering a copy.'

Then, without another word, she disappeared back into the office area, leaving Drew feeling, for no reason that he could explain, like something good might come from his little mishap after all.

CHAPTER 22

The queue at the post office was even worse than the pharmacy had been the day before. Thursday, it appeared, was the day when everyone wanted to post or collect their packages.

'You don't mind if I pay with these, do you, dearie?' Sarah eaves-dropped the old woman in front of her before watching her pay for whatever old lady things she was getting entirely in pennies. 'Forty-eight, forty-nine, fifty..'

Sarah glanced at the register; six pounds twenty. She was going to be there a while.

By the time the woman had paid – having inconveniently discovered that her wallet wasn't just sterling as she had thought, but also contained several Euros, and inexplicably a single Drachma, – Eva was getting restless. Assuming the pick-up would be a one-minute job at most, Sarah flicked her phone onto some video app and handed it to her daughter.

'Can I pick this up please?' Sarah slid the card through the window to the lady on the other side of the glass.

'I know you,' she said, her face widening into a squinty smile.

'Do you?' Sarah asked.

'You're at the Mind Birthing class, aren't you? Don't you think it's great? How long have you got to go now? Only four weeks left for me and this little one.' The woman stopped to breathe and rub her tummy, the already impossibly wide grin stretching even further.

'Oh,' Sarah said, wondering if she was expected to answer all the questions in one go. 'Yes, it's good. Seven weeks for me. Although mine are always late'

'Oh, it'll be so special. I love it when they're tiny. Not that I've had my own yet. This is my first. But I've got three nephews. Here, have a look.' She proceeded to pull her phone out onto the desk when a loud throat-clearing from behind in the queue attracted her attention. She scrunched up her nose and gave Sarah an apologetic shake of the head.

'I'll show you at the next lesson,' she whispered. 'Now, let me go and get the package for you.'

A moment later and she was back at her desk, her grin replaced by a far more morose look.

'Look at this. The delivery people today. No damn respect for people's property.' She lifted up the package to explain what she meant. It wasn't hard to see. One side of the cardboard box had crumpled entirely in on itself, and there were at least two other large dents in the package that Sarah could see. 'You're going to have to open it up,' she said to Sarah, her face still shaking at the sight as if the box had somehow been the victim of a premeditated attack. 'Check that everything works. I can't let you take it like this.'

Sarah eyed the package. Of course, wouldn't that be

typical? The bloody paints finally arrive only to have to be sent back again. Then again, there were twenty-odd in the pack, and she only needed half a dozen to donate to the school. 'Do you know what, don't worry, I think they'll be fine. It doesn't matter if one or two are a bit broken.'

'Of course it does.'

'Honestly. I'll just take them. I haven't got the time to send them back.' The woman's hands were still on the package and showed no signs of loosening their grip.'

'Oh, I can't let do that. What if you come back and say it's broken?'

'I won't.'

'But you might.'

'No. I won't.'

The beaming smile was having a hard time staying in place. 'I can't let you take it like that. I can't. You have to open it up here. Check that it's okay. It's policy. I have to stick to policy.'

'Oh, for crying out loud.' It was the throat-clearing man behind her again. 'Will you just get on and open the bloody thing up, please? Some of us have better things to do than stand here all day listening to you lot jabber on.'

Sarah sighed. He was right. What was the point in protesting? She should just let the woman open it, although she was going to be taking it home even if there were a couple of broken paint boxes. 'Fine,' she said. 'Open up and check.'

Smiling once again, the woman got to work. The standard brown packaging gave way to a neat, small white box that looked far better quality than Sarah had thought cheap paints would come in. However, once again, one corner had been dented in.

'I'll have to open this one too,' the cashier said.

'It's fine.' Only when she twisted it over to get the tape on the side, did Sarah notice the small lilac writing on the package.

'Actually, that's fine. The inside box looks pretty strong.' Sarah's words rushed from her lips. 'I'll take it home now.'

'But we need to see the contents,' she said. 'Check that nothing's broken.'

'It's fine.'

'It's not fine. It's dented.'

With her temperature soaring and a reflexive swallowing motion that she had absolutely no control over in overdrive, Sarah racked her mind for what to do. The item in that package was about as far away from children's paints as you could get. She may not have known anybody standing in the post office queue behind her, but that didn't mean she wanted to share her first glimpse of the Clitomaster sex toy with them.

'Could I open it, please?' she said to the lady. 'It has some sentimental value.'

'That's not policy.'

'Well, it is my item, I paid for it, and my name is on it, so perhaps it should be your policy.' Sarah replied sharply. The woman's lips twisted and pursed.

'Fine,' she hissed, her smile now well and truly gone. Glowering, she slid the glass partition to the side and slid the package over to Sarah.

Now that the box was in her hand, it was obvious to see what good quality it was. The textured cardboard was a nice touch, and the name on the side was embossed. Aware that the queue behind her was growing larger by the second, Sarah peeled back the plastic tab and peered inside.

'Everything's good,' she forced a grin back to the now severely stony-faced cashier. 'All good. Nothing broken'

'You need to get it out so I can see. I have a form I have to sign, see. To say I've seen it.'

'Can you not just take my word for it?'

'No '

'I really have to show you?'

'You do.'

Again came a throat clearing from behind. Well and truly wishing that Wokingham was on some unknown fault line so the ground might spontaneously open up and swallow her, Sarah closed her eyes. She was going to pass out. That's what it felt like. She hadn't ever actually fainted before, but if standing in a packed post office, pregnant with her daughter in her pushchair while she held her newly purchased vibrator out for public inspection wasn't enough to send someone unconscious, she didn't know what would be. With a deep breath, she pulled the item out of the box.

'What is that?' The woman asked.

'It's... umm.' Sarah's voice caught in her throat. Fortunately, someone behind her in the queue already had the answer.

'Is that one of those Clitomaster things?' A voice said. 'The ones that puff out air on your hooha?'

Feeling like she was now going to vomit as well as pass out, Sarah's eyes went to the direction of the question; a plumpish bespectacled lady, older than her mother.

'Yes, I… I think it might be,' Sarah said.

'I hear they're a fabulous thing. Been planning on upgrading myself.'

'Oh, really?' Sarah said, fairly sure she'd slipped into some parallel universe.

'Can you check if it works?' The cashier still hadn't dropped her point. 'We need to see it works.' Sarah looked down at the item in her hand. It was like she had left her body now. She had to have left her body. There was no chance she could still be in it when something like this was happening.

'I still need to sign it off. Can you just give it a quick check?'

Feeling entirely disassociated from the movement of her hands, Sarah pressed the large button on the front. Nothing happened.

'It looks broken,' the cashier said.

'For God's sake, it's not broken.' It was the throat-clearing man. 'It just needs bloody charging.'

'Just pop some batteries in it instead?' someone else asked. 'Has anyone got any batteries?'

'These things don't use batteries now,' the bespectacled woman replied. 'It's all done by chargers. Means they last longer. And they're stronger too.'

'Should you even be using one of those in your condition?' asked the battery lady. 'Can pregnant people use vibrators?'

'It's not a vibrator, it's a Clitomaster,' spectacles reminded them all.

'For the love of all that is holy,' interjected the man directly behind Sarah. 'Please let this woman take her damn sex toy and leave.'

Everyone stopped talking, and Sarah shoved the Clito-master back into the box.

'Fine,' huffed the woman behind the counter. 'But don't even think about returning it.'

Sarah turned and mouthed a silent thank you to the man, who chivalrously averted his gaze as she skulked out of the post office.

The cold air struck her skin as she got outside. That was what she needed. Air. Taking a couple of deep breaths in, she glanced at the object in her hand. Sodding Drew and his hare-brained ideas. She was going to make him pay for this one. Then, searching for her bag, she froze.

'You have to be kidding me.' Steeling herself against the mutters, she marched back into the post office and back to the front of the line, where she nonchalantly placed her hands on the handle of her pushchair.

'What? Like none of you have ever left your child in a post office?' she said.

'Oh, baby.' Drew massaged his wife's feet, failing miserably at keeping a straight face. 'That sounds horrible. I'm sure it was mortifying.'

'It was.'

'But on the plus side, the toy has arrived?' He eyed the package with anticipation, already thinking about how he could incorporate it into the next chapter.

'Can you believe we've only got seven weeks? Seven weeks and this one's going to be here. Unless it arrives early. Christmas day. I bet my money on it. The minute the food comes out of the oven, it'll be there, stopping me digging into my cranberry sauce and pigs in a blanket.

'If that happens, I'll pack you a Tupperware tub so you can eat it on the way to hospital.'

'I knew there was a reason I married you,' Sarah said, managing to angle herself around and kiss him on the lips.

Polly was right, Drew found himself thinking as he pressed his lips into his wife's. She really was incredible.

'Now, I was thinking about this final chapter,' he said, breaking away and nodding his head to the box. 'How about a bit of solo work?'

# CHAPTER 23

She was close. So close. She could feel it building. A few more hours of peace and quiet was all it was going to take. Drew had sent through his final chapter – from his personal email – that morning. Of course, finishing the editing was only part of it, as she had discovered from the millions of weblinks that Drew had sent through to her. Once she'd got it edited, she'd need to format it properly, then get all the page inserts completed. There were margin sizes to consider; correct indents too. Then they'd need a dedication. Who did you dedicate a book like this to, she wondered? *To Mum and Dad, for all your support*, didn't feel quite right. Then there was the cover. She'd searched online and managed to find a couple of places that did them pretty cheap, and it wasn't like they were doing it to properly make money. It just needed to be good enough to keep Drew happy, that was all.

What she really wanted was to get the whole thing fully edited before the Christmas Party on Friday. That left her three days. Provided Drew sorted out the children, and there weren't any major mishaps, it didn't seem impossible. After that, she would get her life back. Whatever that meant. Time to concentrate on things like George's Christmas play costume, for which she was rapidly running out of time, or preparing herself for the nipple-splitting agony that was breastfeeding and the rest of the all-consuming work that came with a new-born baby. An unexpected twinge of sadness struck just around her collarbone. She was sure she'd find a bit of time in there for writing too.

'Three more days,' she said and opened up the laptop, not sure if what she'd just said was a happy statement or not.

'Not long to go now, right?' Heidi said as she stood next to Drew by the sink in the office. 'A Christmas release?'

'I hope so.'

'Well, make sure you send the link through when it's done.'

'I will,' Drew said, not sure if he was flattered or terrified by the proposal of his long-term work colleague reading his lurid prose. And Heidi wasn't the only one.

It took less than a week before news of his dalliance into the literary world spread around the office.

'I just thought people should know you were doing it for a reason,' Barry had said when attempting to explain why he had told the entire team about Drew's enterprise. 'People were gossiping, you know. Saying things.'

'And now they're not?' Drew asked sceptically.

'Well,' Barry tilted his head. 'Most people who mention it seemed to be pretty impressed.'

'Really?'

'Really.'

It had taken a few days for him to believe it, but sure enough, the comments he received were, for the most part, complimentary.

'Good for you,' Andy said when it cropped up out of nowhere in a conversation they were having, about forklift trucks and the need to hire a couple of extra drivers. 'Wish I could get the missus to do something like that. You might end up like that Ernest Jones.'

'You mean E.L. James?' Even before his dalliance into the world of novel writing, Drew was fairly sure he wouldn't have mixed up the most well-known name in erotic fiction with a high street jewellery store.

'Aye, that's the one. She's raking it in.'

'It's a very competitive market now.' Drew tried to sound modest and keep his enthusiasm in check.

'Well, we're all rooting for you here,' he'd replied. And it had been encouraging. Very encouraging. Everything he'd read online said that having a solid fan base to launch your books to was one of the most important factors for being successful. It was a shame he couldn't send out an office memo. Maybe he could put it on the staff intranet instead, although he'd have to check with someone first.

'You need to go home,' Polly said, as she passed his office that Friday afternoon. Friday the thirteenth, although most of the day had gone fairly well. 'You know we've been given permission to clock off an hour early so we can get back for the party.'

'I know,' Drew replied. 'Just got to fill in a couple more of these spreadsheets, and I'll be off.'

'Well, don't be late,' Polly said, swinging around and heading back towards the elevator. 'And I can't wait to talk to Sarah. I have a feeling she and I are going to have a lot in common. She is coming, isn't she?'

'She is,' Drew said.

'Great. Well, I'm sure people will be queuing up to talk to her.'

Only when she had disappeared into the elevator did the weight of Polly's words register with Drew's mind.

'Oh no,' he said.

It wasn't that he was embarrassed. He wasn't embarrassed about any of it. He was proud. Proud of himself and Sarah for what they had accomplished. Proud in some strange way of all his colleagues for the support they had suddenly mustered for his new enterprise. He wasn't embarrassed at all. He was just stuck.

When he and Sarah had first started on their little venture, she had made him promise not to tell anybody about it.

'Why would it matter?' he had said. 'We're grown adults.'

'Because it matters to me,' Sarah had replied. 'I don't want it somehow getting back to the school or the other mums that I'm doing this.'

'Why not? And how would it even get back to them?'

'It would. These things have a way of doing that. Please. If you want me to help you with this, then can you please keep it to yourself? I've got enough stress at the minute without adding that to it. Please, just don't.' And so, he had agreed, mainly because he knew how terrified Sarah was about baby number three coming along, and he didn't want to do anything to rock the boat. Then, as the weeks passed, and the book featured more and more in the conversations, discussions over the baby featured less and less. Given that it was the calmest he had seen her since finding out she was pregnant, it felt silly to disrupt any of that. Unfortunately, he was now in a bind. Technically, he had stuck to their agreement not to tell anyone. After all, she was the one who had sent the email. Had she not, Drew wouldn't have had the situation with Barry, and his whole office wouldn't be waiting to download *Air Hostess Hits Halkidiki* the day it was released.

'Shit, shit, shit.' Drew spoke to himself in a similar manner all the way home. He would have to feign illness. That was the best thing he could do. Only, the hotel had a forty-eight-hour cancellation policy, and they'd already missed that window. Ill or not, Sarah would still make him go, just so they didn't waste the money. Perhaps Sarah would be ill. She had been saying how tired she was all week, and she had been putting every spare hour into trying to get the book finished. Maybe the thought of his Christmas Party would be too much. He could hope. Fifteen minutes into the journey back and his phone pinged with a message.

*Just borrowed a dress from Nelly. Excited.* Followed by various emojis, including a dress and a disco ball.

'Ah, crap.' He pushed his thumbs into his temples and considered the situation. They had the room. They had paid for the room. That was it. The thought struck him like a small bolt of static. He would persuade Sarah that their time would be better spent upstairs in the hotel room – relaxing and chilling – rather than mingling with people they didn't even have telephone numbers for. Comfy mattress, fresh sheets. He could sell it to her. Hotel bathrobes, room service. He shook the idea from his head. There was no way Sarah would fork out for room service when there was a perfectly good and entirely free buffet already waiting for them downstairs. He would have to bring her up a doggy bag. Or several, with the way her appetite was. Still, it was workable. The first option of Sarah not wanting to go still remained most preferential in the situation, but still, he had a back-up plan. He was going to get through this.

Sarah had successfully managed to shave her armpits and approximately thirty-three percent of her legs. Ideally, she would have been able to give her bikini line a bit of a go too, but given that she wasn't even sure where it was, she would more likely end up nicking a region of her anatomy that she really didn't want to have nicked.

The dress from Nelly had been a godsend. Given that she was now less than five weeks away from her due date and exactly zero items in her wardrobe fitted, she had taken to wearing the same black skirt every single day. Top wise, she was also in the dregs of her outfits, which included two stretchy breastfeeding tops. One of them, which was once grey, was now looking decidedly brown, excluding the distinctly yellow circles that fanned out from beneath her armpit. Not exactly Christmas party get up.

Despite it all, Sarah was feeling fairly good about things. The varicose veins that bulged over her calves and around the backs of her knees, the constipation that left her unsure as to whether the gain in bump size was due to baby or bloating, and the acid reflux that left her throat feeling like she had spent a day downing battery acid were all less than ideal, but they weren't the be-all and end-all. Even the sporadic back spasms she had been feeling all morning were just another niggle. Her children were healthy and happy. Her husband was healthy and happy, and for the most part, so was she. Even in a tiny house. As a bonus, the added obsession of completing the book combined with her new antennal class meant she had had less time to fixate on the upcoming trial of labour.

Mind Birthing had become as enjoyable as staring at other women's vaginas could be. The classes had flown by. It had helped a little with the nerves, she considered, during her final session. If nothing else, the naps had ensured she got just a little more rest.

'Breathe in through your nose…' The instructor closed her eyes and inhaled deeply. 'Now breathe out and let the air flow down through your body and out through your vagina, feeling your cervix open with the flow.' She repeated her sentiments again and again. 'In through your nose, and out through your vagina. Let the walls of your cervix expand and grow as the air passes between it.'

'Breathe in —

On the third breath, a small squeak came from the back of the room.

'Yes, Cherie?' The instructor spoke with languorous syllables that filled the room around her like smoke from an incense stick. 'Is everything okay?'

Like everyone else in the room, Sarah's eyes shifted towards the girl at the back. Petite and dark-haired, she had on her face a look of utter bemusement.

'I'm sorry,' she said. 'I just want to check. You don't mean actually breathe out through our vaginas, do you? Only, I didn't know you were able to do that?'

'I think she means in a more metaphorical sense,' Sarah answered the question for her.

'Oh.'

After a question like that, Sarah found it impossible to take anything else seriously, and her nerves at the birthing were momentarily diminished.

'Sarah? It is Sarah, isn't it?'

'It is,' Sarah replied. It took a moment to place the woman, who looked distinctly different now that she was out of her strict post office uniform.

'I just wanted to say sorry about the other week. You know. With the package.'

'I remember,' Sarah said. Three weeks might be enough time to forget some things, but not being forced to unpack a sex toy in a crowded post office.

'Well, I wanted to say I was sorry, that's all. It is just that it is company policy, you see. Anyway, I've wanted to apologise for a while, only, well I was a bit embarrassed, see. But this is the last session, and I didn't want you to think—'

'I understand,' Sarah said. 'Really, don't worry about it. It's all forgotten now.' It was. Five minutes into her and Drew using the Clitomaster, and she had decided she would take the post office scene a hundred times over if it meant not having to give that thing back. Puffs of air; who knew?

A relieved smile washed across the woman's face, although it was quickly replaced by another expression. 'Can I ask you something?' She leaned in as she spoke and lowered her voice to just above a whisper.

'Okay?'

'The Clitomaster. Would you recommend it?' she said.

In moments like this, it was almost impossible for Sarah not to think about the effect Drew's little venture had had on them. Had a woman in a birthing class asked her about the use of sex toys only three months prior, she would probably have run off and locked herself in the nearest toilet and wept in humiliation. Instead, she lifted her head and said to the woman. 'God, yes. Get one now.'

# CHAPTER 24

'Why are you going left here?' Sarah said as Drew veered off the dual carriageway. 'The sat nav said to go straight.'

'I don't think it's right,' Drew said. 'I'm sure this way is quicker.'

'Why would the sat nav tell you a way that wasn't the quickest? That's the whole point of it, isn't it? And you're nearly out of battery. If you keep going the wrong way, it's going to run out before you get there.'

'Trust me,' Drew said. 'I'm sure we can get in this way too.'

Ten minutes later, and they were at a standstill. Clenching her fists, Sarah maintained the air of silence as they waited for the traffic to clear.

'Are you sure you wouldn't just rather head somewhere else to eat first?' Drew said half an hour later as they finally approached their destination. 'You know the food here's not meant to be that great. I was reading some reviews online. It said the portions were really small.'

'It's a buffet,' Sarah replied. 'I'm sure there's going to be enough food. Besides, look at me.' She clasped her hands around her belly. 'I'm pregnant. They're bound to bring me more food. Pregnant people always get more food.'

'But what if they don't?'

'Then we can get something afterwards. There's no point spending extra money we don't have on food we might not even need. Let's see what they've got there first, then we can go and get more if we need to.'

His response came in the form of a disgruntled grunt. Staring out the window, Sarah shook her head and tried to let it wash over her. The entire journey felt like Drew had been trying to put her off going this evening, from the amount of time he took to get ready, to insisting they head inside and have a cup of tea at his mother's when they dropped the children off. At the petrol station, he had dropped his card in a puddle, after which he spent five minutes drying it off before insisting on using it in a cashpoint machine just to check that it worked. Now he seemed intent on slowing down at every set of traffic lights, ensuring he hit them all on red and completely ignoring whatever the sat nav told them.

'Are you all right?' Sarah asked as they took the final turn into a narrow underground spot. The tension in his mood had resulted in a nervous pain rippling through her abdomen. 'Is it me?'

'What?' Drew pulled into a car parking space and cut the engine. 'Is what you?'

'This mood. This silent treatment.'

'I'm not being silent.'

'Drew, you've hardly said two words to me this entire drive.'

As if confirming this, he offered yet another grunting response. Sarah sucked a slow breath in through her nose. 'Fine, be like that. But whatever it is, you need to either tell me or deal with it. I've got enough to think about right now. If you don't want to be there when the baby's born or—'

'No.' Drew showed his first real sign of animation all evening. 'It's not the baby. Of course, I'll be there.'

'Then what?'

A short pause followed. Drew stuffed his keys into his pocket. His eyes looked out the window and back again. 'You're right. That's probably what it is. I'm probably just nervous about the baby. It'll be fine, though. You know that, don't you? It'll be fine.'

'I'm sure it will,' Sarah said. Although for the strangest reason, Sarah was sure he didn't meet her eye as he spoke.

Now that Drew had managed to delay the evening as much as possible – the cup of tea at his mum's was a stroke of pure mastery – he realised he had gone about it all the wrong way. What he should have done was arrive early. Super early. While they were still setting up. Then they could have grabbed some food – using Sarah's pregnancy as a perfect excuse to get the kitchen to whip something up a little ahead of schedule – then snuck off upstairs, while he complained about how sad it was that people never came to support things like this. Then they could have been safe and sound, tucked up in the king-sized bed, and everything would be right with the world. Now, most of the free wine would have been consumed, and tongues were likely to be looser than ever. He was such an idiot.

'You know, I don't think I'm feeling well,' Drew said as, in the hotel foyer, he handed over his details and credit card and waited for them to check the booking. 'Maybe I'll go straight up to the room first. Have a bit of a lay down.'

'Are you sure?' Sarah asked, lifting up a hand and placing it on his forehead. 'You feel okay. Don't you want to show your face first?'

He shook his head, willing his temperature to rise. Saying he wasn't feeling well was one of his first truths all day. He felt like he was about to have an aneurysm. It wasn't the best excuse in the world, but it should at least work.

'I think I'd rather go straight upstairs.'

'Well, I guess I'll go in by myself then,' Sarah said.

'What?' Drew scribbled his name on the piece of paper that had just been placed in front of him. 'Why? Why would you do that?'

'Well, to show we've come. You signed us up for this, didn't you? That means they will have taken our numbers into account. They've probably based the food on who said they will be coming.'

'No one's going to mind about that. Plus, we should probably take the bag up to the room.'

'We can take your bag for you, sir,' said the man behind the check-in desk as he replaced the piece of paper with a key card.

'Oh, that would be brilliant, thank you,' Sarah said.

'Yeah, thanks,' Drew said with a tight smile as he handed the bag to a man in a red waistcoat. His foot had started tapping nervously. There had to be something he could do.

Some way he could get through the night without Sarah coming into contact with anyone from the office. He was about to feign a full-on fainting episode when something behind Sarah's head caught his eye. His lips twitched in a smile.

'Have fun at your event,' the man at the check-in said. 'The party's in the —'

'Yes, we will,' Drew said, whipping his arm around his wife and steering her back toward the lift and away from the screen that boldly displayed all the event locations at the hotel that night. A quiver of excitement rattled through him. After all, one Christmas party was as good as the next.

'Do you know what? You're right. I should go for one, at least.'

Sarah gave him a puzzled look. 'Are you sure?'

'Yes, definitely. Come on then,' he said, casting one more look at the screen to make sure he knew where he was going. 'It's this way. On the second floor.'

Using the elevator ride as a moment of respite, Sarah propped herself up against the side. The back spasm she had been experiencing was still going, although it had swapped sides now. Maybe one day, when they didn't have a mortgage on a house she hated and barely enough money to treat the kids to a day out, she would see a chiropractor or a physio. She wasn't exactly sure what the difference was. Meanwhile, Drew was turning his phone over and over in his hand like it was some kind of card trick. Wouldn't it be just their luck for him to drop it just after they'd spent all their money on the kids' Christmas presents? At least his mood had changed. He was chirpier than she'd seen him all night.

'Do you want to put that in my bag?' Sarah said, reaching out her hand. 'And you can give me your wallet too? There's plenty of room.'

His eyes went down to the phone in his hand, as if surprised to find it there.

'Okay. Thanks,' he said and handed her the items.

The elevator doors pinged opened.

'After you,' Drew said, stepping in front to hold the doors.

A smell of freshly baked bread drifted in from the hall around them as men and women with wine glasses stood at tall tables speaking in subdued voices. It was a pleasant enough foyer with large windows, ornate ceiling, and large double doors that lead through to another room. Her first impression was that it wasn't the most jovial of office party atmospheres. Then again, who had the energy for that on a Friday evening after a full week at work?

'I guess the food must be in there,' Drew said, pointing to the double doors. 'Shall we?'

'You lead the way.'

Tugging at her dress, Sarah followed her husband towards the main room, where if anything, the atmosphere was even more unsettling than outside.

It was the quietness that was unnerving her, she realised. No one was talking at anything above subdued whisper. Glancing at her watch, she frowned. At this time, she would have expected half the people to be shouting across the room at one another. Or at least laughing. Hardly anyone appeared to be laughing. And where was the woman who always tried to drag everyone along to do karaoke after these things? Was her name Trish? Surely, she would be somewhere singing along. Only there wasn't any music at all. Slowing her pace to a stop, she looked around.

'I don't think I recognise anyone,' Sarah scanned the room in search of a familiar face.

'Of course you do. Look, there's Jo from accounts.' Drew lifted his hand and waved at someone Sarah couldn't make out. Whoever it was, they didn't appear to respond.

'Come on, let's grab some food.' Drew said, taking her by the elbow and leading her to the doorway. 'I'm sure there'll be some more people you know here, somewhere.'

With an unidentifiable feeling of trepidation, Sarah headed through the double doors. 'There,' Drew nodded across the room. 'There's the food. Why don't you grab a plate, and we can take it upstairs to the room.'

'Really?' Sarah was having a hard time trying to piece together what exactly about the situation was causing her to be so on edge. 'You don't just want to say hello to a couple of people first? Have a couple of drinks?'

Wrinkling his nose in a most peculiar manner, Drew shook his head. 'Honestly, I speak to these people every day. I spend all day in the office with them. It's you I want to be here with. You that I want to spend time with.'

He lifted his hand to her cheek. A warming sensation bubbled through her. With all their time spent on the kids and now the book, it was sometimes tough to remember how sweet he could actually be. And he was right, of course. He probably spent far more time having one to one conversations with these people than he ever did with her.

'Fine,' she relented. 'We'll grab a plate. But if someone

wants to stay and chat with you, you have to be polite, okay? You can't use me as your excuse.'

'It's fine. Honestly. Look, everyone's already talking to each other anyway.'

Sarah cast her gaze across the room as she moved towards the buffet table. He was right. Everyone in the room seemed to be deeply engrossed in one conversation or another. Dozens of little clusters were spread out around the space, including a small group by the door and two or three more propped up against the wall. They were a very huggy bunch, Sarah thought, noting one particular woman who seemed to be going around squeezing everyone in sight. More a family than an office. She had never realised how close Drew's working environment was before.

When she placed her second shrimp satay onto her plate, it hit her.

'Drew,' she hissed. He was going ahead in front of her, piling up his plate like it was the last time he expected to eat for a month. 'Slow down. Come here.'

He stopped and glanced over his shoulder, at which point, Sarah beckoned him back towards her.

'What is it?' he said, his eyes darting around in their sockets. 'You need to come down this end. Have a look at some of the bruschetta. And we should probably grab an extra plate for desserts too. We don't want to forget those.'

'Drew, look around,' she said, putting her plate down on the buffet table. 'Don't you notice anything odd here?'

'Like what?'

'Well, firstly, I still don't know anyone. Not a single person.'

With a jowl wobbling shake of his head, Drew grunted

his response. 'It'll be all the pickers and drivers. They have a massive turnover every year. You know that. Probably half the staff are new. More even.'

'Maybe.' Sarah was having a hard time shaking the scepticism in her voice. 'But then that doesn't explain why every single person in the room is wearing black. And why nearly half of them are crying. Drew, I think we might have got the wrong floor. I think we're at a funeral.'

# CHAPTER 25

What type of hotel held a bloody wake that close to Christmas? That was what Drew wanted to know. And how the hell could somebody even manage to get a booking like that so last minute? The Home Crew had booked this place months in advance, with a hefty deposit if rumours were to be believed. Yet now it appeared that any Tom, Dick, or Harry could simply pop their clogs and have a room ready to go.

'What are you doing?' Drew asked as he watched Sarah slip her plate onto a table. 'You can take it with you.'

'I'm not taking a dead man's food with me.'

'Why? He's not going to know. And what's going to happen to it otherwise? Just take it. No one will even notice.'

As the words escaped his lips, Drew realised they might not be as true as he had hoped. Several pairs of eyes were looking in their direction. One particular pair of eyes belonging to an unusually tall man in a mourning suit offered them a quizzical glare. Drew smiled before remembering that this very much did appear to be a wake and turned the smile into an over exaggerated sad face. God damn it. Why did Sarah have to wear that damn turquoise dress? She stood out like a bloody sore thumb. Slowly, they edged their way out of the main room and back towards the elevator.

'How the hell did you not realise?' Sarah said as the lift doors closed around them. 'I thought you said you worked with these people.'

'Obviously, I just got confused,' Drew said, wishing like hell that he'd just managed a mouthful of guacamole and nachos before they had fled. Dealing with this situation was hard enough as it was, without adding the fact that he was growing hungrier and hungrier by the second. 'There are a lot of people I don't know.' Drew attempted to defend himself. 'They should have had clearer signage. Look, why don't we go up to the room now. Just order room service.'

Without any warning, at least not one that he saw, Sarah slammed her palm against the edge of the elevator.

'God damn it, Drew, I just want to go to a Christmas party. Just for half an hour. The only people I ever speak to are other mums. Mums I don't even like. My conversations revolve almost entirely around the topics of phonics and reading level and why the hell my kid insists on putting every damn object in her mouth while having to hear about how bloody Philomena is already reading sodding George Orwell. I just want a normal conversation. A normal night where I can see people drinking wine and talking about holidays and adventures and believe that I'm one of them. That I still have a life. Would that be too much to ask for just one night?'

Stunned by the reverberation that continued around the lift wall after Sarah had expelled her last breath, Drew twisted his lips together in an awkward roll.

'I guess we could check one of the other ballrooms?' he said.

This time, the elevator opened to *Last Christmas* by Wham! Choruses of laughter and chatter swilled around them, and as much as Drew wished otherwise, there was no denying the obvious differences between here and the previous gathering, although, in his defence, he didn't feel like he recognised any more people; with the men now dressed in casual coloured shirts and jeans, and the women dressed in anything from jeans and vest tops to full-on sequinned gowns. Several pairs of eyes moved towards them, which were followed by hurried whispers. He attempted to loosen the collar on his already unbuttoned shirt. It was feeling terribly tight all of a sudden.

'This looks more like it,' Sarah said, a wide smile on her face. 'Now, why don't you ring your mum and check that the kids are all right? That way, you can stop worrying and start enjoying yourself. I'll go get us some food.'

Jumping in front of her, Drew blocked her way. 'No, don't be silly. You don't want to be walking around. You need to sit down. You've already been on your feet too much today. And you said your back was hurting. You've only got three weeks to go. Remember what the doctor said about not being a young mum this time.'

Her eyebrows rose in a clear indication that she was not impressed. 'It's four weeks. And I'll remember the doctor said that when I'm standing up doing dinner or running after Eva when you're at work too.'

Drew inched himself away. Whether it was his imagination or not, he couldn't help feeling that people were closing in on them. He had already noticed Heidi, waving from one side of the room, trying to catch his attention, and Barry was bound to be lurking around somewhere. It wasn't like Barry had much in the way of boundaries when it came to the office; God knows what he'd say if he'd had a few.

'There.' Drew spotted a sudden escape plan, all by himself in the corner of the room. 'You can sit down and chat with Stu. I'll get the food.'

'Stu?'

'You know Stu. From accounts.'

Sarah took a moment, after which her face frowned considerably. 'You mean the weird one with all the conspiracy theories who refuses to go on the internet or use email?'

'See, you do remember him. Come on. I'll take you over there.'

Then, narrowly avoiding two of the lads from marketing, he swept his arm over her shoulder and guided her across the room to Stu. After five minutes with him, she'd be begging Drew to leave.

It was easier to agree than object, and as much as Sarah didn't want to admit it, her legs were starting to ache, and her back was starting to throb with a bit more ferocity. She would have a word with him later, though, she thought, as Drew flung his arm around her and steered her towards a far corner of the room. Probably not tonight; there was no point ruining everything when they had a room paid for, but she would definitely be having a word.

'Stu,' Drew said, as he pulled out a chair for Sarah. 'You remember my wife, Sarah?'

Stu's eyes darted suspiciously around the room. 'You know it's an unsecured wi-fi network in this place?'

'Is it?' Sarah took out her phone.

'No!' Stu's hand flew into the air. 'Are you crazy? Turn that thing off. You don't know who will be listening.' Sarah turned back to Drew for support only to discover that he had high-tailed it and was already halfway across the room. She placed her hand on her bump and took a deep breath.

'So, Stu,' she said. 'Have you got any exciting plans for over the holiday?'

'You know that some people believe Christmas celebrations are just a societal response to seasonal depression?' Stu responded.

'Oh, really?' Sarah's eyes went across the room to where Drew was now at his second buffet table of the night. He was going to pay for this.

'It makes sense. When you think about it.'

'I'm sure it does.'

Over the next few minutes – that felt substantially more like hours – Sarah learned various other titbits of information she had previously been oblivious to, including the fact that governments were controlling the countries through the use of fluoride in toothpaste and water and that Paul McCartney actually died in 1985 and was replaced by a man who looked and sang exactly like him. Stu did start to list the evidence that supposedly substantiated this claim but, by that point, Sarah had already switched off.

Deciding that she was going to go insane listening to any more drivel, and suddenly aware of the fact that her bump had shifted position so that it was now sitting on her bladder and squeezing it like a water balloon, she pushed herself out of her chair.

'Sorry,' she said. 'I just need to head to the ladies. I won't be a minute.'

Her first instinct was to head back towards the elevators but, after a few steps, realised that if the toilet was in that direction, she would probably have seen it. So she stopped, turned around, and tried to take stock of where it could be.

'Are you all right?'

The voice caught her off guard.

'Oh, sorry, yes. Just in a world of my own. Looking for the ladies.' The lady she found herself face-to-face with looked barely old enough to be out of university. Her ripped jeans and white vest top looked infinitely more stylish and sophisticated than the majority of the women around her. Despite her earlier confidence, Sarah found herself feeling like a beached sperm whale by comparison.

'They're just around the corner,' the girl pointed, before changing her look to a far more concerned one. 'You're Sarah, right? Drew's wife?' she said.

'Yes.'

'I'm Polly.' She leaned in for what Sarah assumed was going to be a handshake but actually resulted in kisses on both cheeks. 'I am so pleased to meet you. Drew's so incredibly proud of you.'

'Is he?'

'Of course, he talks about you all the time.'

'Thank you. That's nice to hear.' It was. Sarah felt bad now. How many times had she imagined Drew typing away at his computer, getting his coffees from the coffee machine, and enjoying his Monday fry up without even a second thought towards her trying to juggle housework and the kids without going entirely insane? The fact he appreciated it so much that he spoke about her to his colleagues meant something. Maybe she would let him off the hook for his weird behaviour tonight. A sharp pain shot through her side, just below her ribs. Wincing, she placed her hands on the spot.

'Is everything okay?' Polly rested a hand on her shoulder.

'Oh, yes.' Sarah shook the pain away. 'All three of them have been kickers. I suppose I should be grateful, really. They've certainly got some strength.'

'Why don't you come and take a seat?' Polly hooked an arm around Sarah's back, offering support that she was annoyingly grateful for. 'Do you want me to get you anything? Food? A glass of water?'

Sarah shook her head. 'Honestly, it will pass. I'm guessing you haven't gone through this yet?' It was part age, part the fact that the girl had a waist similar in thickness to one of Sarah's thighs that led her to the assumption. Fortunately, Polly didn't seem to take offence at the comment.

'Oh no, I'm miles off. Very much single. And no intention of going down that road until I'm a hundred percent sure it's what I want. There's no going back once they're out.'

'You can say that again.'

The girl smiled back. She had one of those infuriatingly effortless looks about her. Like she was the type of person who could wear a white dress without the constant fear of spilling something down it. By contrast, Sarah had once managed to get ketchup on her bra, despite being fully dressed at the time.

'But you and Drew have got things great between you,

right? I mean, from what he's said, you guys sound like the most picture-perfect married couple of all time.'

'Really?' The compliments were starting to get confusing. Maybe she was thinking of someone else. There was another Andrew in the department. Perhaps she had got them confused. Her sudden pause for consideration did not go unnoticed.

'I mean it,' Polly said. 'I don't know another couple that could do what you two do.'

'What we do?' Sarah tilted her head, even more confused than ever.

'You know,' Polly leaned in as if she was about to tell her a secret. 'Writing the book.'

It had to be the music, Sarah thought as she blinked repeatedly in hopes that they may somehow improve her hearing.

'Sorry, the book?'

'Well, you know,' Polly looked at her with something akin to reverence. 'To be comfortable enough to let your husband spend all his time writing away about what a dirty air hostess gets up to in her spare time.'

'All his time…' Sarah found the rest of the sentence swallowed up by the large lump that was swelling in her throat.

'Oh,' Polly's eyes widened. 'Sorry, I didn't mean to offend you. I mean, the chapter you wrote… Wow. Seriously wow.' She leaned in closer, seemingly oblivious to the sheer feeling of horror suddenly engulfing Sarah. 'I mean, I know you've got this one on the way.' She gestured to Sarah's oversized belly. 'But you know, if you and Drew ever fancy re-enacting that cockpit scene, I'd be more than happy to join your flight crew.'

CHAPTER 26

Had she had the ability to run, she would have run. The spasm beneath her ribs had been joined by a trembling in her legs and a tightening in her throat that was getting worse and worse by the second.

'I'm sorry,' Polly said, raising her hand and placing it against her shoulder. 'Is everything okay? You look rather pale.'

'I just need some air, that's all.' Sarah managed to stumble forward. Her elbows jostled a person in front of her as she tried to make her way to the elevator.

'Please,' Polly said, grabbing her hand. 'Let me help you.' Sarah shook her away.

'I'm fine. I'm fine.'

'Honestly, it's no bother,' Polly said.

'Really, I'm —'

'Please, I can —'

'Will you just *fuck off?*'

She hadn't planned on the words coming out quite so loud. She hadn't planned on saying them at all. She didn't even know this woman. This woman with her unfeasibly long legs and perfect skin who just offered… who just suggested that…

Sarah's head was swimming. Everything was swimming. She couldn't have offered what it sounded like she just did, could she? Because it very much sounded like a proposition. The tightening in her throat had been replaced by an impossibly large lump that refused to be swallowed back down. Whether she had proposed what Sarah thought she had or not was irrelevant. She knew about the book. Drew had told her about the book.

Sarah's eyes scanned the room. Faces had turned towards her, all with a mixture of expressions. Some offered glances of concern with worried creases on their foreheads. Others appeared to be smirking behind their glasses.

'Sah,' Drew appeared at her side, his hands laden with two plates piled high. 'Are you okay. Is everything okay?'

He couldn't understand what had happened. One minute he had looked at Sarah, and she was sitting happily by Stu, listening to him jabber away – most likely about the Paul McCartney cover-up that he talked about constantly – then two minutes later, she had silenced the whole party with her screaming. By the time he had put his spoon of spicy jalapeno salsa onto his plate, Sarah's face had turned purple with rage.

'Sah.' He realised a bit too late that it was impossible to

comfort someone when both his hands were full. 'Are you okay? Is everything okay?'

'I don't know. Why don't you ask her?' Sarah pointed her chin at Polly before slamming her fist against the elevator button.

'Shit.' He wasn't sure if he muttered the words or said them out loud. Either way, it didn't make any difference. It all meant the same. Sarah knew. *How much* was the first question that sprang to mind. Exactly how much did Sarah know? His eyes momentarily left his wife and darted around the room. There was Heidi, staring straight at them. Andrew and Trisha. And dozens of other people whose names he didn't know. All of them were staring at Drew and Sarah, waiting to see how the scene would unfold. Only when he turned back did he see that somehow, in that blink of an eye, the elevator had appeared and Sarah had slipped inside.

'Sah!' Drew lunged towards it and tried to jam his leg in the narrowing gap, but his foot scuffed against the metal. He kicked the closed doors with his shoe, which had absolutely zero impact on the elevator, but – judging from the pain that was searing upwards from his big toes – may well have broken something.

'Drew?' He turned behind him to where Polly's face crumpled in concern. 'Is she okay? What's wrong? Do you need to go after her?'

The air quivered in his lungs. 'What did you say to her?' His words came out as a hiss as he placed the plates on a table. 'What did you just say to my wife?'

'Nothing.' Her face still a picture of innocence. 'I didn't say anything. Not anything bad, at least. I was full of compliments.'

'About?' A squeezing twisting motion was laying claim to Drew's intestines. 'What were you complimentary about?'

'About you. How great you are. How good your marriage is. Her writing.'

'Oh, Christ.' He brought his palms up to his temples. 'You mentioned the writing.'

'Only in passing. I told her it was hot, that was all. Seriously hot.'

He knew they shouldn't have come. They just shouldn't. He beat his fist against the elevator button. Why the hell was it taking so long to come? She could be anywhere by now. And she had the freaking car keys too. Damn it. Drew looked at the number above the elevator. 'Where the hell is the staircase?'

Humiliated didn't even come close. Sarah had been humiliated before. Like the time she had gone to Philomena's birthday party at the swimming pool and discovered only at the end that she had had her bikini bottoms on inside out the entire time. All of Justine's posh friends had seen her Asda-brand label sticking out the back. And that was before Eva had decided to take off her swim nappy and poo right on the edge of the pool. Then, of course, there was the time only recently at the post office. That had been humiliating. But this… this was something altogether different. This was mortifying. This was demoralising. This was her husband's doing. She could hear him still shouting for her as the elevator door closed on his foot; she hoped he'd broken a bloody toe at least.

Letting her read what she had written, without her permission. How could he have even thought that was all right? And not letting her know afterwards?

The thought caused bile to rise up and hit her in the back of the throat. The attractive, young childless woman with her perfectly-applied makeup and stretch-mark-free stomach. The way she spoke about it like it was some casual matter she and Drew chatted about in the staff room each morning. Or maybe they didn't. A worse thought entered her mind coinciding with a stomach-searing pain. Maybe he hadn't told her at the office at all. After all, her invitation wasn't the type of comment you'd make if you weren't sure it would be reciprocated. Images swirled and spiralled in Sarah's head. Lunchtime rendezvous; Polly and Drew clocking off early to head back to her impeccably decorated LEGO free flat. How was that even possible? After all they had been through together, would Drew really do something like that to her? A stabbing pain, this time at the base of her spine, brought her thoughts back to reality just as the elevator slowed to a stop.

With a steadying breath, she stepped outside into the foyer. His phone was still in her handbag, she realised, as was his wallet and car keys; standard protocol for a normal night out – when they used to go out that was. Well, sod him. He could make his own way home. He could walk if he had too. That should give him a bit of time to think about what a prick he'd been.

'Sarah, wait!' A door to the left of the elevators flung open. Through it came a panting, red-faced Drew. 'Please, wait. I can explain. I can explain.'

The blood pounded in her face as she spat the words at him.

'You can explain how someone – some pretty young woman I might add – managed to read a personal email that I sent to you? *The* most personal email.'

'I can. I can.' He paused and rested his hands on his knees while he panted. By the looks of things, he had run down the stairs, although given that it was only three floors, his displaying a clear lack of fitness did nothing to soften her mood. 'I'm sorry,' he continued. 'I didn't want to tell you. It was Barry.'

'Barry?' Sarah lifted her hands with the question. 'What the hell has Barry got to do with this?' Her heart tripped over in her chest. 'He's read it too? Are you serious? How many people, Drew? How many people have seen it?'

She watched as his Adam's apple rose and fell.

'It was an accident,' he said. 'He thought he was closing the window. He didn't mean to send it.'

'What? What are you on about?'

'Barry… he used my computer. Just after you sent it through to me… He accidentally forwarded it.' Drew's words tumbled out between pants.

The air in the room was growing more oppressive by the second. 'Who did he forward it to?' she whispered, although, in her heart of hearts, she felt like she already knew the answer. 'Drew?' She questioned again when the pause had stretched out so thin it felt like it might splinter in the air around them. 'Who did Barry send the email to?'

'Everyone,' Drew said, his voice almost as quiet as hers. 'He forwarded it to everyone.'

Something more physical than the stupidity of Drew's words walloped Sarah firmly in the stomach.

'Jesus!' she said, doubling over and grasping her bump. Drew jumped to her side.

'Sah, are you okay? Is it the baby? You need to sit down.'

With gritted teeth, she breathed out, partially against the pain, partially to stop herself clobbering her husband in public. Now that they had stopped arguing long enough for her to take stock of her surroundings, she could see the people at the check-in watching them, waiting to see what the crazy pregnant lady did next. At least she had that on her side.

'Get off me,' she said, flicking his arms off from around her shoulder.

'Sarah, please. Let's just go up to the room like I —'

'Ohhh.' Sarah let the vowel resonate around her as more of the puzzle pieces clicked into place. 'So that's why you wanted to skip the party altogether? Nothing to do with spending a bit of quality time together like you'd said at all, was it? It was all just part of the plan to make sure you didn't get caught.'

'Sah, there was no conspiracy. I swear. It was all just a terrible accident. I promise, if you sit down and take a minute to calm down, you'll see that this is actually quite funny.'

He realised afterwards that that might not have been the best choice of words. Yes, he now managed to find the event moderately amusing, but he had had two weeks to process it all. It was likely to take a good long while before Sarah could see the funny side of it. Judging by the purple hue that was currently flourishing on her cheeks, she was most definitely not there yet.

'You find this funny? You find every person in your office talking about me behind my back funny?'

'Look, I didn't mean that.' He tried to backpedal. 'I should have told you. I know I should. I just didn't want to upset you. You've already got enough going on with the baby and the others.'

She was still shaking. Her fists were alternating between clenched, unclenched, and grabbing her side where the baby was performing parkour against her kidneys.

'You thought it was okay? Just letting people read my personal writing.'

Drew opened his mouth to respond before changing his mind, and then his tone. 'That was the whole point, Sarah. That was the whole point of doing this. We wrote this book so that people could read it. So what if it happened a little earlier?'

'A little earlier and without my consent. We hadn't even discussed this, whose name it would go under. Who we would tell about it.'

'I assumed we would tell everybody.' Drew felt like he had been fired back to a couple of months earlier. 'I assumed the whole point of this was to sell books. People need to know about it if we're going to sell it.'

'Well, how about instead of *assuming*, you actually talk to me about things instead. Or is that what you've got Polly for?'

'For God's sake.' This had been going on too long, Drew thought. People were starting to look. 'Sah, please, can we just go upstairs and talk about this?'

'The only place I'm going is home.' As he spoke, her

hand reached into her bag. Drew felt his pockets, realising where this was going next.

'Sarah, you can't possibly think of driving like this.'

'Like what? Pregnant? You don't seem to mind when I'm lugging groceries here, there, and everywhere.'

'I mean this upset. You can't drive this upset.'

'You think I'm upset? I'm not upset.' Her eyebrows rose as she sneered. 'I'm bloody furious.' With the keys in her hand, she turned around to go. Drew squeezed on the bridge of his nose as he tried to work out what the hell to do next. He was in a no-win situation. Insisting she stayed would be a disaster. There was as much chance of trying to persuade Sarah to see his side right now as Barry getting promoted to CEO. What she needed was a bit of time to think this through and realise it really wasn't as bad as all that after all. But he couldn't just let her go. Not the way she kept clutching at her sides.

'I'll take you home,' he said, reaching over and taking the keys from her hand. 'We'll go now.'

Sarah spun around as fast as her bump would allow. 'Give those back.'

'Sah, you're being ridiculous.' He twisted his arm behind his back, placing the keys out of her reach. Still, she lunged for them. 'Sarah, stop it.'

'I said, give them back.'

'Just let me drive you home. Please. You're upset. There is no way I'm letting you drive home in this state.'

Something venomous flashed across her face, and for a second, Drew assumed she was going to make another bid for the keys, but instead, she took a step backwards.

'Fine then. I won't drive. I'll get the train home.'

'Sah —' The impulse to object flickered through him as she glowered. At least a train journey home would give her time to think about how unreasonable she was being, he considered. At least there was that.

'Fine,' he said. 'Do what you like.'

# CHAPTER 27

She shouldn't have been surprised that he let her walk out like that. That was Drew to a tee. Backed into a corner, and somehow, he turned it around so that she was the unreasonable one. Well, screw that. She was right in this situation. A hundred percent right.

Considering the watermelon-sized protrusion from her belly and the fact that she was ravenous with hunger, she was walking at an impressive pace towards the tube station. A clearness to the air hinted at an icy night to come. This was the moment she wished she had brought a coat. Or a jumper. Damned Drew. Why the hell would he let his pregnant wife storm off into the middle of London mid-winter with no coat. No doubt, he would go upstairs and have a good old giggle with Polly and Barry and polish off whatever free booze was left. Well, good luck on buying a round once it was all gone. She smiled inwardly as she headed towards the underground. His wallet was still in her handbag, as was his phone. Maybe she could see if his credit card could stretch to a first-class train ticket home.

Drew didn't care about the looks he got as he sidled up to the bar. When he finally got the barman's attention, he ordered himself a large whisky. He would put it on the room. Just another massive waste of money when they barely had enough to get through Christmas as it was. He should have known Sarah wasn't really on board with the project. Not like she said she was. Even now, even after all the time they had invested in the book, she still didn't think it would work. Not that she'd ever say that, of course, but actions spoke louder than words and, right now, her actions were singing from the rooftops.

He took a sip of the drink and let the heat burn the back of his throat. Talk about an over-reaction. Anyone in their right mind would have seen that he did what he did to save her some embarrassment. That was all. Okay, in the long run, it hadn't worked out quite the way he had hoped, but really.

'I've been looking for you.' Drew didn't bother turning his head as Polly slipped onto the barstool next to him. 'Is everything okay? Where's Sarah?'

'Somewhere on the underground by now, I expect.' Drew took another mouthful of drink.

'I'll have the same as him,' Polly said when the barman appeared in front of them. Drew snorted into his glass. Of course, he would appear to serve her a drink without her so much as nodding in his direction. Drew had needed to wave his hand and bob up and down on his stool for the best part of five minutes before anyone took his order.

'I'm so sorry,' Polly rested her hand on Drew's knee. 'I

had no idea she didn't know. Honestly. The way you talked about it. About her. I assumed you didn't have any secrets like that.'

'Well, you assumed wrong,' Drew said, still not moving his gaze from the rust-coloured liquid at the bottom of his glass. His heavy sigh dissipated into the air around him. What was he even doing there? He thought to himself. He should at least head upstairs to the party and commiserate with the free booze. The thing was, he didn't feel much in the party spirit now.

With a broad smile that was entirely different from the nonchalant apathy with which he had looked at Drew, the barman placed Polly's drink down in front of her, along with the black, folded wallet containing the bill.

'I'll get it,' Drew said, sliding it over to him.

'You don't have to do that.' Her hand went on top of his. 'I feel terrible enough as it is.'

Drew snorted. 'It's not your fault. Trust me, this whole disaster is of my own making. Well, mine and Barry's. I owe you a drink. It was my wife who swore at you in front of the entire staff.'

'To be fair, I did already know she had a way with words.' Polly gave a short chuckle that Drew just couldn't find it in himself to reciprocate. He slipped his hand out from under hers and moved his attention across to the barman.

'Just put her drinks on my room,' he said.

The barman smiled. It wasn't exactly genuine, with his pulled tight lips and smarmy glint in his eyes. If anything, it was more of a sneer than a smile. But what did Drew care about a barman? He didn't. He didn't care about anything right now.

'You got a room?' Polly said, bringing Drew's thoughts out of his pit of misery before they could slump down any lower. 'Fancy.'

'A waste of money more like.'

'You planned a romantic night?'

'And look how well that turned out.'

'Look,' she said, pushing at his knee and causing the stool to swivel around so that Drew was now looking her square in the face. 'Maybe it isn't a bad thing that everything came out like this,' she said. 'For Sarah, that is.'

'Really?' Drew took another mouthful of his drink. He'd be needing another one in a minute. 'How do you figure that?'

'Well... think of it this way. Why did you lie to her in the first place?'

'I didn't lie.' Drew was staunchly defensive on the matter.

'You didn't tell her that everyone had read her email. It's lying by omission, Drew, but it is still lying.'

'I only did that so she wasn't hurt.'

'Really?'

'Why else?'

A pause lingered and expanded as Polly held the question without an answer. Slowly, she ran her tongue around her lips before opening her mouth to speak.

'Don't take this the wrong way, but the way I see it, and I could be wrong and everything. I just think not telling her about email was a pretty big thing to hide from her. I mean, you could have got fired. You nearly did get fired. I'm guessing you didn't tell her that part either?' Drew pressed his lips together, giving Polly the answer she already knew was coming. 'Exactly. You see —'

'You've got to understand —'

'Oh, I do. I understand.' Polly's hand landed back on his leg, an inch or two above his knee. 'I completely understand. I do. And I think you're amazing. The way you tried to protect her from all that. It's what a great husband does.'

A guttural grunt spluttered in Drew's throat. He was pretty certain that wasn't how Sarah was seeing it right now. With a squeeze on his thigh, Polly brought him back to the moment. 'Sometimes, you need to step back from it all. Drew. You need to take time away. You need a chance to be yourself.'

'You think I'm not myself?'

'To be honest, sometimes I even wonder if you know who you truly are anymore.'

There was something about the way she looked at him as she spoke that prickled the hairs on the backs of his neck. Her words, soft and languid, just like that was how words were supposed to be spoken. And she was right. For all Sarah complained about not knowing who she was anymore, it wasn't like this was exactly the life he would have mapped out for himself either.

'With all the children and everything at work, when was the last time you actually got to cut loose?' Polly questioned. 'Really enjoyed yourself?'

'Cutting loose isn't really my thing.'

'Cutting loose is everyone's thing. You have to. At least once in a while. Go on, think about it. When did you last have fun?'

Drew thought it over. He had gone for a steak with one of his old friends at the beginning of the year. It was a great steak, and the ales were good too, even if they were extortionate, but that probably wasn't what she meant by cutting loose. The problem was that the next day he had needed to look after George while Sarah ran Eva over to some club or another, so a wild night just wasn't on the cards. He was pretty sure wild nights were never on the cards anymore.

'Exactly.' Polly spoke as if she had somehow managed to read his thoughts. Another shift in her fingers meant that her hand was now definitely above the knee. If anything, it was encroaching on the groin region. A lump formed in Drew's throat. Anyone's hand that high on his leg was a little uncomfortable, let alone a work colleague. She probably hadn't noticed, though, he thought. Maybe she had had a few too many, although she was perfectly articulate. Some people were just like that, though. Drunk yet articulate. What he needed to do was find a way to make her notice where her hand was without making her feel awkward about the situation. Swallowing profusely, he shuffled slightly in the hope of loosening her grasp. To his surprise, her gripped tightened, moving up again. She squeezed gently into the top of his leg.

'You still have the room booked, don't you?' she said, leaning in and whispering in his ear. 'How about I show you what it really feels like to cut loose?'

A cooling sensation prickled across Drew's skin. It turned out she knew her hand was there after all.

# CHAPTER 28

The underground had been a piece of cake. Several side-stabbing ninja kicks from the bump accompanied by surprised yelps of pain from Sarah ensured that she was quickly offered a seat to sit down on. However, when she reached Paddington Station, her good fortune dried up.

'You have to be joking,' she said. A large sign by the entrance to the station informed her that the line was currently undergoing repair work and, therefore, a replacement bus service would be put on for all passengers.

'And how long's that going to take?' A man behind her spoke the exact words she and probably everyone else on the platform was thinking. He was sharply dressed in a suit, with coloured brogues and his top button undone and tie pulled loose. He looked like the type of man who spent his weekdays in a London studio and his weekends in a large five-bedroom detached all with en-suites and walk-in wardrobes.

'The buses are over there.' Someone pointed in the direction of the carpark. 'It says they'll be leaving at the same time. I guess we'd better get going.' Following the masses, Sarah headed with the crowd towards the carpark, where a large coach had an A3 piece of paper taped to the inside of its front window.

'This is probably going to take the whole night,' Brogues whinged as he headed up the steps in front of her. Using the handles on both sides, Sarah lifted herself up the steps, pausing at the top to speak to the conductor.

'Any idea how long it will take to get to Wokingham?' she said. Behind the steering wheel, the driver began a long inhale before she noticed the excessive bump beneath Sarah's dress. Her look changed to one of more wearied pity.

'Still gotta do all the other stops first, love. And there's the road works. Wish it could be quicker, but there's nothing I can do.'

'I understand,' Sarah replied, aware that she hadn't actually got an answer, but even if she had, it wouldn't have made any difference. She didn't have any other way home. So, whether it was one hour or five, she was on this bus for the long haul. Feeling like there was a long night ahead of her, Sarah slumped down into a seat and pulled out her phone. No missed calls. No messages. Of course, there weren't; she had his phone, she reminded herself. Still, he could have rung her from someone else's phone – it wasn't like her number was hard to remember, and she'd had it for long enough. Smacking her lips in annoyance, she held down the button on the side of her device and switched it off. It wasn't like he would say anything that could put this right anyway.

'Is it okay if I sit here?' A young woman asked, indicating the seat beside Sarah on the aisle. Sarah nodded, despite the fact she had absolutely no say over where anyone sat at all. The girl smiled sweetly.

Another five minutes passed before the bus finally pulled away from the station, timed perfectly with another lurch of Sarah's stomach. Clenching her jaw, she inhaled and tried to suck the pain back down. She had thought Eva was bad, with all the twisting and turning she did, but this one was giving her a run for her money. If it kept on behaving like that, she didn't know how she was going to last another four weeks with it inside her.

'Are you all right?' the girl next to her asked. 'I've got some water in my bag if you'd like?'

Sarah began to shake her head before changing her mind. 'Actually, would that be okay?'

'Of course.' She reached down into her bag, pulled out the metal bottle, and passed it to Sarah, who quickly unscrewed the lid and took a drink.

'Thank you,' she said, passing it back.

'No worries. Keep it. I've got another two in here. I hate paying for bottled water, don't you? I mean, water? Seriously? How dumb do companies think we are?' The girl's eyes moved to her bump momentarily and stopped her rambling. 'Is it your first?' she said.

'Third,' Sarah replied.

'Oh, wow, you look so young.'

'Thanks?' Sarah said. Although she wasn't sure if it was meant as a compliment or not.

'How much longer have you got to go? Can't be that long, can it? I mean, you're pretty big. The bump that is. It's a great bump.'

'Umm, thank you.'

It was apparent the girl wanted to keep talking; no wonder she had asked if it was all right to sit there before she sat down. While Sarah wasn't much in the mood for conversation, it was probably better than sitting and fuming over what a complete and utter dick her husband was.

'Four weeks,' she said. 'I've got four weeks to go. A bit less actually. Assuming he comes on time. My other two were late.'

'Wow, that's not long. My sister had a baby boy last month. My third nephew. Third, can you believe that? She was trying for a girl, you know. That's why she had a third. She won't say that, of course, but I'm her sister. I know these things. She says she's stopped now and everything, but she ain't. I told my mum, I said "*I bet you, she's gonna have another. And I bet it'll be a boy too.*" Look.' The girl's hands were back in her bag, this time feeling for her phone. She handed it to Sarah. On the locked screen was a photo of her sitting on a sofa with the tiniest of new-borns on her lap, and two other children, similar-looking in age to George and Eva, were sitting on either side.

'He was eight weeks early,' she said, taking the phone back to gaze at the picture herself. 'He was well tiny.'

'God, that must have been terrifying.' Sarah had never particularly enjoyed the delay that had come with both George and Eva, but she would have rather had it that way than the other.

'Yeah, I mean it was. But my sister, she's well chilled. And he was super strong. Like, she was worried a bit and stuff, but she knew, you know. He's doing really well. Home and everything. Although he still can't fit into any of the clothes I bought him. It's cool, though. I just bought him more.'

Sarah chuckled. Despite her loquaciousness, she was warming to the girl. Partway through her chuckle, another searing pain around her diaphragm struck. She clenched her jaw and fist simultaneously.

'Are you sure you're okay?' the girl asked. 'That's the second time you've looked like that.'

'It's fine. It's just pre-labour, that's all.' Or *surges* as her Mind Birthing class would call them. 'They happen all the time.' A small twinge in her abdomen warned her that another one was likely incoming. She had suffered days of them with George, a full forty-eight hours of expecting him to drop any minute; she wasn't going to fall for that again, although they hadn't been quite so painful or close together back then.

For half an hour, Sarah let the girl natter away to her, telling her about the date she had been on the night before and the college course she had just started. She was endlessly forthcoming with information, from the pictures the guy had sent her before, to the meetup and to the allergy issues she had with dairy. Despite the oversharing, it hardly felt like Sarah had her undivided attention. It was a sign of the times, she thought, how the girl, midway through the conversation, would constantly glance down at her phone. The first two or three times, Sarah thought that maybe a message had come through, but after the fourth or fifth time, she concluded it had to be some kind of nervous tick. Like the planet might suddenly implode if she went too long without checking it. *It's just a way of life,* Sarah thought, suspecting that she was scarily similar in her inability to go more than four minutes without checking social media.

'I know I want to do something with people, but I just

haven't worked out what type of people.' The girl was now talking about why she had switched her college courses three times already. Sarah grimaced as she nodded, trying to smile her way through the current pain that was searing its way through her sides. 'I thought that maybe I'd work with little kids and stuff, you know, like in a kindergarten or something. But then you have them all day, you know. And kids can be freaking annoying. It's different when they're your own, I bet.'

'I think you get sick of them faster,' Sarah replied.

The girl opened her mouth as if to speak, although before any words escaped, her eyes were back on her phone again. When her face came back up to Sarah, it had paled slightly.

'I know you're the expert at this,' she said. 'But I've been timing and stuff. You seem to be having one of those pains every five minutes. Are they normally as regular as that?'

Sarah clicked her neck from one side to another, trying to bring a little relief to her muscles. Everywhere had been cramping since she sat down.

'What was that?' she said.

'Those pains. They're every five minutes. Real regular. Aren't they meant to be random if they're the other ones? Those pre-labour ones?'

Sarah frowned and looked at her phone. While she was certain the girl meant well, it was almost impossible that Sarah would have found herself in the early stages of labour without realising it. And not all of the pains felt like that anyway. Some were almost certainly the bump shifting around and practising tae kwondo. No doubt, the baby would tire itself out soon enough. 'Honestly, it's fine. This isn't it.

I've done it before.' An awkward silence grew between the pair. 'So, tell me about the courses again…' Sarah tried. It didn't take much. Soon, the girl was talking about the possibility of moving into hospitality. When she felt her stomach muscles tighten exactly five minutes later, Sarah gritted her teeth. As silently as she could manage, she dragged in a lungful air through her nose, which she expelled in an extended hiss.

'Was that another?' The girl had unclipped her seat belt and crouched in the aisle by Sarah's feet in a manner that made Sarah feel about a hundred times more awkward. 'Is there someone you need to call? Is there anyone you need me to call?'

'No, no, it was just wind,' she lied. 'I've just had a bit of indigestion recently. That's all.'

Sarah swallowed. There. It was fine. There was no way she'd have been able to just breathe down through it if it had been a real contraction. Not even with all the Mind Birthing bullshit in the world on her side. She'd get home, get out of the ridiculous dress, and make herself a cup of tea. A cup of tea would help.

# CHAPTER 29

D rew was suffering from extreme light-headedness. Although not an expert, he was pretty sure it was the type of light-headedness that always came when a beautiful, smart, young woman suggested they head up to a hotel room together and cut loose.

Polly was sitting back in her seat, the twinkling in her eyes even brighter than the glass in her hand.

'You don't need to worry. No one needs to know.' She had a confidence about her. Or was it arrogance? At that precise moment, they were hard to distinguish. 'No one would ever know. We could keep it a secret. My little Christmas present to you for all your hard work.'

There was a standard reply he was meant to give at that moment, but given the massive lump that had swollen in his throat, he was having rather a hard time remembering it.

'Sarah,' he managed to choke out.

'How would she find out?' Polly whispered. 'I'm not going to say anything.'

Drew shook his head. It couldn't be real. It just couldn't.

Things like this didn't happen to average-looking middle-managers. They weren't the type of men who had attractive young women throwing themselves at them and begging them for a night of adulterous passion. And yet it was happening.

'So?' Polly said, her hand back on his leg, causing a series of chills to run up and down his spine. 'Shall I order us a bottle of wine to take up to the room or not?'

'It's just —'

'What have we got to lose?'

Somewhere, a switch flipped. Of course. Polly was care-free with the whole world in front of her for the taking. She had nothing to lose. But he already had everything. Every-thing he wanted, everything he needed. And all of that could be ripped from him in one single night. Jumping up from the stool, he banged his knee on the bar as he moved.

'I… I… no. Sarah. I mean, thank you, but no.'

'Sorry.' Polly's cheeks were flushed. 'I just thought you and her —'

'We're married. We're good. We're better than good. We're having a baby. Shit. Shit. What am I doing? What the hell am I doing?'

A delicate hand rested once more on his shoulder. 'Drew, you didn't do anything. Really.' The pink blush was gone. She was back to cool, sophisticated Polly. Unflappable Polly. Unlike Drew. Drew was most very definitely flappable. And flapping.

'I need to go. I need to find her.'

'She'll be fine. She was getting the train home, you said. Why don't you just come up to the party for one drink? A *work* drink. The others were asking where you'd gone to. And

I promise, no funny business.' She winked. It was probably a sexy wink, probably another attempt at seduction, only he didn't have time to give it any attention. He needed his phone. Where the hell was his phone? He scanned his eyes up and down the length of the bar, then checked on the floor before re-checking his pockets, even though he knew the phone couldn't be in them. He never put his phone in these pockets. Whenever he wore these trousers, Sarah always carried his phone in her bag.

'Noooo.' He turned around in a circle like somehow he might find the answer to his issues walking through the revolving doors. When that didn't happen, he ran for the elevator.

'Wait, where are you going? I thought we were going to the party for a drink.'

Drew shook his head as he pushed the button on the elevator while simultaneously searching for his keys. 'I need to get going. I need to find Sarah. I need to put this right.'

'Shall I call someone? A friend? Your mother? A priest. Some people like to have a priest by their bed when they're giving birth, don't they?'

'I think that's just when they're dying,' Sarah replied.

'Oh. Maybe not a priest then? How about a sister? A cousin?' The girl was doing a stand-up job at sounding chirpy. If anything, she seemed excited by an event Sarah was still almost positive was not going to happen. For twenty minutes, she had been doing her best to swallow down the contractions like spasms in the hope that the girl wouldn't notice. It hadn't worked.

'It's fine. Honestly. It's just pre-labour. They'll stop soon enough. Actually, I think they may have passed…' She paused, holding her breath while it passed.

'I think they might be getting a bit closer.' The girl bounced on her seat. 'I love this bit; don't you love it? You must be so excited. God, I'm excited, and I don't even know your name. My name's Jenny, by the way.'

Another spasm timed itself perfectly, causing Sarah to bite down on the sides of her cheeks.

'Sarah.' She spoke through clenched teeth, relaxing her muscles a fraction of a second too early. The pain burned through her.

'Drew,' she yelled at the air. Actual labour or not, what kind of dick husband would let their heavily-pregnant wife storm out of a hotel in the middle of London?

'What's the noise? What's going on back there?' The bus driver called up from the front.

'I think she's having a baby,' the girl replied before Sarah could open her mouth.

'I am *not* having a baby. It's not due for another four weeks.'

'Three and a half.'

Sarah growled. Defending the fact that she was not in labour was not how she had planned her evening. 'This is my third.' she said. 'And my others were all late. I know what labour feels like.'

'Your third?' The driver met her eye momentarily in the mirror before shaking her head, satisfied at the response.

'The woman knows what she's talking about. If she says it ain't coming, it ain't coming.'

'Thank you,' Sarah exhaled, feeling the weight in her stomach drop down as she breathed.

'But I've been timing.' Jenny wasn't going to give up yet. 'And they're currently all under five minutes. I'm not sure if she's dilated yet. I could check on Google. I bet Google can tell me how to check if she's dilated.' She began typing. 'Oh, apparently I'd need access to your vagina.'

Sarah hoisted herself up, putting her weight on the seat in front. 'No one is going anywhere near my vagina.' She glared up and down the aisle. 'I mean that, no one. Including this baby. I am not in labour. So, if we can just get to the next station and all get home, that would be just great.

Ignoring the various looks – that ranged from sympathetic concern to extremely nervous judders – Sarah sank back into her seat.

It was Drew and his stupid toxins that had caused this to happen. My god, she was going to give him an earful when this was over. And the yelling was only going to be half of his punishment. She wasn't going to change a single dirty nappy when this one arrived. No way. Not one. Not an ounce of baby vomit either. Nor the disgusting little black ball of vileness that formed when their belly button went all crusty and dropped off. Drew was going to have to deal with it all. With a ripple of regret, her thoughts flickered briefly back to Drew alone at the hotel. He probably thought he was doing the right thing, not telling her that people had seen the book, she realised sadly. It wasn't the right thing. It was definitely *not* the right thing to do. But he would have *thought* it was. That was typical Drew. Botching things up because he was trying to make life easier.

With her anger waning ever so slightly, Sarah considered whether or not she should ring him. It had been over an hour since she had left the hotel. He was probably worried. He'd probably realised she'd got his phone by this point too. Then again, he deserved to be worried. It was him who had put her in this situation. Him and his stupid lying and emailing. She would let him stew for a bit longer. While still deliberating how long she would draw his punishment out for, her thoughts were interrupted by the sudden spasm of pain which rippled around her belly and back. This time, she clawed her hands as she waited for it to pass.

'That's four minutes now,' Jenny said. 'Isn't it funny how it's so different in real life compared to the movies? Like your waters and stuff. Do you know that a baby can actually be born in its sack? The amniotic sack, that's what it's called, but you probably know that already, don't you? Anyway, I saw it on YouTube. This baby came all the way out, and it was still in the bag. Didn't burst or anything. Looked like an alien. Was well weird. My sister's water broke on our mum's sofa. She was well cross about that. 'Til she found out the insurance covered it. Imagine that.'

Sarah's inhaling and exhaling echoed loudly in the air. It was hard to decide if Jenny's jabbering was meant as a deliberate distraction, or she really was incapable of not talking. From the seat behind came a hard throat clearing.

'I'm sorry, but would you mind keeping it down a bit?'

'Sorry?' Sarah said.

'Well.' He coughed again. 'Some of us here are trying to get on with some work. Would you mind talking a little bit quieter?' It was the man with the brogues, she realised. Tie still hanging loose around his neck.

'I didn't realise we were being loud,' Jenny joined in.

'No? Well, at the very least, could you change the topic to something more… civilised?'

A shudder ran down Sarah's spine. Grinding her teeth together, she prepared herself for a fight only to find herself beaten to the post.

'Civilised? She's pregnant, you twat.'

'I can see that. All I'm saying is that perhaps the conversation you're having is not ideal for a public forum.'

'What public forum?' Jenny was now off her seat and standing in the middle of the aisle, her head a full foot above his. 'You're the one listening in on us. And while we're at it —'

'It's fine,' Sarah said, flinching as she twisted around to face him. 'We'll keep our voices down.'

'Thank —'

'The hell we will. How do you think it happens, you twat? It happens like this. She's having a bloody baby.'

'I'm not having a baby now.'

'You bloody are. I bet you five quid it's on the way.'

Sarah was about to accept the bet when the pain struck again. It wasn't a pin point this time. Not beneath her ribs or on her diaphragm. It was everywhere. Every muscle in her abdomen all coming together at the exact same point. Like they were all trying to push something out.

'Oooooh bugger,' she cried

'I bloody told you, didn't I?' Jenny said with a smirk.

# CHAPTER 30

I f nothing else, Drew had learned this; if they ever had enough money to purchase a new car, it would be a car that came with an inbuilt satellite navigation system. Without his phone, he was completely lost.

'I've already been down this road!' he yelled, thumping his fist against the steering wheel as he was forced down yet another one-way street. Who designed these roads? That was what he wanted to know. And did they design them with the sole purpose of making life as difficult as possible for anyone who didn't have a smartphone or a photographic memory? All he wanted was an exit sign. A big, EXIT LONDON, sign. Would that have been too much to ask for?

Thirty minutes after leaving Polly at the bar and dashing for the car park, he found himself driving once again past the grey stone building of the hotel. 'You have to be kidding me,' he said. Inhaling through his nose and trying his best not to beep the hell out of his car horn, he approached the next junction. 'Let's try right this time.'

It was the fact that she had gone off with his phone that infuriated him the most. What the hell was she thinking? She was less than four weeks away from her due date. And hadn't both of the others been born early? Or was it late? They had definitely been either early or late. With a sigh of relief, Drew turned off the one-way road onto something with an inkling of familiarity. When he got home, she was going to get an earful for this. That he promised.

It was as though a switch had been flicked in her brain and her uterus simultaneously. She was in labour. Actual, physical, baby-on-its-way labour. The moment she had been dreading from the moment she first realised she was pregnant was here, and she was on a bus.

'Try the hotel again. It's been fifteen minutes. He might be in the room now,' Jenny said helpfully. 'Why don't you try the hotel again?'

'If he had gone to the room, he would have seen the messages by now,' Sarah replied.

There had been no answer in the room the first time she rang, and the person on the other end of the line hadn't sounded too happy about going upstairs and crashing the party to find a guest, even when Sarah stressed how important it was.

'I'm afraid guest privacy is paramount to us here at Eden Garden Hotel,' the woman had said, all toffee-nosed and elitist. 'But if you would like to leave a message, we will be certain that it gets to them.'

'I'm having a baby. I'm having a baby in the back of a bus in the middle of a dual carriageway, and I swear to god, if you do not go upstairs and find my husband, then I will be ringing every paper from here to bloody Inverness about your customer service.' She was then put on hold for a full ten minutes before the woman came back online.

'I'm very sorry. He doesn't seem to be at the party. And there's still no answer from his room. I can leave a message for him if you'd like.'

'Yes, if you could leave him a note saying his wife is about to give birth in the back of a bus, that would be great.'

To give the woman her due, it did sound like she wrote it down. Now, of course, Sarah had drained her battery entirely. Perfect. Just perfect.

In the madness that was realising she was actually in labour, Sarah had failed to notice that the bus had gone from a slow crawling pace to completely stationary.

'What's the holdup?' Brogues called up to the front. 'Why aren't we moving?'

'Road works,' the driver called back.

The man's grunt snorted only inches from Sarah's ear.

'If I'd known we were going to be stuck in traffic all night, I'd have waited for the next train.'

'You're more than welcome to get off at the next stop,' was the reply that came back.

Beads of sweat had started to gather on the back of Sarah's neck. At least this one was being born in winter. Those last months with George in her felt like she had a toaster oven inside of her. But still, she had been ready and waiting for him. She had had a *go-bag* waiting by the door.

Snacks and clean clothes for when it all got a bit messy. She picked up her phone and stared at it blankly. There was no point in trying the hotel again.

'Is there someone else you can call?' Jenny was back to making suggestions. 'What about your home phone? Maybe he went straight home?'

'We keep it unplugged. I don't like all the cold callers.' Sarah realised for the first time how ridiculous that was, forgoing one of the key home safety items for the sake of not having to hang up on a salesman of questionable intentions. Still, Jenny wasn't done with suggestions.

'How about calling someone using his phone, maybe? You said he was at a party, right? Is there anyone he would be with that you could call?'

Sarah considered it. It wasn't a bad idea. Just because the woman at reception hadn't found him, it didn't mean he wasn't there. He could easily have slipped into the toilet when she went upstairs. Or been chatting away and not heard her asking over the music. She picked Drew's phone out of her bag. The stunt with the sat nav meant that the battery on his phone was down to a single line of red. Still, she figured it would be enough to make one phone call. With her heart having inched its way up her throat, she typed in his password. It would have to be Barry. Barry was the one she had known the longest. A second after finding the number, the phone was ringing. Picked up in two rings, a chorus of Wizzard rang down the line before Barry started to speak.

'Drew, where are you? You haven't left, have you? We saw you and Sarah have a bit of a barny; that wasn't to do with the book, was it? You know it's probably just her hormones playing up. Women and their hormones. Bloody nutcases the lot of them. I don't know how you do it if I'm honest. Living with a pregnant woman. I imagine it's like sharing your space with a starving hippo.'

'It's Sarah, Barry.' An awkward silence punctuated the air.

'Oh.' She could hear the swallow down the line. 'I mean… I just meant. You know, pregnancy, hormones. I didn't mean I wouldn't want to live with you. I'd love to. Not that Alice and I —'

'Look, Barry, is Drew there with you? I can't get hold of him. It's rather important.'

'I haven't seen him,' Barry answered. 'That's why I thought you were him.'

Sarah's stomach plummeted again. Or at least it would have done, had it had anywhere to go. Instead, a low groan rattled from her throat.

'Could you just check? Please. See if anyone might know where he's gone? He's not in our room, and I need to get hold of him.'

'Hang on a minute. I'll ask if anyone's seen him.'

While Barry disappeared, leaving a chorus of White Christmas buzzing fuzzily down the line, Sarah noticed that the volume in her own environment had increased substantially too.

'What's going on?' She said to Jenny as it became apparent that a large number of people were grizzling and snapping complaints at one another and, most of all, at the bus driver. 'Did I just miss something?'

'Apparently, these roadworks go on for another two miles. Means the people getting off from now on are going to miss their connections.'

'Have they not put buses on for that too?' Sarah asked.

'Apparently not.'

She glanced around the room, noting the annoyance on people's faces. Two rows behind her, a young girl had fallen asleep on her mother's shoulder while Brogues now had his phone plugged into the largest power bank she'd ever seen. Unless he was planning a four-day hike across the Sahara, it was difficult to imagine anyone going that long without being able to find a plug socket. A wave of contracting muscles rolled through her when she caught the sound of someone calling her name, faintly, as if miles away.

'Sarah? Are you still there? Sarah?'

'Barry.' Sarah pressed the phone to her ear. 'Barry? Have you found him? Do you know where he is?'

'Sorry. A couple of the lads saw him downstairs at the bar about an hour ago with Polly.'

'Polly?'

'Yes, but no one's seen either of them since. They seem to have both disappeared.'

The petulant grumbles from the bus, along with the tinny music from down the phone line all drifted into the ether as Sarah repeated what Barry had just told her.

'Polly and Drew,' she said. 'They disappeared together?' Her chest felt like it had just been attacked by some rib split-ting monster. 'Barry, is that what you said?'

Whether Barry answered or not, she didn't hear. The pain shot through her from all points simultaneously. Unable to hold any of it back, she let out a god almighty scream.

'Argh!'

'Okay.' The bus driver was looking back through her rear

review mirror. 'That is not sounding good. Is everything all right back there?'

'Not really!' Sarah heard Jenny say beside her. 'Where's the nearest hospital?'

'You want to go to the hospital? This isn't a taxi. This is a public bus.' Brogues was out of his seat. 'Do you want everyone to miss their connections?'

'Do you want to catch your connection with a sackful of amniotic fluid and a recently ejected placenta all over your shoes?' The girl replied. It was a good enough question to have him fall back in his seat.

'Honestly,' Sarah pushed herself up on her elbows to stop the dizzy spell that followed. 'I'll be fine. Honestly. I've got plenty of time. I just need to get home. Get to…'

She couldn't even form his name in her mouth. It didn't make sense. It didn't. Drew and Polly. Polly and Drew. They couldn't have left together. Polly was so young and leggy and beautiful. And Drew was… well… he was hers. He wouldn't have done that, surely not?  But then if he could lie to her about people reading the book, what else would he lie about? 'I'll be fine. Honestly,' Sarah repeated the words breathless and frail. 'It'll be fine. It has to be. It has to be.'

While Jenny responded by leaning over and rubbing her arm, Brogues was on his feet.

'I've had enough of this. I'm not going to sit back here any longer.'

It was possibly the worst timing anyone could have had. A shift of her pelvis, him bending down to get his briefcase. That split second was all it took. It did at least show that on some occasions, waters could break just like they did in the movies; in one massive rush that flooded from Sarah, straight to the ground and all over a pair of perfectly polished brogues.

'What the f—'

'Well, at least you know your baby's got a sense of humour,' Jenny said.

# CHAPTER 31

**D**rew flung open the front door
'Sarah!' he yelled up the stairs, flicking on the lights and dropping his keys into the bowl. 'Sah, I'm sorry. I am so, so sorry.' He raced upstairs into the bedroom. The bed was still made or as close to being made as it ever really got. Running back downstairs, he opened the door to the living room.

'Sah?' His pulse, which had maintained a fairly high pace since he left the party, kicked up another notch. 'Sah?' The room was in darkness. He began scrambling around on the floor to try and plug the phone lead into the wall socket. Once that was done, he scooped up the receiver. 'Shit,' he said out loud. What the hell was her phone number? He squeezed his eyes closed as he tried to remember it. There was a double four in their somewhere, he thought. Maybe a four, zero, four. Or four, four, zero, four.

'Buggering hell.' Why did he not know his own wife's telephone number for crying out loud? He could still remember the number for the house he lived in until he was thirteen and the number of Steve Moore down the street. He could even remember the number of his Aunt June, who had moved three times and died since. 'Stupid technology,' he screamed at no one in particular. He would go around to his parents, that was what he'd do.

Still busy swearing to himself, and only half a mile away from their house, Drew lifted his foot off the accelerator. Would Sarah really have gone to his parents? He considered. She had to be dragged there under duress at the best of times. And where would she have slept? On the sofa? And then there would be all the questions about why she wasn't with Drew. The car slowed to a crawl as he realised there was no way in hell she could have put herself through that. But where else did she have to go?

'This is ridiculous. You do realise you have taken us hostage? Do you hear me? Hostage.' Brogues was near apoplectic with outrage. 'I'm going to call the police. I'm going to. If you do not turn this bus around this instant, I am calling 999.'

Sarah had been moved to the back seat of the bus; the place where all the cool kids sat. She didn't feel like one of the cool kids right now, though, with her dress up around her hips and her feet pressed against the window.

'Perhaps you ought to draw the curtains,' someone said as a lorry beside them beeped their horn. Even in her state of shock and denial, she could see it was probably a good idea.

'Does anyone have any more water? We're all out of water here.' Jenny asked, having already used her own supply along with her scarf to mop up the mess on the floor.

From somewhere up front, a bottle was passed back to them. Sarah gulped as much down as she could manage. Several big contractions had already come and gone, and while the baby and its health were highest on her list of priorities, there was another more immediate issue to deal with.

'Plastic bags,' she said, during a break in the pain. 'You need to cover the seat with plastic bags.'

'Don't worry, we'll make sure you're comfortable,' Jenny replied.

'I don't care about comfy. I just don't want —' She stopped herself. 'Just put some damn plastic bags down, will you?'

Involuntary bowel evacuation. Another part of that whole process Sarah had wished to suppress; the act of crapping herself, repeatedly, in front of whoever happened to be present in the room at the time. She had thought the second time would be better for some reason, that she would be able to feel the difference between a baby and dropping a massive one in front of a midwife. Nope. With Eva, she had been letting it all go and not giving a crap. Literally. And it was going to happen again. All over the cool kids' back seat. Well, that would stop them wanting to sit there again in a hurry.

'Jenny, you won't leave me, will you?' Sarah clamped onto her new friend's hand. 'I'm not very good at this.'

'You'll be fine. You've already had two.'

'And it was horrible. I didn't want to do it again. I don't want to do it again. Please don't make me do it again.' Pressure surged down her stomach, momentarily distracting her and causing her to remember her more immediate fear. 'And will you get me some damn plastic bags?'

Due to the complete middle-classness of her fellow

commuters, only one plastic bag could be found among the group. She was instead lying upon a mix of hessian, canvas, and organic cotton totes, one of which was so horrendously placed that the handle was chafing her backside. She would have complained, but it wasn't like the rest of them were having a particularly pleasant journey either.

'Did you not hear me? I'm going to call the police.'

'Will someone shut him up? Because if someone does not shut him up soon, I am going to pull up on this lay-by and push him out myself.' The driver was keeping her eyes forward on the road, despite the standstill.

'We're already late. Won't make any difference now,' someone said. 'Let's just make sure she gets to the hospital. Get this bubba out safe.' A general hum of agreement buzzed through the bus.

'Shouldn't we call an ambulance?' Someone else said. 'Wouldn't it make sense to call an ambulance?'

'You think they're going to be able to get here any quicker?'

Sarah let all the conversations fall into her periphery. That was for someone else to deal with. The bus, the journey; they could argue over that. Her job was to keep the damn baby in until they reached the hospital. And try not to have any panic attacks in the meanwhile.

Sodding Drew. The lying, cheating idiot of a man. Could he not have just been by her side for this and then gone off and screwed the intern? Would that have been too much to ask for? The thought went around and around in her head. Of all the nights.

'How far away are we?' Jenny yelled to the front. 'Contractions are at three minutes this end.'

'ETA of ten minutes,' the driver called to the back. 'Just hold it in a little longer.'

Jenny's hand came across and rested on her shoulders. For all her youth and constant nattering, Sarah was thankful there was someone here to hold her hand through this.

'You can do this,' Jenny dropped her voice to a low resonance. 'Breathe in through your nose and let the breath go out and down through your vagina.'

'Sorry?' Sarah blinked, alerted to her words.

'In through your nose and out through your vagina. Feel the surges blooming through your body.'

Sarah reached up and grabbed Jenny's hand.

'You did Mind Birthing?' She twisted her head up, not sure if this was an auditory hallucination she was hearing and whether that was even possible.

'Did I not mention I was my sister's birthing partner for all three?' she grinned. 'She's all about the hippy nonsense.' Then, for a hundred reasons, each of which was entirely deserved, Sarah burst into tears.

In less than ten minutes, Drew had found the crazily painted fence. Never again would he comment on its ridiculousness. There was no way he'd have been able to tell the house apart from the other hundred identical new builds without it. He might even paint his own that colour when he got through this. Not that they had a fence, they had a wall. They could paint that instead. Leaving the engine running, he raced through the gate and hammered on the door.

'Drew?' Nelly answered the door in what he assumed were pyjamas. 'What are you doing here?'

'Is she in here? Sah!' He called over her shoulder and into the house. 'Sarah, I'm sorry. Honey, I'm sorry.'

'Drew!' Nelly placed her hand on his chest and pushed him outside. 'What are you doing? It's half ten.'

'Is she here? I can't get hold of her.'

'Who? Sarah? I haven't seen her since she picked up the dress. I thought you were staying the night in London?'

'We were. It's just… it's well… look…' Drew peered over Nelly's shoulder into the house, wringing his hands as he spoke. 'Can you just call her, please? Find out where she is?'

'Why don't you ring her?'

'She took my phone. And I don't know her number.'

Nelly looked at him sceptically, which he really didn't feel like he deserved considering his panicked state and the fact that no one actually knew anybody's number by heart anymore. 'Please, can you just ring her?'

At the most disturbingly slow place possible, Nelly ambled back into the house, pushing the door close in a manner that indicated to Drew he probably wasn't welcome to join her inside. Looking down, he noticed he was standing on a brown doormat with the words *I like it dirty* woven into them. Beside it, two garden gnomes were copulating. Sarah did have the strangest taste in friends. A moment later, Nelly reappeared with her phone in her hand.

'It's going straight to voicemail,' she said.

'What? Give that to me.' Drew snatched the phone off her and hit the call button himself only to find it was, as Nelly had said, going straight to voicemail. 'It must have run out of battery.' The realisation hit him like a train. 'She's got your phone, you damn idiot,' he said to himself. He might not be able to remember Sarah's number, but he could remember his.

'I know it ain't ideal timing, but you should really have a few pictures to remember this moment by,' Jenny was saying as she picked up Drew's phone and flicked it to camera mode.

During the impromptu photo shoot, Sarah realised there was only one thing for it. She would have to call Drew's mother. She desperately didn't want Amanda with her during the birth, probably any more than Amanda would want to be there, but it did look like her only option.

'Oh, that's a smashing one,' Jenny said. 'And this one. Here let me show you.' She turned the phone around so Sarah could see the screen. It was possibly the worst photo Sarah had ever seen of herself. Her hair was matted to her forehead, she had a pained grimace on her face, and her eyes were like those of a cornered wild animal. Fortunately, she didn't have to look at it for long. The moment she went to take the phone so she could call Amanda and Neil, the screen went completely blank.

'I think the battery might have gone,' said Jenny.

With the call going straight to voicemail, Drew handed the phone back to Nelly. If only he hadn't used the sat nav on his phone all the way to London, he thought.

'Look,' Nelly said, coming over and placing a hand on his

shoulder. He didn't need a hand on his shoulder. He needed to know where the hell Sarah was. 'Maybe she's just gone for a walk. Or to a bar. Or just have some space outside of that crappy little house of yours she hates so much.'

Drew stepped back. 'She doesn't hate the house. She loves the house.'

'She loved the house years ago when you bought it, Drew. Now she hates that house. And she hates that you don't even see she hates it.'

'She says it's cute.'

'When Drew? When was the last time she said that it was cute?'

He bit on his bottom lip, attempting to chew over all the things he was hearing. Only, after a minute, he realised it didn't matter.

'Look, she wouldn't have gone for a walk. She wouldn't. No matter how pissed off she is with me.'

'Exactly how pissed off was she?'

'Please, Nelly. Can you just help? I need to find her. I need to know she's okay. I'm begging you.' And he was, he realised. Hands clenched, leaning forward, begging for all he was worth.

Nelly's gaze went back to her house, a pinched lined creasing in her brow.

'I suppose we better start by calling the hospitals.' She disappeared into the house for a second time. Wearily, Drew followed her in.

# CHAPTER 32

She really didn't want to scream. She didn't. What she wanted was to be in a nice soft hospital bed, gulping back a lungful of gas and air with Drew rubbing her back until his hand cramped. Permanently. With Eva, he had decided three hours in that he needed a bit of a break and headed down to the hospital cafeteria to fetch himself a cup of hot chocolate. Really, Drew? She had wanted to say to him. *You* needed a break? But, despite it all, she desperately wished he was there with her. The contractions were now interspersed by spasms of uncontrollable sobs.

How was it possible that he could do this to her? How? And what would happen next? How were they meant to afford marriage counselling with nappies and breast pumps and cracked nipple cream all piling onto the shopping list a month before they were supposed to? She gasped, her muscles squeezing at the exact same moment a new thought struck. What if he didn't want to go to counselling? What if this thing with Polly was more than just a fling? And even if he did want to work it out, how could she stay with him after this? Cheating on your pregnant wife. That really was about as low as you could go. Did she really think that lowly of herself?

'You need to keep breathing,' Jenny was telling her. 'That's it. It's nearly passed. Just keep breathing. Remember, your body is a vessel —'

'I don't want it to be a vessel. I want it to be filled with drugs.'

'Turning off now,' the driver called from the front. 'Five more minutes.'

'You said that fifteen minutes ago!' Sarah screamed back.

'Yes, well, I lied then. I'm not lying now.'

Sarah clawed her fingers into the seat cushions. How the hell was she going to do this on her own? She asked herself for the hundredth time. Maybe she could get a magazine deal in one of those crappy papers Nelly always read on the sly. *I found my husband cheating the day our baby was born*. It wasn't nearly as catchy a title as some of them, but maybe they'd pay her a bit of money. And if by some stroke of luck that book of his did sell more than half a dozen copies, she was keeping every damn penny of it.

There were only two hospitals in the region that were open at that time, and according to them, Sarah hadn't been admitted to either.

'Can I leave my number then? Can you call if she comes in?'

'This isn't a hotel, sir.'

'No, I know. Only it's my wife. I can't find her.'

'Then maybe you should try missing persons, sir.'

'No, you don't understand. She's pregnant. I just need to know if she comes in. Please, can you just —' There was no point carrying on. The line was already dead. After that, they tried further afield, using the map on Nelly's phone to find all the hospitals in the region that she could have possibly gone to. He had tried his parents too, although he had called under the ruse of checking that the children were in bed.

'All tucked up and asleep,' his mother had said. 'I take it you two are having fun? It doesn't sound like you're at much of a party.'

'Oh. I'm just outside,' Drew said. 'Well, I should get back. We'll see you in the morning.'

'No worries. They've already made enough mess. You might as well take the day.'

So that was it. Sarah wasn't home, she wasn't at his parents'. She wasn't at her best friend slash the only person she could stand in a hundred-mile radius. Wherever she was, she either didn't want to be found or couldn't.

It was past midnight now, three hours since Sarah had stormed out of the hotel.

'I should go to the police station,' Drew lifted himself up from the sofa.

'Look, you'll sort this. Whatever it is. I'm sure she's fine,' Nelly said, doing her best to reassure him. 'Maybe she just checked herself into another hotel room. Maybe she just wanted to give herself a little peace.'

'Maybe.'

'And if she's not back by lunchtime, then I'll do another ring round with you. Head to the police station too.'

'Thanks,' Drew muttered. He should have been able to

give her more thanks than that, he thought, as he dragged himself back to the car. She had just spent two hours with him, making one pointless phone call after another, but he just didn't have the strength. What was he meant to do now, he wondered, slipping into his car. Just go home? Just go home and pretend his wife wasn't missing? Go home and pretend she hadn't stormed off with a look of absolute hatred in her eyes?

The sting of bile struck once again at the back of his throat. You read about it, didn't you? He thought. Those couples who have a massive argument only for one of them to get caught up in a terrible accident before they can make up. What if that had happened? How would he ever look the children in the eyes again? But then she wasn't in a hospital, he reminded himself.

When he finally opened the door to the house, he headed straight to the living room, where he stretched his legs out on the sofa and moved his head from one side to the next. Sarah obviously hadn't had much of a chance to tidy before they went out. Books were stacked on one end of the table, mounds of clothes on the other. There was a pile of children's toys that had been swept into the corner of the room and two plates that he had a vague recollection of Sarah asking him to put in the sink yesterday. His stomach sank. Maybe Nelly was right. Maybe Sarah had been screaming about the size of the house all this time. He had just chosen not to hear it.

From somewhere outside came the screeching of tyres. Drew lifted his head for a fraction of a second before moving over to the bookshelf. Their wedding photo was masked in a thin layer of dust, which he liberated from the surface with a gentle blow of air. He tried to remember the last time he had looked at it. The last time he had even thought about his wedding day. Probably when Facebook pinged up that he had a memory to look at. He had thought he was getting it together, the job, and then the book. How had he managed to make such a mess of everything without even trying?

In the end, he fell asleep in front of the television. A particularly bloody horror film – the type he would have revelled in normally – provided a cacophonous accompaniment to his shallow snoring. Only when the remote fell from his lap and clattered to the ground, well after the film had finished, did he jolt awake.

'Sarah?' He asked, before shaking himself awake into the moment. His stomach plummeted. Outside, it was still dark, although the stars had faded the way they did just before dawn. In another hour, he would start ringing the hospitals again.

# CHAPTER 33

'She's ever so peaceful, ain't she?'

'She is.' Sarah tilted her chin and lightly kissed the newborn's forehead. She had that perfect smell, the creased skin, and the scrunched up little fists that she wanted to remember forever.

'Have you got a name?' Jenny asked, her hand gently stroking the baby's back.

A smile graced Sarah's lips as she looked at her youngest daughter.

'Elspeth,' she said. 'I think I'm going to call her Elspeth.'

'Great name.'

'It is, isn't it?' Sarah had always loved the name. There was something so gentle about it, yet at the same time, regal and creative.

'Do you think she'll remember me?' Jenny asked. A moment later, she shook away the question. 'That's stupid, ain't it? Ignore me. Only, it's really special, you know. It's really something, seeing them come into the world like this. I thought it was because it was with my sister before. You know.

They were my blood and everything. But it's the same. This little baby… I, I…'

'I know,' Sarah said, and she did. The fact of the matter was there were simply no words that could do justice to the moment she was feeling right now.

'Jenny,' Sarah reached up and took her newest friend's hand. 'I know what you should do. Train to be a midwife.'

He hadn't waited for the elevator. It was taking too long. Instead, he had raced up the stairwell. It felt like a good idea on the first floor and still so on the second, but by the third floor, Drew's legs were starting to burn, by the fourth, he had substantially slowed, and by the fifth floor, he was wondering if they kept defibrillators in the stairwell as well as on the main floor, and whether or not he could use them on himself. Lungs heaving, he dragged himself up the final flight and flung himself into the maternity ward.

'Sarah. Sarah Morgan.' He panted at the desk. From behind a computer, a nurse lifted her eyes. Her jaw jutted outwards, a distinct look of disapproval in her eye.

'You're the dad?'

'I am. Oh, thank God she's here. Where is she? Can I see her? I need to see her.'

'That's up to Mum,' the midwife replied. Hoisting herself up out of her chair, she moved wordlessly through the hallway, Drew hot on her heels.

'She's in there,' she said. 'But if she doesn't want to see you, that's up to her.'

While Drew wasn't sure what situation Sarah would be in

when he entered the maternity ward to see his wife, he knew there were certain things he hadn't been expecting. Like a young girl with her hands on her hips, blocking the way for him to get in.

'Drew, I take it?'

'Sorry, I…' Drew rubbed his eyes. The sleeplessness from the night before was clinging to his temples, slowing all comprehension. 'Where's Sarah?'

'You don't deserve to see them. Either of them. You lying, dirty —'

'It's all right, Jenny.'

Drew peered behind the angry young woman. Draped in a green hospital gown, Sarah pushed herself up to a sitting position. If he had thought he was tired, it was nothing compared to how she looked. Despite the dolling up for the night before, there was not a scrap of makeup on her face. Her hair clung to her cheeks and her neck, and all in all, she looked the most beautiful he had ever seen in his entire life. He was moving towards her when he stopped in his tracks.

'Oh my god. Is that…. is that….' Tears clouded his eyes.

'Drew, meet Elspeth,' Sarah said.

'Elspeth?'

'Elspeth.'

Every emotion he had ever known flooded from his body as he fell onto his knees beside the bed. 'Oh, my goodness, she's beautiful. She's so beautiful.' A full head of dark hair covered her crown, her closed little fists tucked up beneath her chin. 'Elspeth,' he whispered. Still panting, he landed his lips on the top of his wife's head. 'Sah, I am so sorry I wasn't there. Please. Please forgive me. You took my phone, and I didn't realise. And then I didn't have sat nav, and then I tried at Nelly's. Oh my god, I am so sorry, you know that, don't you? I am so sorry. I am so proud of you.' He kissed her again. Then the baby again. 'You are so perfect. Isn't she perfect? I am so sorry I wasn't there to meet you straight away. You were fine though, right? She's fine, isn't she? She looks fine?'

It took a moment for Drew to realise he was the only one speaking. Other than saying the baby's name, he didn't think Sarah had uttered a single word since his arrival. He shifted his body back and looked at the pair together. The sense of unease deepened. It wasn't so much Sarah's lack of speaking that was unnerving him. It was something else. Her whole body language was rigid and tense as if she wasn't actually pleased to see him.

'Sarah? Is everything okay?' A wave of fear struck. 'It's not Elspeth, is it? Everything's okay, isn't it? She's okay, isn't she?'

He moved his hand down to his baby, searching for some kind of indication. They didn't leave babies with their mum if they were sick, did they? No, of course not. Unless they were really sick. And she was breathing, stirring, so surely not.

'Elspeth is fine,' Sarah told him.

'Thank god.'

So why did it feel like something was wrong?

'Sah, what is it?' A trembling formed in his hands, which quickly rose up through his chest. Slowly, and with tears in her eyes, Sarah twisted her head around to face him.

'You lied to me, Drew. You manipulated me. You made a fool out of me.'

'This is about the book!' A sigh of relief floated within

him. 'Sarah, I know. I was completely wrong. I just thought…
I just didn't want to stress you out. That's all. You understand
that, don't you? I thought I was trying to protect you. I was
wrong. I realise that now. Please, I don't want to fight about
it. I don't, not now that Elspeth's here. Please, you do believe
me, don't you?'

She nodded slowly. It was barely a single nod, during
which her cheeks remained sucked in the entire time. For
some reason, it made him more nervous, not less.

Sarah's eyes met his. Deep sallow bags highlighted the
maze of capillaries that wove around her pupils. Still, there
was something unsettling about the way she held his gaze,
with coldness and fire that didn't make sense together.

'Honestly, I thought it was for the best,' he repeated, his
words sounding lamer and lamer by the second.

'I understand,' she said. 'And what about Polly? Did you
think that was all for the best too?'

'Polly?' Drew's head began to spin. It was like dozens of
strands of a conversation were whirling in the air around
him. 'You know about Polly?' He felt the blood rush from his
head.

'I know it all, Drew.' A stray tear escaped down Sarah's
cheek. A single sniff sounded as she wiped it away with the
back of her hand. It felt as if a chasm had formed within
Drew's chest.

'I didn't know it was going to happen like that. I didn't
ask her to do it.'

Sarah snorted. 'Oh, great. And you couldn't possibly have
stopped her, could you?'

'I didn't know.' Drew lifted his hands into the air. 'I swear,
I didn't know. When I left, she was talking to Barry. Then she

appeared in Casper's office, and I was sent out. I didn't even know what she'd done until afterwards. She thought she was doing the right thing. She was just trying to stop me from getting fired.'

'Fired?' For the first time, Sarah's unflappable demeanour faltered. The surprise in her voice registered with their daughter as a small whimper floated up from Elspeth's lips. After hushing the girl with gentle rocking motions, Sarah lowered her voice into a hiss. 'What the heck, Drew? How much have you been keeping from me?'

'Nothing… Well, a couple of things, but only because —'

'Because you were protecting me?' Her face indicated how much she thought of that reply. 'Seriously, Drew, that line's not going to cut it this time. I don't think I even know who you are anymore.'

Drew was scratching his head now, trying to make sense of the jumble of words going in, none of which appeared to be linked. There was no way he was going to manage to get through any more of the conversation without a little bit more clarification. He took a step back and looked at his wife. 'You're mad because of the email, right? Because Barry forwarded the email, and I nearly got fired?'

'And I'm mad because you spent the night with poxy Polly!'

'What?' Drew's face scrunched up. 'No, I didn't. I spent the night with Nelly.'

'Nelly?!' The vein was now bulging in Sarah's forehead. 'What the hell were you doing with Nelly?'

'What do you think? Ringing around every bloody hospital and police station trying to find out where you were.'

Elspeth began to cry. Sarah shot Drew a look. The venom in her eyes had only multiplied.

'I rang Barry, Drew. I tried to get a hold of you when this —,' she nudged her chin towards Elspeth, '— happened. He said you'd been at the bar with Polly. That you left together.'

'Ahh,' Drew nodded as one by one, the pieces fell into place. 'We were at the bar, but then she… she…'

'Yes?' Sarah said. 'Then she what?'

It was mean. Laughing at him was mean. But it was funny. She could picture the scene in her head. Patient Drew. Sweet Drew, who hated to cause a scene, completely oblivious to this young twenty-something throwing herself at him. It was a miracle he hadn't gone all the way upstairs before he'd realised. 'You thought she'd put her hand there by accident. You can't be serious?'

'I am. I thought she was just being friendly, that was all. Comforting, you know.'

'Oh, she was trying to be comforting, that's for sure. I guess she has a bit of a daddy thing going on.'

'What do you mean by that? I look very good for my age.'

'You do.' She twisted her lips in an attempt to suppress her smirk. She was still mad. Unbelievably mad. And the rules about the nappy changing and belly button yuckiness were still firmly in place. But the dread that had been swirling around her stomach had been replaced by something else. Something comforting.

'You did it. I told you that you could. All by yourself.'

'Now is not a great time for an *I told you so,*' she said, rein-

270

forcing the point that there was a long way to go before complete forgiveness was achieved. 'And besides, I wasn't on my own.'

'Well, you're incredible. The pair of you, you're absolutely incredible.'

Sarah closed her eyes and sank down into the pillow. Elspeth was in Drew's arms.

'I was thinking,' Drew cleared his throat. 'I was thinking that I'll talk to Mum and Dad.'

'About what?'

'About money.'

Sarah shifted herself in the bed. 'Really?'

'Why not? What's the worst they can say? I'll ask for it as an early inheritance. Then maybe if they'll lend us enough, we can put it down as a deposit on a bigger place.'

Sarah studied his face, searching for some kind of proviso. But none came. 'You're sure? I thought you didn't want to move?'

'I think it's time. We can put our house on the market as soon as you feel ready.'

A lump swelled in Sarah's chest. 'You mean it?'

'Well, it will only be a loan, of course. Until the book royalties start coming in.'

I t had all happened quickly. Elspeth, for all her charms, wasn't much of a sleeper, although she was very useful when it came to softening-up Drew's parents. They agreed immediately to a loan, just as Sarah had known they would, and the house was on the market before Elspeth was a month old. It was now just a waiting game. Waiting for the right place to come along and waiting for the right person to discover their house. Fortunately, they had a few things – besides the three children – to keep them occupied in the meanwhile.

'The cover looks good. Don't you think the cover looks good?' Drew ran his hand over the screen like it was something more tangible than pixels on a piece of glass.

'The cover looks good. Nelly has done a great job,' Sarah agreed. 'It all looks good. Are you sure you're ready? No last-minute changes you want to make?'

Drew shook his head. 'Nope, this is it. *Adventures of an Air Hostess, Book One: The Hostess Hits Halkidiki* is going live.' His grin was contagious. Even if the whole thing had been ridiculous, it was worth it to see that grin. 'Do you want to press *Publish?*'

Sarah shook her head. 'You do it.'

'We do it together?'

It was probably a bit silly, both of them there, their fingers on the touchpad of the computer, ready to press, but there they were.

'Three, two, one…'

The End

## ACKNOWLEDGMENTS

Massive thanks must go to both Charmaine and Vector Artist. To Charmaine for her amazing skill in helping me get this book edited, and to Vector Artist for taking on board all of my ideas to create yet another dynamic cover.

Thank you to all of my beta readers who take the time to read early drafts and offer valuable feedback, especially the eagle-eyed Kath, Lucy and Carol as well as support and encouragement. Please know that every recommendation to a friend, share on social media or kind message, means so much to me.

Thank you to my husband who helps me find the time to write and tirelessly checks and double checks and keeps me on track.

Lastly, thank you to every reader who has taken the time to read my work and listen to my stories, and to the amazing bloggers who have done so much to help me along this journey.

## ABOUT THE AUTHOR

Hannah Lynn is an award-winning novelist. Publishing her first book, *Amendments* – a dark, dystopian speculative fiction novel, in 2015, she has since gone on to write *The Afterlife of Walter Augustus* – a contemporary fiction novel with a supernatural twist – which won the 2018 Kindle Storyteller Award and Gold Medal for Best Adult Fiction Ebook at the IPPY Awards, as well as the delightfully funny and poignant *Peas and Carrots series*.

While she freely moves between genres, her novels are recognisable for their character driven stories and wonderfully vivid description.

Born in 1984, Hannah grew up in the Cotswolds, UK. After graduating from university, she spent ten years as a teacher of physics, first in the UK, then in Thailand, Malaysia, Austria and Jordan. It was during this time, inspired by the imaginations of the young people she taught, she began writing short stories for children, before moving on to adult fiction.

Nowadays you will most likely find her busy writing at home with her husband and daughter, surrounded by a horde of cats.

ALSO BY HANNAH LYNN

PEAS, CARROTS AND AN ASTON MARTIN

E ric sighed heavily. Suzy took his empty glass from his hand and swapped it for a full one.

'Maybe I should give it up. Let the church have it. I mean it's just a car. After all, we can always go and buy another vintage DB4,' he said.

Suzy gave him a withering look.

'I mean, we'd have to re-mortgage the house,' Eric said. 'And Abi would have to go to that school down the road where all the kids smell like baked beans and do their homework on used kitchen roll, but we'd get by.'

'You're not going to give it up,' Suzy said. 'We both know that.'

Eric thumbed the rim of his glass until it let out a deep, low hum. 'No,' he said. 'I guess not.'

'So, I guess we're all heading to Burlam this weekend?'

Twenty minutes later, Eric was sitting at his desk with Suzy peering over his shoulder. His laptop was open on the *Burlam Village Website*, specifically the Classifieds. The page contained various lists and headings in colourful blues and greens with a serene picture of the river and sailing boats set as the background.

'I'm not sure this is what he meant,' Suzy said. 'I thought you said *you* had to maintain the allotment?'

Eric continued typing away in the little rectangular box. 'This is just a short-term solution to buy us a little time. Anyway, I'm maintaining it. I'll just be paying someone else to do the digging.'

'I'm not convinced.'

'Trust me. This will see us all a lot happier. Mr Eaves included.'

With a satisfied smile, Eric clicked enter.

'There. All done.'

Half a second later his succinctly worded advert appeared on *Burlam Village Classifieds* page. "*Gardener wanted for allotment plot. Can grow anything. Will pay good money.*"

'Now all we have to do is wait for the applicants.'

Peas, Carrots and an Aston Martin is a heart-warming novel from the Peas and Carrots humorous fiction series. If you like crazy capers, quirky characters, and brilliant second chances, then you'll love Kindle Storyteller Award winner Hannah Lynn's madcap tale.

Buy Peas, Carrots and an Aston Martin to ride into the weeds today on Amazon!

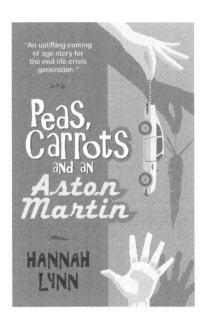

"**I absolutely loved this book**! It's funny, uplifting, contains a whole host of unforgettable characters and I can't wait to read the sequel! I was looking for something to cheer me up and this fit the bill. **A highly recommended 5 star read**."

"Peas, Carrots and an Aston Martin was **brilliant from start to finish** just downloaded the second book would **definitely recommend** to anyone."

"Will have you laughing one moment and misty eyed the next. This was **a joy to read**. Her characters a vividly drawn and strangely relatable. **Recommend**."

"**I loved this book**! Had me gripped from the first page. A real feel-good factor. Might need a tissue at some points. **Hugely recommended**."

## STAY IN TOUCH

To keep up-to-date with new publications, tours and promotions, or if you are interested in being a beta reader for future novels, or having the opportunity to enjoy pre-release copies please follow me:

Website: https://www.hannahlynnauthor.com/

Alternatively sign up to my newsletter and receive a free book.

Sign-up to Newsletter

## REVIEW

As an independent author, I do not have the mega resources of a big publishing house, but what I do have is something even more powerful – all of you readers. Your ability to offer social proof to my books through your reviews is invaluable to me and helps me to continue writing.

So if you enjoyed reading ***Erotic Fiction?***, please take a few moments to leave a review or rating on Amazon or Goodreads. It need only be a sentence or two, but it means so much to me.

Thank you.